DOW   Downey, Timothy.

         A splendid
           executioner

$17.43

DATE			

© THE BAKER & TAYLOR CO.

A SPLENDID EXECUTIONER

Timothy Downey

A SPLENDID EXECUTIONER

E. P. DUTTON ● NEW YORK

Published in the United States by
E. P. Dutton, a division of New American Library,
2 Park Avenue, New York, N.Y. 10016.

Library of Congress Cataloging-in-Publication Data
Downey, Timothy.
A splendid executioner.
I. Title.
PS3554.0934S6   1987   813'.54   86-16644
ISBN: 0-525-24486-7

Published simultaneously in Canada by
Fitzhenry & Whiteside, Limited, Toronto.

COBE

DESIGNED BY MARK O'CONNOR

10 9 8 7 6 5 4 3 2 1

First Edition

TO LINDA

The reward of empty words is always punishment.

—AESCHYLUS

Part One

One

The truth made a splendid executioner.

Fact: The City of New York Mortgages and Conveyances identified the Mortgagee of lot number 4333 as one Sahara Enterprises, Inc.

Fact: Sahara Enterprises, Inc., was a wholly owned subsidiary of Quotidien Co., the Mortgagor.

Fact: Quotidien was controlled by a holding company, Dinah, Inc., itself an operating arm of the Next World Foundation, A. Fitzwater, Chairman.

Fact: A. Fitzwater was Brother Atwood Fitzwater, local TV evangelist and spokesman for Decency In New York (DENY), a single-issue group opposed to the granting of civil rights to homosexuals. Brother Atwood lobbied for mandatory prison terms for "sodomists" and consistently referred to AIDS as "divine retribution" in his televised Sunday sermons.

Fact: Occupying lot number 4333 was the Ramjet Theater, known for its chicken hawks working the balcony, and the Speedway Lounge, famed for its backroom rough trade.

3

So the truth, just as Pete Killharney's "knowledge-able source" had promised, the clear, career-killing truth was that the righteous Brother Atwood Fitzwater held well-hidden ownership over a couple of Times Square sleaze joints.

"I'm going to crucify the pervert," Pete muttered cheerfully, earning a scowl from Miss Jergens, the fossilized librarian of the New York County Surrogate Court.

Only a life spent reporting the sins of the powerful prepared him to believe such enormous hypocrisy. But the even greater stupidity of leaving a traceable paper trail—that had a suspicious neatness. Such tidy damnation was the signature of Red Ethel. Fitzwater had been set up for this fall.

Killharney looked around the second-floor archive room for someone to share the revelation with. Not Miss Jergens, she hadn't spoken to him since an anti-Lindsay piece he wrote two decades ago. Nor the two giggling paralegals sharing a joint by the corner windows. Indignation appeared beyond them. And the always busy Pelicans—the Legal Aid lawyers—were too inured to perfidy to be properly receptive.

Luckily, Shulman was in his usual corner. Tax lien ledger propped against his hemispherical gut, the senior partner of Shulman & Shulman shoaled for bankrupt properties as he licked his lips with dainty, vulpine flicks.

"Find any SROs begging for condo conversion, Irving?" Pete asked.

"I don't know why I bother," Shulman complained about the activity that had made him a disgustingly rich man. "I should be like my brother Georgie. One Rockefeller infarction is worth six months of this shit."

"Rockefeller infarction?"

"It's what they call it when you check out while still in the saddle. Georgie has a client now, pulled a Rockefeller, and son of a bitch if the girl didn't know that CPR, saved his fucking life."

"So George is handling the divorce."

"Better. He's got a twin bill going on it. There's the divorce, sure, plus the client's suing the bimbo for practicing medicine without a license. Me, I think the guy's a little ungrateful."

"I got some company for him. You know Brother Fitzwater?"

"That schmuck."

"What if I told you that schmuck owns a leather bar off Eighth Avenue?"

"I heard you been hitting the hard sauce lately." This was not appropriate audience reaction.

"At least you don't have to worry about going the Rockefeller route. With that fat pot of yours, you could never get it near enough to raise your blood pressure." Pete left the lawyer to his failure-filled ledgers.

Waiting for the elevator, Killharney considered the crack about drinking, then dropped it. The reporter's creed: There are no secrets. He held no exemption.

The elevator's ornate brass doors creaked open, and Pete began a glacial descent while he pondered the secret of Lot 4333. For Brother Atwood's ownership was truly the least of the preacher's sins. Fitzwater had a morally fatal affinity for callow young men who would administer hot lunches and the odd B-and-D. And one of them had apparently sucked him into buying the building, then betrayed the infatuated demagogue to Pete's source, who by no coincidence worked downstairs, in the Municipal Research Center, for Red Ethel, its director.

An old Trotskyite, Ethel Rosenbloom had survived strikes, beatings, and her husband, Max, who died in '37 after picking up pneumonia in the Tombs while doing a week for unlawful assembly. For forty years since, she had been underground, filing and remembering, until now as its director she and her stable of angry, mostly gay assistants used the Municipal Research Center to help subvert the power elite.

Killharney had to admire Red Ethel's most recent setup. It was entrapment that hid itself, for the evidence damning Fitzwater was the property ownership, not the self-destructive cravings that had led to it. But it was enough. As sure as the rich got richer and the poor died young, Pete was going to nail the sanctimonious hate-monger.

The elevator opened onto an unfamiliar world.

"Where the hell am I?" he asked, and listened to his question echo down a dim, empty hallway.

The basement. He had pushed the wrong button. Killharney stepped back into the elevator, then returned to the incongruously shabby corridor. The marble and brass opulence of the upper floors hadn't made it to the basement. Here, brick replaced marble, painted pine the polished mahogany found above. Curious, he wandered down the hall, peering into dark rooms stacked with cartons, tin file drawers, dusty antique wooden cabinets. One room was filled from floor to ceiling with stacks of teacher payroll cards going back fifty years.

A picture came to Pete of records silting downward as more were piled on top. Upstairs, lawyers and bureaucrats and columnists kept the current files churning. But down in the basement, back through history, all these records eventually came to rest, forgotten, abandoned, never to be seen or cared about again. Room after subterranean room was crammed with the moldering rolls of dead men, defunct alliances, and the undiscovered evidence of countless crimes. Pete wondered if he could eke a piece out of the image. Probably not.

Seeking an exit from this bureaucratic graveyard,

Killharney followed the corridor to a connecting hall, at the end of which a marble staircase obviously led to the first floor. He took the stairs two at a time, reaching the building's enclosed inner courtyard with the same guilty relief he often felt when leaving a cemetery.

The last light of the feeble March sun barely penetrated the grimy skylight three stories above. He stopped, and listened. From somewhere he could hear the sound of typing. Then it too stopped, and the building seemed to plunge into a morguelike stillness. In the sudden, frozen silence, Pete sensed he wasn't alone. His eyes searched the shadows.

"Who's there?" he demanded, his words quickly swallowed by the enveloping gloom. What ghosts had followed him up from the basement? What wrongs were they crying for him to expose?

Reason returned. The silence thawed. The building's natural noises clattered to life once more, and Killharney reached for his cigarettes with sweaty, shaking hands.

Hitting the hard sauce. It was a hell of a time to be talking to ghosts. He had a story, a great story to break. Worthy of the Hit List. Yes, yes, and by all the avenging angels in heaven he deserved a drink.

"Seamus, drinks all around!"

"And may I draw yourself a draft, Peter?" asked Seamus O'Brien, the hearty, florid-faced, snow-topped owner of the County Cork Bar and Grill. "You're looking as dry as a Methodist camp meeting."

"It would be an act of mercy," Pete agreed. "Let me wash up."

He wrestled the men's room door (there was no women's) as closed as its decades-old warp would allow. The thick stink of disinfectant and old men's piss briefly dampened his thirst, but as he lathered his hands Pete considered how much that smell defined, even circumscribed his adult life. The first week at his first newspaper job, running copy at the old *Herald Tribune*, the night rewrite man had introduced him to flaming chartreuse, and Killharney's last memory of the evening was of rolling in his own puke on the filthy tile floor of some Twenty-third Street Irish bar. Then there were the longshoremen's hangouts he had inhabited while doing research for his Pulitzer series on mob control of the waterfront. And the countless, purposely anonymous dives where, raging and wounded, he had sought respite from the pain of Margie's infidelities and eventual abandonment, now two years ago. Disinfectant and old men's piss, Killharney's scatological madeleine. Proust he wasn't, he thought, kicking the door open and ducking to fit his six-foot-five frame through a door fitted to an earlier and shorter generation of Irish drunk.

"Finished your devotions?" Seamus asked, drawing the draft and setting it with a sturdy thump next to a shot glass lipped with scotch.

"A toast to all God-fearing men," Killharney called to the bar, and popped the whiskey back. As the poison disintegrated his digestive tract, he settled on the leather swivel stool with a sigh of contentment.

"Amen," responded the one-legged Hanratty from his perch by the front window, where the sooty neon Rheingold sign washed the disabled veteran in a diabolical red. Hanratty had been transformed in Killharney's column into the Doughboy, whose garbled sensibility of an earlier age nonetheless showed up the shabbiness of the present.

"Hypocrisy, said some dead frog," continued Pete, "is the homage vice pays to virtue."

He let beer chase the scotch. Ah, the sweet slaking

of thirst. Ah, sanctuary. The County Cork Bar and Grill was one of those neighborhood pocket bars on Eighth Avenue, invisible and cheap, in the heart of what used to be Irish Hell's Kitchen, now surrounded by *bodegas*, thrift stores, and Chinese take-outs. Killharney lit a Lucky Strike and let his gaze glide approvingly down the long teak bar, its rail worn to the wood by unnumbered forearms. Above the bar, hanging from the stamped tin ceiling, fly-spattered chandeliers barely illuminated the signs pushing dollar shots of Mount Vernon whiskey, notices of reluctance to extend credit, as per state law, or to cash checks, as per the wisdom derived from forty-five years of pouring booze. A chalkboard menu at the end of the bar announced the daily special, corned beef and cabbage, not a radical culinary departure at the County Cork. Killharney hated corned beef. Killharney hated cabbage.

"Hungry?" asked Seamus, seeing Pete scowl at the chalkboard.

"How about a burger and some onion rings," Pete ordered. "And another White Label."

He pivoted around on the stool to head for his booth. His was the middle of five, away from both the front-door drafts and the men's room traffic. Pete knew every varnished check in the grain, every scrawled phone number (he had called them all once and gotten a column out of it), every piece of petrified chewing gum stalactiting the underside. And tonight, tonight when he burned to nail together the Fitzwater exposé, when he was righteously angry for the first time in what seemed months, his booth was occupied by . . . a couple. Jesus save us sinners. The boy was a button-down type, the girl looking Seven-Sisterly, yuppies slumming for local color before retiring to his renovated brownstone or her doormanned high-rise for a bout of cautious fucking.

"Say, you want to try the corned beef and cabbage?" he asked his date.

"Puke," she answered. "Would you actually eat something that came out of there?" she inclined her pony-tail toward the kitchen kept immaculate by Seamus's spinster sister Kate.

"Garrgh," said Pete, swiveling back to his refreshed shot glass. As he tossed back the second scotch, he glimpsed his reflection through the bottles picketing the mirror behind the bar. A number of distinguished enough wrinkles. A less distinguished stitching of burst capillaries across his pug nose. Full head of once-black hair, now salt-and-pepper. He could stand a trim. And he needed a shave. Hell, he needed a new face, and a new life while he was ordering.

The pay phone rang, and Svenson picked it up. A sinecured sandhog for the perpetually unfinished Manhattan water tunnel number 3, Svenson in Pete's column was the Swede, the voice of hardhat America.

"Killharney," he called in his flat Bronx honk. Pete shook his head no, he wasn't there.

"He ain't here," Svenson duly lied, then listened. "Hold on," and he covered the phone. "It's the city desk, says Lopiccolo just got iced."

"Christ, it's Judgment Day," Killharney said, feeling that confusion of fulfilled expectation and generalized regret he always experienced when violent men died violently. He opened his notebook to the "Murder" divider, which was epigraphed, "Any man's death diminishes me, because I am involved in mankind." Would Donne really have felt diminished by the news of the Icepick's death? Did Killharney? Yes would be a lie. No wouldn't be the truth.

He wrote down directions from the editor, signaled to Seamus a shot for the road, grabbed his hamburger, and twenty minutes later Pete was at the murder scene in Brooklyn, wearing a properly mournful expression undercut by a smear of burger grease streaked across his face from a pothole jolt in the taxi ride down.

Thorkington was leaving as Killharney arrived, and grabbed the vacated cab.

"Get all you needed, Herb?" Pete asked the veteran police reporter for the *News*, who had the routine of sensationalism down to a five minute drill of who, how, and when. Thorkington regarded him with the weary red eyes of the habitual drunk.

"Wait till you hear about Saint Francis," he said, and collapsed into the back of the taxi.

Saint Francis?

The paraphernalia of police work were already in place. Thick, oiled rope stretched across the street, signs stuck to it proclaiming KEEP OUT! CRIME SCENE. A crowd of the curious pressed against the thin barrier, politely craning to catch a gruesome glimpse. Just inside the restricted area was Forensics' battered black station wagon. With the methodical restlessness that marked good evidence-gatherers, they scurried about drawing lines, taking measurements, snapping photographs, dusting for fingerprints and shoe impressions. A half-dozen other bored policemen, calamity their routine, maintained public order by doing nothing whatsoever. Pete didn't linger on these standard sights; he had already devoted two columns to the subject.

Where was he? Chapel Street, the night desk had said. The Brooklyn Cathedral. He looked around for a suitable edifice, but the only close qualifier was this small, sooty brownstone church surrounded by warehouses. Yes, this was it; a historic marker proclaimed it the second-

11

oldest diocese in the country. Killharney looked closer. It was a very old church. The acid air of the city had pocked and pitted it everywhere, and splotches of plaster repair work gave its side a leprous appearance in the harsh glare from the anticrime streetlight on the corner. There was a postage-stamp cemetery behind the church, its tilting tombstones covered with moss, one with spray-painted graffiti.

It started to snow.

He took out his notebook and wrote down details about the church and surrounding area, then approached his favorite homicide detective. Lieutenant Dombowski and a solemn row of cops stood staring at something on the cathedral's front steps. The detective saw Pete and waved him over.

"You drunk yet?"

What was this about his drinking?

"You take the pledge, Dombowski? Turning temperate to atone for past binges?"

The detective shrugged. "It's your dinner," he said, and stepped back.

And there lay Lorenzo Lopiccolo, longtime member of the Killharney's Bar Hit List, quite emphatically and violently deceased. The slumlord's bulging eyes and bloated purple cheeks spelled strangulation, and Pete glimpsed the metallic glint of a gently waving wand of piano wire leading from the blood-ribboned neck.

But there was something else, a lumpy, bloody mess crammed into Lopiccolo's puckered mouth. Reflexively, Pete looked down to the trousers, the bull's-eye of blood where the genitals had been hacked away.

Oh God. Oh God.

Pete looked away, fighting for control, as close to sick as he had been since that day-care center fire and the sight and smell of its dozen charred little corpses.

12

Another remembrance of death surfaced, a face dripping blood, his father's. No.

Get away. Escape. Look at the pretty snowflakes. Think of basketball. Payroll records. Better. He swallowed, set himself, turned back, regarded the body with a show of clinical detachment.

"That knee broken?"

"Both knees, both shattered."

"Jesus."

"Yeah."

"Mob job?" Pete asked, fishing.

Dombowski snorted ambiguously, then they were all lit by the bright lights that accompany video minicams.

"What the fuck?" the detective bellowed, wheeling around to the nearest uniformed patrolman. "What is this, fucking 'Candid Camera'? Get them across the street, now!" he jerked his thumb at the camera crew. Pete himself retreated from the detective's side, knowing Dombowski's rages were short-lived but nondiscriminatory.

"You still dusting for prints?" the cop shouted. "What have you been doing, pulling circle jerks in the back of your wagon? You, did you sign for what you just bagged there? Where's the goddamn square who found the stiff?"

Killharney blended into the small crowd of onlookers, searching for usable reactions, but found only the typical range of horror and fascination plastered on their cold-reddened faces.

"I hear it's Mafia," said a short grandmotherly type with gleaming eyes, a mole the size of a dime on her left cheek.

"Definitely drug-related," said a man whose bathrobe trailed beneath his ski parka.

This was not the stuff of snappy columns.

"Killharney!"

Dombowski's summons indicated that the storm of abuse had passed, and Pete returned to the steps. It was snowing much harder, a swirling haze of large flakes that melted immediately.

"Look at that arm," Dombowski said, and Pete looked at Lopiccolo's outstretched arm, frozen by death into a perpetual pointing gesture.

"Yeah?"

"What's it look like?"

"Like he's pointing."

"No. Jesus, Killharney, you're a Catholic. What's it look like?"

Pete remembered Thorkington's parting words.

"Saint Francis?" he guessed.

"Fucking right. There's a statue at Mercy, where my oldest daughter goes, Saint Francis, arm out just like that, except there's some bird sitting on his finger, the statue's."

"How about that," Pete said evenly.

"I saw it and thought of you, those little details you like to throw in. Help you out with your job."

"Speaking of jobs, why are you here, Dombowski? You think Lopiccolo qualifies for Major Case Assignment?" MCAs were Dombowski's province; the sarcastic SOB solved homicides. "Wait, don't tell me. The way landlords contribute to Hizzoner's campaigns, the mayor wants them to feel confident they'll get first-class attention in case one of the bastards gets blown away."

"Fuck that. I don't want people thinking murder's the way around paying the rent on time. Fad like that gets started, we'll all be swimming in blood."

An ambulance arrived, and attendants eased the mutilated corpse into a body bag, struggling to zip it over the Saint Francis arm.

"But it might be a mob hit?" Killharney suggested again.

"Anything's possible with those sweethearts," the cop answered, unconvinced. Pete thought out loud for them both.

"But the damage doesn't fit together. Like the knees. If an enforcer's breaking knees, he wants something, he's not going to snuff the guy. And if it's a contract, why waste time busting knees? Not to mention . . ."

Out of the corner of his eye, Pete saw a priest approaching, black overcoat flapping like the wings of some great bird that feeds off death. Was that the angle?

"Disgruntled tenant, then?" he wondered.

"Disgruntled, that's good. Think I'll use that in my report. 'The victim's knees were disgruntled into many tiny pieces.' " The cop contemplated the possible addition to the jargon of police reporting. "Guess you got an opening in your Hit List now."

And Pete saw it, saw it all, intro, setup, tag line, tomorrow's column as neat as a proof sheet in his mind's eye. God, he needed a drink. He turned to go, but Dombowski detained him with his Polish ham of a hand.

"You know something?" Dombowski said with a quietness that made Killharney listen. "This ain't no mob hit. This ain't your typical jerked-around tenant neither."

"I hear there's been an accident," said the priest.

Warmup for writer's hell was announced by a telephone that wouldn't stop ringing. Go away. Please. Anything, he'd do anything for another hour's sleep. Please.

Killharney knew it was useless, knew Wilson had ordered some assistant to keep trying till he answered. Pete sent a hand out on blind reconnaissance, slapping a hard object off the nightstand. The explosion of broken glass jarred his scummy teeth apart. A second sweep knocked the receiver off the phone, and the ringing stopped. From somewhere underneath the bed a tinny voice squeaked upward.

"Mr. Killharney. Mr. Killharney? Are you there, Mr. Killharney? Mr. Wilson would like to know if you have your copy for . . ."

There was a grateful pause, then another, considerably more compelling voice ascended.

"Pick up the phone. Now!" said his editor. Killharney picked up the phone.

"Hell . . ." his vocal chords balked at the effort. Where were his cigarettes?

"Where's your column, Killharney?"

"Well, Chief, let me think," and Pete lit a Lucky, which triggered a coughing fit. When he finished, the editor spoke again in soft, dangerously considerate tones.

"If you're entirely finished with your Camille impression, I was wondering whether you could cast around to see if, say, last night perhaps, you managed to write anything at all I might just possibly be interested in. Could you do that for me?"

"Ah, hold on."

Pete swung his feet to the floor and promptly ground his big toe into a glass shard.

"Fuck, shit, piss, cunt!" he swore, and inspected the damage. Bloody, but not life-threatening.

"I'm waiting," said Wilson, still ominously polite.

Pete hopped over to the Formica table and pawed through the morass of candy and cigarette wrappers, crumpled typing paper, bent beer cans, pretzel pieces, moldy TV dinner tins, and four empty scotch bottles. Four?

A wave of nausea nearly floored him, and he grabbed the table for support, burying his left hand in green mashed potatoes. The place could stand a little tidying. He wiped his hand on a piece of ceiling plaster that had fallen off the week before.

He knew he had written a column, written something at least. Phrases drifted back to him. Bigotry and religion. Boss Tweed. Something about the Hit List. And there it was, sitting on top of his old Royal, neat as could be. Pete might be a drunk, but he was a goddamn professional one.

He brought the column back to the bed, trailing a thread of blood through the new archipelago of broken glass.

"Got it right here, Chief," he said. Wilson hated being called Chief. "Killharney comes through again. Want me to run it downtown before deadline, do you?"

That did it.

"You scotch-sodden moron, deadline's in twelve minutes. Why the hell else do you think I'm wasting my breath asking a second-rate drunk for fourth-rate filler he probably wrote in his sleep? I'm attending the birth of a new literary genre, somnambulistic journalism. The Killharney School of Automatic Writing. Of all the worthless, degenerate . . ."

Wilson sputtered into incoherence. He had been appalled to discover how little Killharney remembered of what he had written when drinking. "Scotch-sodden moron" was a bit harsh, though. The first voice came back on the line.

"Mr. Killharney? Mr. Wilson suggests you read me your copy. I'll take it down and type it up, and we'll meet that old deadline. What do you say?"

Pete swallowed the gibe that rose to fill such an easy opening. Wilson was fiercely protective about his assistants. "Great idea," he said instead, and read her the copy for his column, "Killharney's Bar."

17

" 'Killharney's Bar is in deep mourning tonight. Hiram the bartender has broken out the black crepe that hasn't been hung since Meyer Lansky's passing. The jukebox will only play "Wedding Bells Are Breaking Up That Old Gang of Mine," the closest its playlist gets to a dirge. And the Doughboy swears he saw a tear trickle from the watchful eye of the Boss Tweed portrait over the cash register. Hatred, as with so many of the very best things, must halt at the grave.' Paragraph.

" 'Lorenzo Lopiccolo is dead. Known affectionately as the Icepick from an occupational tool he favored in his salad days, this pillar of the real estate establishment was gruesomely murdered last night and dumped at the steps of the Brooklyn Cathedral. It's the closest he got to church since Joey Gallo's funeral. His own is likely to be a closed-casket affair.' Another paragraph.

" 'Tenants who somehow managed to survive the Icepick's stewardship may discover that those metal ornaments in their apartments are capable of giving off heat. For the uninitiated, they're known as radiators. And those two cold-water taps? Try the left one. I know, it's hot. Oh, there's a whole new, post-Lopiccolo world for the families who had to inhabit his slums. Safe stairs, patched roofs, no rats, and yes, even heat!' Make that an exclamation point. New paragraph.

" 'However, the Icepick's hastened demise has punctured the Killharney's Bar Hit List. Since typically only the good die young, this mid-term vacancy is as rare as a Russian envoy paying his parking tickets. Consequently, I have spent ten dollars on boilermakers while contemplating a suitable replacement, and at a buck a shot, this qualifies as deep thinking.' Paragraph.

" 'The press of eligible candidates is, as ever, prodigious. Any one of last year's Dishonorable Mentions amply deserves our opprobrium.' Parens. '(The Swede

asks if that's some type of cancer. Look it up, Swede.)'
Close parens. 'But I can't seem to find the proper enthusiasm for censuring corrupt judges or condemning
contractors who build hospitals on hazardous-waste land-
fill. No, the Icepick's icing has inclined me toward mat-
ters religious. Hence, the following nomination:' Colon
and paragraph.

"'I hereby submit Brother Atwood Fitzwater for
membership in the Killharney's Bar Hit List.' Paragraph.

"'For you connoisseurs of Sunday sermonettes,
Brother Atwood is a familiar figure, with his carefully
wild hair, unblinking, indignant bug eyes, and preaching
filled with the coarsest kind of calculated demagoguery.
Some of the faithless have wondered which Gospel of
Christ Jesus this minister exegetes for his unswerving
advocacy of the death penalty. But no decent Christian
could object to Brother Fitzwater's favorite crusade:
making the world safe for heterosexuals.' Paragraph.

"'According to Fitzwater, fags are everywhere.
They're teaching our children. They're running the army
and the EPA. They've infiltrated Hollywood and the NFL
and the halls of Congress. That's right, most politicians
are faggots. And all reporters.' Paragraph.

"'A scourge on our society! Oh, Wickedness! Oh,
Sodom returned!' Exclamation points and initial caps
scattered through there, if you would. And paragraph.

"'It is my confessedly gleeful duty to report that,
like Lot's wife, Brother Atwood has permitted himself a
rearview peek at our own Sin City. But unlike that sadly
salted matron, he has been able to turn this regard to
profit. For Atwood Fitzwater owns a building whose two
businesses cater to homosexuals. The Speedway Lounge
is a bar whose house special can't be described in a family
paper. No, Doughboy, it doesn't have anything to do with
the Indy 500. And according to the current listing in *Gay*

Times, the Ramjet Theater is running that chicken classic, *Penetration Point,* starring every inch of Rod Long, twenty-four hours a day. Pretty regular testifying, that.' Paragraph.

" 'As Heraclitus says, bigotry is the disease of the religious. And no, Swede, Heraclitus isn't that new unisex hair salon near Bloomingdale's.' Paragraph.

" 'Brother Fitzwater, you're not only a bigot, not only a peddler of hatred and intolerance, you're a hypocrite and profiteer in degradation. You stink. If there is that hell you've consigned all those preterite leather-lovers to, your trip ticket is already punched. Until then, welcome to the Hit List.' End copy. Any questions?"

"What are your sources?" demanded Wilson, from another extension.

"Public record. City Mortgagors for 1986, liber 817, page 192. It's a lock."

Wilson didn't immediately accede to this opinion, and in the pause that ensued, Killharney noticed his cut toe had bled a small pool of blood onto the floor. His mind flashed back to last night's bloody circle of castration. Then the hangover reasserted itself with stomach-churning vengeance, and he collapsed helplessly onto the bed, soiling sheets and blankets with his still-leaking wound.

"It's about time you stooped to facts," the editor grumbled at last. "Good column, Pete," he conceded, and hung up on the prostrate reporter.

Killharney dropped the receiver to the floor and considered whether fetching first aid was worth the strong possibility of vomiting. No. He needed a drink.

It was St. Patrick's Day in New York: frigid, wet, and unrelievedly miserable. The parade was likewise its typical, exuberant fiasco, ten thousand Irish too dumb to get out of the rain and a million more willing to watch. The cheerleaders' bare thighs burned red from the afternoon cold. Tuba players kept their bells covered. Drenched flags and pompoms drooped listlessly, and the phalanxes of marching cops and firemen maintained set expressions of gruff or grudging stoicism. Even the usually spirited police horses keeping Fifth Avenue clear looked like glue-bait in the freezing rain that lacquered their flanks. Everyone, except of course the dignitaries who had long since fled the covered reviewing stand on the cathedral steps, suffered.

Luckily, Killharney was drunk. Guardedly drunk, about halfway to gloriously drunk. One more stop and he would have his yearly St. Patrick's Day column complete; he already had the centerpiece. Between bands, Killharney had witnessed a shabby black derelict on the other side of the avenue, weaving among the shamrocked housewives, businessmen on breaks, and doped-out adolescents. The bum's drunken rambling had caused the crowd to edge away and two foot cops to move watchfully closer. His message, however, was entirely apt.

"Go, Irish!" he had bellowed, over and over. "Today's you' day. Erin go fucking bragh!"

It was, Pete thought, a noble benediction.

Killharney jostled his way up to Fifty-seventh Street, where Assistant Inspector Francis X. Herlihy presided over the pandemonium wishfully called the Crowd Control Center. When Pete worked the police blotter fifteen years ago, he had met Lieutenant Herlihy, whose cherubic face and cheerful manners were almost grotesquely out of place at the old Centre Street headquarters. A sure burnout, Pete had predicted, but Herlihy had confounded him by not only surviving but quickly moving up to attain command rank. Pete had followed and occasionally chronicled the rise, and only once, after the

21

gang rape of a nun, had he ever seen him show anger. On that occasion Herlihy had taken a nightstick and snapped it in two with his hands, which is impossible. Inspector Herlihy enjoyed near universal respect.

Ear pressed to a walkie-talkie no doubt squawking the most horrendous villainy, watching a child throw up over one of his captain's parade-polished shoes, Herlihy's watery blue eyes never lost their mixture of resignation and surprise, even after spying Killharney swaying nearby.

"Peter, how good of you to stop by," he said. "Come for the body count?"

"Can't disappoint the reading public, Francis. They've grown accustomed to my pandering."

"Peter, now Peter," the cop said, "you and I deal with the muck, for whatever private purposes compel us, but we're neither of us muck ourselves. Sinner though you are, you're still on the side of the angels."

Herlihy's unflappable optimism always made him feel nervous, unworthy, and shamelessly proud.

"Erin go fucking bragh," Pete replied, sounding like some coarse buffoon. Herlihy smiled.

"I like that," he said, and lifted the plastic off his clipboard to recite the rain-spattered statistics beneath. "Let's see what we have so far. Twenty-seven purse-snatchings, looks like an organized operation. Twelve pickpocket reports, three arrests there, believe it or not. Must be the rain making wallets stick. Forty-six public intoxications. A dozen or so brawls, one arrest when a disputant broadened his quarrel to include the officer on the scene. Two armed robberies, probably coincidental. Oh yes, and one homicide, almost certainly parade-related."

"Why's that?" asked Killharney, furiously transcribing in his battered, soggy notebook.

"The victim had a bottle of Jameson's rammed up his asshole."

"What?"

Pete looked up to see if he was being kidded, but Herlihy's pale eyes stared back, unblinking, with a sadness unusual even for this constant witness to depravity.

"Jesus," Pete muttered, and shivered, and the saturated notebook cover shredded off in his hands. First Lopiccolo, then this poor slob. Was it all getting worse, or was he losing his capacity to tolerate the sadism that so often embellished murder? Killharney felt dirty, tired, dissatisfied. This was not the only truth worth reporting. "I hope at least it was empty," he said, the wisecrack congealing humorlessly in the freezing rain.

He felt horrible. A chill picked up at yesterday's parade had settled in his chest, and if it weren't payday, Pete would never have stirred from his bedside bottle of medicinal scotch. But his ex-wife, Margie, had promised court action if he was late with another support payment, so he had made the pilgrimage to the paper's headquarters, an art-deco abomination on Fourteenth Street ugly enough to have earned historic-landmark status. Once there, Killharney was good for nothing and accomplished it.

Sneezing and coughing, Pete picked up his "To Be Checked" folder and leafed through the reminders that demanded his urgent attention. His enthusiasm wasn't sparked. He glanced at the police report on Lopiccolo, where Joseph Owens, shield number 1132, described the strangled, bludgeoned, and mutilated corpse as an "apparent homicide perpetrated by unknown assailant." Who else but cops kept the word *perpetrate* current?

The precise anatomical jargon of the autopsy report was chillingly impenetrable. The shattered knees became "multiple fracturing of the patellas, with resulting traumatic perforation of surrounding ligature and fragments penetrating the membrane of the femoral sockets." And the castration was transformed into "incisions on the anterior and lateral walls of the penile protuberance resulting in global amputation." The exhaustive technical detail made the deranged slashing both impersonal and painfully real. Global amputation did not sound like fun.

This was not making Killharney feel any better. Nor was contemplation of the list of sources he was supposed to call each week and hadn't. Or the other list of story ideas he hadn't followed up on. All in all, Pete doubted he could feel worse.

"Killharney!"

The summons of James McNaughton Wilson rolled through the newsroom. Thank God he had finished his column. Clutching the copy as a talisman, Pete headed for the glass-walled office that afforded the editor an unobstructed panorama of his domain. Pete's fellow reporters followed his progress with the curious or commiserating looks commonly viewed from a tumbrel.

"What about Murry?" Wilson snapped.

"What about Murry?" Pete echoed, following one of his own guiding principles: play dumb if you're dumb.

"Dead."

"Dead?" Another? Something was going wrong.

The editor's thick gray eyebrows twitched once with disdain.

"Sit."

Pete sat, peeling off a Kleenex to staunch his dripping nose, and Wilson responded with appropriate compassion.

"It must be payday," he said. "For your information, Mr. Killharney, Congressman Murry was assassinated yesterday afternoon shortly after leaving the reviewing stand in front of St. Patrick's Cathedral."

"That's a shame," Pete said, trying to summon some

respect for the dead man that he had never felt for him alive. Murry had made the Killharney's Bar Hit List by being the most corrupt congressman in the New York delegation. He was universally reputed to have taken bag money from the mob, the ILA, the shipping lobby, an assortment of foreign dictators, and anyone else interested in buying into the deliberations of the maritime subcommittee he chaired. "How did it happen?"

"Someone stuck a forty-four into his mouth and pulled the trigger."

"Tough break."

"And inserted a full bottle of Irish whiskey up his anus."

"What!"

The last sentence in today's column had been "I hope it was empty, at least." But Killharney had no idea the victim was Murry. Why hadn't Herlihy told him? Respect for the dead, no doubt. Francis probably pictured the picnic Pete would have had with it. Such predictable callousness didn't say much about either his ethics or his writing.

"Full?" he asked, quickly rewriting the end in his head.

"Did you attend the parade yesterday, Mr. Killharney?"

"Where do you think I picked up this walking pneumonia?"

"And you missed any mention of this little incident, any whisper whatsoever of the murder and defilement of a member of the United States Congress?"

"I heard about the Jameson's," Pete admitted.

"Yes, a cute touch. No need to find out facts. String together some juicy particulars, drink yourself into a trance, and next morning you wake up to find another thousand words written. Hell, you're a columnist, you don't need to clutter your style with solid reporting."

"Wait a minute."

"I've waited minutes, Mr. Killharney. I've waited days and months and I am most heartily tired of the occupation." The editor leaned forward. "You have become a drunk. I don't care. Dress up in women's clothes. Paint your balls red. Drink yourself cirrhotic. I don't care. I am not a priest or a psychiatrist. I am an editor, your editor, and I put you on notice: I will not longer or silently endure the horseshit you've been handing in lately, your guaranteed contract notwithstanding. I demand daily competence, and if you don't deliver, I'll pull your column. Do I make myself clear?"

"Jesus, I hope you don't think you're being oblique," Pete said wearily. He felt mired, wrapped in an enormous fatigue that muffled the sting of Wilson's scathing censure. What were the symptoms of walking pneumonia? Or clinical depression? Killharney blew his nose with a self-pitying honk.

"You look like death, Pete," his editor remarked. "Hand in your copy, pick up your paycheck, and get the hell back to bed. And for Chrissakes, clean up your act. I hate firings and funerals and I expect you to spare me from attending to either."

It was a good start. In one corner garbage, in another laundry. On the bed was the shopping bag of essentials: new handkerchiefs, two new white shirts, package of three pairs of Fruit of the Loom jockey shorts, typing paper, beer, a snack-size cherry pie, handful of TV dinners, and a carton of Lucky Strikes. Killharney opened a pack and lit one up, cracked a Rolling Rock, tore the crinkly cellophane wrapping off the typing paper, fed a bright white sheet into his Royal, found his notes, and sat down to write.

He jotted down a rough outline of the column on a legal pad.

He finished the beer and opened another.

What was the lead? Something about violence, about the gratuitous brutality that now seemed obligatory. Where had he put those medical examiner's quotes?

Pete lit another Lucky and searched through the laundry pile for the message slip containing his notes from the coroner's report.

A third Rolling Rock.

He wrote, "The Swede tells me that knee-breaking has become passé." That might work.

He stood, paced the twenty-foot length of his small studio apartment, kicked the pile of dirty clothes into a more compact mass. He sat back down and studied the label. Latrobe, Pennsylvania. Arnold Palmer's hometown. He finished the bottle and opened a fourth.

Killharney loved to write. Killharney was a writing fool.

The building buzzer sounded. Thank God. Pete reached over the garbage and depressed the intercom button.

"Daddy?"

Lamb of God. Peg.

"Uh, what?"

"What do you think? Let us in, dummy."

He buzzed in his daughter and quickly chucked the new empties into the trash corner. Killharney smoothed back his hair and listened to three sets of footsteps thunder up the four flights to his bachelor digs.

"Hi. This is Muffy Patrick and this is Leslie Statler-Stevenson and you look crummy. Yuk, how can you live in this dump? Why don't you get a cleaning lady or something?"

His daughter Peg swept into his tiny apartment, trailing along behind her a pudgy, freckled redhead and a tall, horsy girl who stopped at the door in undisguised horror. It wasn't that bad, Killharney took silent exception. Was it?

"Hey, slow down, motormouth," he said.

"I told you he'd call me that." She rolled her eyes extravagantly. In the three years since Peg had turned twelve, nearly everything Killharney said mortified her. "So what do you think, Muff?" she asked her fat friend.

"It's even better than I imagined. I mean, an actual writer's garret. Look, even paper in the typewriter. God, I can't stand it!"

Garret?

"Oh God," Muffy continued, "we're not disturbing your writing or anything, are we?"

"Hardly," Pete honestly replied. The other girl took a tentative step into the apartment, eyeing all surfaces as sites of contagion.

"We've just come from a matinee at Lincoln Center. We heard Emmanuel Ax play the *Pathétique*," said Peg.

"It was super." Leslie spoke for the first time, trying to sound bored and succeeding.

"And some Bartok thing."

"Barf," Leslie said.

"I liked it," said Muffy.

"You would," Leslie said, tersely establishing the hierarchy of friendship.

"So you thought you'd drop in on the old man while you were in the neighborhood," Pete said, smoothing over the gibe.

"Some neighborhood," said Peg, who had a point. One thing Hell's Kitchen was not was neighborly. "Muffy wanted to meet you. She wants to be a writer."

Pete glanced at the single sentence he had written in an hour. "Good luck."

A long pause followed. Pete saw Leslie Hyphen-Name staring at the piles in each corner. Muffy tenderly touched his typewriter.

"Well," Peg said edgily.

"Why don't we go out for a bite to eat?" Pete suggested.

"I know a café with decent cappuccino on Lexington Avenue," Leslie said.

"Super," said Pete. The phone rang.

"I'll get it," Peggy said. "I bet it's Mom. Hello. Obviously I'm here. Oh, Mother! Of course not. Of course. No. Worse than you could begin to imagine. Hold on. She wants to talk to you." She passed Killharney the phone.

"Hello, Marge."

"Thank you for getting the check on time for once."

"You're wel—"

"Do you know those girls walked down Ninth Avenue to get to you? Three teenage girls. Every degenerate for blocks must be panting outside waiting for their reappearance. I expressly forbade Margaret, I'll have you know."

"Margaret?"

"She's fifteen, Pete, old enough to be addressed by her full name. Have you already called her 'motor-mouth'?"

"Once."

"She hates it."

"I'll stop."

"I bet."

"Margie," he said in a tone that made Peggy look worried.

"Would you at least make sure they take a taxi to Grand Central?"

"Anything for my child bride," he said, beginning to

29

feel the familiar belligerence that had regularly blemished their domestic life. Peg twitched in shame.

"And warn her about the Hare Krishnas and the rest. Adolescents are so susceptible to that sort of thing."

"Jesus, if she's old enough to handle her Christian name, she can cross the waiting room without being tempted to shave her head and live on brown rice."

Mortification was palpable. He desisted.

"Honestly," Marge said, unfazed, "you really should do something about your rage levels. This Type-A hostility has you on the fast track to a massive myocardial."

Margie had once fucked a heart surgeon.

"I'm taking medication," said Pete, remembering with some surprise that he had just drunk four beers. You're not supposed to forget drinking four beers. "Is that all?"

"How are you?"

"Crummy, I'm told."

"Same old Pete," she said, and hung up.

"My mother's so dumb," Peg explained to her friends, who nodded knowingly.

"So," said Pete, "why don't we fast-track it over to that super café?"

On the street, they were slapped by the frigid wind off the Hudson River that sucked away warmth. No perverts were apparent. The girls talked horses as Killharney steered them past SRO hotels and storefront missions, piles of garbage that dwarfed Pete's, and a clump of jobless blacks huddled around an oil-drum rubbish fire, passing a pint around. The simple pleasures, thought Pete, whose force of habit led his charges past the County Cork.

"Oh my God, that's it! That's it, isn't it?" squealed Muffy.

"What?" asked Killharney in alarm.

"Yes, Muffy," Peg said with a vast weariness.

"Can we go in? Please? Just for a minute. Please?"

Pete realized they were talking about his bar, and his thirsty soul thrummed in sordid anticipation.

"Well, it's not really the place for young women," he dutifully warned, holding the door for them. The bartender looked up in surprise at the flushed female faces approaching him, then recognized Peg and broke into a broad, warm smile of welcome.

"Margaret Eileen," Seamus greeted her. "My, but you're a ray of sweet Irish light come to brighten an old sinner's day. Thank the Lord she takes after her mother in looks, eh, Peter?"

"Hi, Mr. O'Brien. This is Leslie and Muffy and we just surprised Daddy. You wouldn't believe what a mess his apartment is in."

"But I would, darling. A man without a wife is like corned beef without cabbage."

Killharney scowled and signaled for a Dewar's.

"Oh my God, this is it, this is *the* booth! Oh God, I'm going to die!" Muffy squealed as she sat in Pete's favorite booth, reverently stroking the scarred table and bench.

"Aspiring writer," Pete explained as he tossed the scotch back and pointed for another with the same motion.

"Which one is the phone number for the transvestite hooker?"

"You're sitting on it."

"Peg, darling, you're turning into a beauty, you are," Seamus said, gracefully changing the subject. Killharney was surprised to see his daughter blush.

"Oh, Mr. O'Brien, go on with your blarney," she said, turning deep red.

Pete saw it was true. She was indeed a beautiful young woman. Perfect, creamy skin and thick dark hair, the contours of a stunning figure, and her mother's eyes that mixed mischief and innocence with the same clear gaze. He felt his chest seize in paternal pride, was overcome by boundless, useless love. He was almost drunk.

Suddenly an alternate idea for tomorrow's column began to form in his distracted mind. Horses and rubbish fires, studying the *Racing Form* over a pint of Night Train, the stench of burning varnish and rubber coloring a heated discussion over the finer points of thoroughbred breeding: the search for quality while trapped in a world devoid of it. Yes.

"Enough local color," Killharney announced. "Time for decent cappuccino."

Seamus stared at him.

"I think we should really be heading for the station," Leslie spoke up for the first time in the bar. "If we catch a cab, we can make the 5:15."

Muffy looked greatly disappointed, which made one out of four.

"I think that's best," Peg agreed.

Killharney flagged them a cab, slipped Peg a ten over her protests, gave her a fleeting kiss she deflected to the outer limits of her cheek, and watched the Checker disappear into the downtown flow of traffic. He felt dumb and bereft. He hadn't called her Margaret once.

What did she think of her slovenly, drunk father? And what else but Peg really mattered to him anymore?

Not Margie. She had grown tired of the time and attention Pete's career took from their marriage. After too many nights spent alone while Pete chased a new story—and there was always a new story—Margie had turned elsewhere for attention. *Many* elsewheres, as she had made it plain in the scene that followed Pete's finding her in a good-bye embrace outside a Manhattan hotel known for its matinee rates. And she was the only woman Killharney had ever loved. No longer.

And writing? Pete remembered a colleague once saying that desire was the first to go for reporters like themselves. And somewhere Pete had misplaced it, somewhere back during the divorce, perhaps. Or before. Maybe the routine of four columns a week had caught up with him, had exhausted his ability to see and describe the new. Now he so often settled for playing changes on his fictional stable of barflies, hustlers, court watchers, cops.

Wilson was right. Pete took cute details and stitched together columns utterly lacking in journalistic justification. Truth had degraded to style, a style easily and rightfully parodied. He had let the fire that once fueled his career fade to an unthreatening glimmer.

Pete wanted a new life. Or his old, indignant one back. This present Killharney quite frankly sucked.

He kicked the icicle off a slowly dripping hydrant and turned back into the stabbing wind, toward his filthy apartment and the shabby remnants of a once productive life. The bums were still huddled over the smoking drum, trying to warm themselves with garbage and the imagined memories of yesterday's winners. And so was Killharney.

Two

The subway hadn't been fun. Crowded and filthy, of course. But then Killharney was elbowed in the ear on the Times Square shuttle. At Grand Central, a woman getting off the Lexington Avenue express had turned around and slapped him, for a reason that only became clear from the leer on the fat face of the man pressed next to him, waiting to board the downtown train. A definite perpetrator. Happily, just before Fourteenth Street the subway blacked out, and Killharney took the opportunity to sink a knee into the creep, who remained doubled over as Pete stepped off.

Life was filled with such small victories. A column done before deadline. An unseen act of revenge. A controllable hangover. Payday. Yes, the signs were in place; it was going to be a good day.

Pete threaded through the crowds shuffling along the underground arcade lined with newsstands and locksmiths, shoemakers, florists, stores selling T-shirts and discount jewelry, and Pete's favorite, the popcorn stand that filled the passageway with the compelling odor of its inedible product.

Progress was slow because of the bottleneck caused by two bag ladies, one black, one white, who always positioned themselves across from one another in the aisle. The ancient black bag lady, huge in her dozen layers of rags and newsprint, was muttering her usual guttural imprecations, which would become frantic screams if anyone spoke to her. The second societal defeat, a younger, frighteningly skinny white woman with wild white hair, was marginally more approachable but still way over the edge. This morning, she was packing and unpacking a Bendel's shopping bag with shreds of foam rubber.

"I didn't do anything. How can they elevator me?" she asked no one. "Rich people don't die. It's their own fault. I'm taxi. Read my rights. Read me. I don't answer news."

"Good morning, Mildred," Pete said, giving her the daily dollar. She left off rambling to stare with suspicion at him, her face trembling with the effort of recognition. Then the light faded from her eyes.

"Your hands are caked with blood," she said, and scurried behind the levee of junk-stuffed bags she had built to keep the flood of pedestrians from overwhelming her.

Pete decided to ignore the curse. Some cigars are simply cigars, Freud said, which was good enough for Pete Killharney. He emerged from the subway into blinding sunlight streaming down Fourteenth Street, transforming the tacky thoroughfare into a canyon of sparkling brilliance, of clean edges and promise so bright it hurt to look. It was going to be a good day.

"Pete Killharney?"

He looked around, blinking stupidly as he battled the sun, finally bringing into focus a pretty redheaded woman, flushed with cold.

"No autographs, please," he said.

"Autographs? I'm freezing out here forty-five minutes waiting for you to show up for work. I've been approached twice to buy illicit drugs, been hit on a half-dozen times by businessmen looking for a morning quickie, and you tell me no autographs? Wilson will love this."

"I had no idea my editor had expanded into escort services."

"Our editor. Buy me a cup of coffee and I'll explain this mission of mercy."

Steering them toward the Greek coffee shop off Fourth Avenue, Pete sneaked appraising glances at his apparent colleague: shoulder-length red hair blown all to hell by the wind, arched eyebrows that gave her an expression of continual surprise, freckled pug nose, the beginnings of laugh lines at the corners of strikingly emerald eyes, down coat, good calves, sensible shoes. A daughter of Erin for sure. An unanticipated shiver of lust shook him as he held the door for her, and he wondered what she saw when she looked at him. A dissipated, middle-aged man who had kept her waiting.

"You should work on your first impressions," she said, glancing around the dingy Aegean Restaurant. "My name's Sheila McGrath and I think I'm frostbit."

They took the table farthest from the door. One of the Greek countermen sauntered over, swiped at the table with an evil-looking rag, and slapped down two plastic menus.

"Coffee," Sheila McGrath ordered.

"Two."

The Greek pursed his lips, swept up the menus, and brought back two cups of excellent coffee. Pete lit a Lucky, while the woman pulled out a photocopied proof sheet and tossed it to him.

"Read it," she said, and turned her attention to the hot coffee.

It was Bisceglia's "Ombudsman" column, his weekly recital of his fellow reporters' sins. Underneath the vastly flattering head shot of "The People's Watchdog," the headline read, HIT MAN KILLHARNEY ADDS ANOTHER NOTCH.

My fellow reporter, Pete Killharney, annually publishes the 'Killharney's Bar Hit List,' his personal and highly idiosyncratic choice of the ten worst New Yorkers. This heralded column is an entertaining mixture of justifiable outrage and potshots at his many enemies (one of whom has been dead for thirty years). The Hit List has become something of an institution, but Killharney himself would never claim for it the status of Final Word. Unfortunately, he doesn't have to.

Someone, some madman, has chosen Killharney's celebrated column as a shopping list for socially useful homicide.

"What the hell!" Pete bellowed, pounding his fist on the Formica and spilling his coffee. The woman deftly avoided the flow and smiled sweetly at the surly Greek until he came over and mopped up the mess. Livid, Killharney read on.

Three weeks ago, real estate developer Lorenzo Lopiccolo was murdered and violated. This past St. Patrick's Day, Congressman Michael Murry met a similarly gruesome end. Both men were members of the Killharney's Bar Hit List. Both men are now dead.

A coincidence? Consider this: both victims died as a result of neck or mouth wounds. Admittedly, different weapons were used, but both were effective silencers in the metaphorical as well as physical sense.

"Metaphorical fucking sense," Pete said. "I'll metaphor that wop rat bastard."
"Keep reading," Sheila suggested.

The postmortem mutilations likewise may have a symbolic element to them. Mr. Lopiccolo allegedly had a weakness for women. And on at least three separate occasions I've personally witnessed the late congressman in a state of acute inebriation. The atrocities can therefore be related to each victim's rumored failings.

"Acute inebriation," Pete repeated scornfully.
"Drunk," she explained.

Let me hasten to say that Killharney never aired the dead men's personal foibles. His indictments centered on what he took to be grave sins against the city. To Pete, Lopiccolo was a slumlord and Murry a politician on the take, and this paper's columnist has backed his judgments with enough solid evidence that he has never been successfully sued for libel.
But let me also stress that neither victim was ever tried and found guilty of these crimes. In the eyes of the law, these men were innocent. But that didn't matter to whoever took Killharney's column at face value, as a literal hit list. Two men, so far, have fallen prey to some psychopath whose warped sense of justice has been shaped by the Killharney's Bar Hit List. A bloodbath may have begun.
If I were one of the nine surviving members of the Hit List (a replacement for Lopiccolo was picked the night of his murder), I would fear for my life.

If I were Pete Killharney, I would seriously examine my possible culpability in two men's deaths.

And since I'm a reporter, I'm going to spend some time examining the responsibilities of my privileged profession. I hope every member of the Fourth Estate will do the same. We now all have blood on our hands.

Where had he heard that before?

The truth was, Pete had heard it all before in that part of his conscience which harbored dark inferences. He had suspected something was wrong when Wilson told him about Murry's murder, but to read his worst misgivings in his own newspaper struck with the force of personal ravishment.

"Why's that SOB out to nail me?" Killharney asked.

"He has company. All three networks are waiting outside the paper's headquarters to videotape your reaction. Which is why I'm here. Oh, and this."

She handed him a business card.

"What is it?"

"The paper's law firm. Brother Fitzwater is suing you for five million dollars."

"Libel?"

"Reckless endangerment."

"What?"

"And the police want to chat. A Lieutenant Dombowski, I believe he said."

"Jesus, you're a bundle of glad tidings."

"What I am is a reporter, seven years with the *Boston Globe*, two days with the *Apple*, and so far I've yet to see your face on premises. I volunteered for this errand thinking it might be my only chance of ever meeting the great Pete Killharney. My life is now complete." Then she leaned forward and touched his arm in an unexpected gesture of tenderness that disconcerted him. "I'm sorry for your trouble," she said. The universal Irish refrain.

"I wonder which disaster I should deal with first?"

"The lawyer. Five million is a lot of paydays."

"Payday? Sweet tears of the Virgin, what about my check? Margie will murder me."

"Margie?"

"My ex."

"Child support?"

"You got it."

Sheila reached into her handbag and passed him his check.

"It's an editor's job to stay a step ahead of the soap-opera lives of his reporters. Quoth J. M. Wilson," Sheila said, then narrowed her green eyes gravely. "Pete, what if it's true?"

Killharney felt two contradictory sparks flare in his heart. He felt first a powerful surge of affection that at an earlier age he would have called a crush. And, simultaneously, he was scared. People were going to die.

"Pete, great to see you again."

Hadden Pomerantz, Esq., escorted Killharney into his butternut-paneled office twice the size of Pete's studio. Pomerantz was five years older, looked ten years younger, and loathed Killharney, who had always returned the sentiment.

"Always a pleasure," Pete lied, sprawling in the Brancusi chair that clients were only supposed to admire. "Guess I'm stirring up more trouble for you."

Pomerantz chuckled. "We're not the ones being sued for five million. We get paid for bailing out you free birds. You know that song?"

"Song?"

" 'Free Bird.' My daughter plays it so much I asked

40

her if it was the new national anthem. And you know what she said?"

"No, Hadden, I don't."

"She said it was her personal national anthem. Can you understand that? And all those electric guitars screeching at each other. I swear, it makes me wish I hadn't eighty-sixed my Valium."

Killharney lit a Lucky and drew in an abrading lungful of smoke to bite through the unctuousness thickening the office air. A nonsmoker, Pomerantz refused to permit ashtrays in his office, so Pete let the match fall to the plush, pearl carpet. The lawyer didn't blink.

"We have a new twist this time. Not libel, no, you really hammered Fitzwater with that homo link. His program's been canceled. The Moral Majority shoved him overboard. His wife Dinah's filed for divorce; it seems she didn't appreciate having her first name used for one of the dummy corporations."

"I'll pray for his immortal soul. What about the fucking suit?"

Pomerantz picked up a tennis ball and began squeezing it rhythmically, popping the veins on his tanned, sports-hardened hand.

"Word has it his counsel has been directed to get you."

He switched hands.

"And?"

"And your colleague, Mr. Bisceglia, appears to have furnished what they obviously believe is a satisfactory pretext."

"Bullshit."

The lawyer ignored the interjection, returning the ball to the first hand.

"In his suit, Brother Fitzwater maintains that elevation to your Hit List has recklessly exposed him to the danger of unprovoked psychotic assault."

"Bullshit."

"It's a variation of the old 'shouting fire in a crowded theater' principle. Your right to publish stops short of advocating execution."

"Disregarding the fact that I've never advocated anyone's execution and that Bisceglia's full of crap, the bottom line is that I can write any goddamn thing I feel like, excluding provable libel, H-bomb secrets, and threats on the President's life."

"A rather sweeping claim, Pete." The bastard wanted him to squirm. "Sweeping and dubious."

"Christ, Hadden, this is a dime-a-dozen nuisance suit. One of your blow-dried Harvard drones could quash it in an afternoon and still have time to toot up."

"I'm flattered by your confidence in my firm," the lawyer said. He stood and walked over to a gleaming chrome exercise bike enthroned on a corner platform. He frowned as he tested the tension knob. Pomerantz always frowned before uttering banalities.

"Reckless endangerment," he intoned somberly. "It could be your Dunkirk. Your Dien Bien Phu. I'm not snowing you when I say they have some heavy wood. For starters, there are two brutal murders to grab the jury. Plus the religion angle to play for sympathy. Compared to preachers, reporters are about as popular with the general public as car salesmen or politicians."

"Or lawyers."

"And they have a couple of very slick lawyers gunning for you. The partners at Nashua, Stearns put their kids through college with their take from damage suits like this. Add the corroborating testimony of your fellow journalist, and Fitzwater may just have a case. Seriously. And I'm not even mentioning eight other possible litigants waiting for their shot at you."

Something wasn't being said. "What are you getting at?"

"Your publisher telexed this morning to personally express his deep concern over this situation."

Closer.

"What are you getting at, Hadden?"

The lawyer stroked the bicycle's worn leather seat with obvious affection. "The thing is, your columns are so damned inflammatory. A little help from you could make my job a whole lot easier."

"Help?"

"I know those lawyers. They're real sharks."

"Help, Hadden?"

"All I'm asking for is something to fight back with, to cover your Irish ass, if I may be blunt. A column or two about your journalistic principles, and I'd have some ammunition to prepare a defense for you. You believe in freedom of the press, right? First Amendment *uber Alles*. So help me out and cite some higher authority than your own damned prejudices. Is that such a terrible thing to ask?"

Killharney walked over and draped an arm around the lawyer's shoulder.

"Are you telling me the problem's bad enough to employ platitudes? Jesus, I had no idea. I naturally find this deeply troubling. And you can quote me."

Pomerantz kicked viciously down on the bike pedal, almost toppling the apparatus. He carefully righted the bicycle, strode back to the desk, and resumed his tennis-ball exercises. They weren't sufficient for self-control. Pomerantz went through a series of thumb-jabs into his temples, against his closed eyelids, along his cheekbones, and down his windpipe and the back of his neck. It apparently worked.

"Acupressure," he explained in a normal tone. "Releases the tension that accumulates in facial tissue. You should try it."

"I like tension."

The lawyer studied the tennis ball meditatively.

"It's not just the lawsuit. I know I'm not the ideal person to be giving you advice, but please listen to me a minute. You've just become a celebrity. You're now a media star. If you sail into all this with nothing but a few boilermakers and your ready supply of obscenities, you'll get eaten alive."

"You know, I'm half convinced you do care, Hadden, and you're not just barking when Murchison says bark. But I've got more going for me than a strong stomach and a gutter mouth. I work hard and I write the truth." He hoped. "And if the DA did his job a quarter as well, all those hateful scum would be behind bars instead of suing me."

"Says Pete Killharney."

"Fucking right. Take care of this dipshit suit for me. I have to go talk to a Polack."

Pomerantz didn't get up.

"Always a pleasure," he said.

"You remind me of a bad dream, you know that? I see you coming, I pinch myself, try and wake up."

Dombowski was not in a good mood.

"Didn't you get laid last night?" Pete asked sympathetically.

"Last night, last month," he answered, filling the duty-stained Mr. Coffee reservoir. A pool formed at the base of the appliance and quickly fanned out over the detective's desk.

"What the fuck!" he said, and disappeared for something to soak up the leak. Killharney took the moment to scan Murry's autopsy report. Cause of death, if he correctly read the turgid jargon, was the disintegration of the cerebellum. Some memory arose regarding the cerebellum and the mouth. A killing shot. That was it. Firing upward into the mouth was one of the nonreflex killing shots that precluded any reaction by the victim. Insert barrel, pull trigger, end of story.

"Goddamn cheap piece of shit," Dombowski said on his return with a stack of paper towels. "No wonder the fucking Japs are taking over. I got that for Christmas, can you believe it?"

"People seem willing to believe a lot less lately."

"Bisceglia's piece? Where'd I put that?"

The cop shook off the damp paper and studied the column admiringly.

" 'Metaphorical as well as physical sense,' " he quoted. "That's good. Why don't you write like that?"

"Pride."

Dombowski pulled out a soiled handkerchief and carefully swabbed each nostril, then remembered he was angry.

"So I get a call this morning from the commissioner's office. And to what do I owe the honor of such attention? To you, Killharney, to the fact I tell my priest at confession I know you. The commissioner's office suggests I talk to you about the Murry homicide."

"So talk."

"What the fuck's going on?"

"Good question," Pete said.

"You had any contact with the killer yet? Postcard? Thank-you note in the personals?"

"The only response so far is a call from you. And a five-million-dollar lawsuit."

"What's that?"

"Brother Fitzwater alleges he's been recklessly endangered."

"That shit-eater has more to worry about from bacteria than from any psycho."

Outside Dombowski's office, three hookers shivering from the cold were herded into the holding pen. They must have been working the lunch crowd and were probably grateful for the heated respite afforded by the arrest. Pete toyed with the idea of interviewing them, but the arrival of a black gentleman in a white, ankle-length, mink-trimmed leather coat canceled that. No pimp would let his fleet idle unless the meter was running, and Pete had yet to find a line on the expense sheet for such incidentals.

"What about a late valentine?" Dombowski prompted.

"You know I wouldn't withhold material evidence in a homicide."

"No, not Citizen Killharney."

"You got something you're not telling me?" Pete asked. "Matching prints, an eyewitness, anything to connect the two killings besides Bisceglia's drivel?"

"What I got are two stiffs and no killer. I don't give a fuck if you fingered them. But if you find out something, I want to hear it first. I don't want any more calls from the commissioner. You got that?"

"Cross my heart."

"Yeah, lift and separate." Dombowski stared despondently at his cracked coffeemaker. "You know that bottle of whiskey that buggered Murry?"

"I heard. Full."

"It *was* full. The killer twisted it until it cracked. Shredded his bowels."

"Jesus."

"This is one vicious nut we're after. And if you ask me, he ain't done yet. Willing to lay a pound note on it?"

Killharney met the detective's challenging glare. He silently shook his head.

The TV showed a very furtive-looking Killharney, beneath which the caption promised, COMING NEXT: HIT MAN KILLHARNEY.

"Jesus, Pete, you look like you just got caught with

your thing in some twelve-year-old's mouth," said Hanratty as Pete's scowl was replaced by an antacid ad.

"Guilty," seconded Svenson.

"A definite perpetrator," agreed Killharney. A swarm of reporters had caught up with him at Police Plaza after he had finished talking with Dombowski. He was not looking forward to viewing what resulted.

"Columnist Pete Killharney was questioned by the police today in their efforts to establish the connection between his notorious 'Killharney's Bar Hit List' and the recent deaths of two prominent New Yorkers, including the late Congressman Michael Murry, murdered last St. Patrick's Day on the steps of the Cathedral. Let's look."

Killharney filled the screen again, hemmed in by minicams and microphones as unseen voices bombarded him with questions.

"Do you believe the Lopiccolo and Murry murders are the result of their both being on your Hit List?" someone asked. The on-camera Killharney snorted derisively. Off camera, he winced at how his nervousness was coming across as conceit.

"The police say the allegation hasn't the support of a single known fact."

"Then why were they questioning you?"

"You can find out by reading tomorrow's *Apple*," said Pete with a wink, and began to edge away.

"What about the lawsuit filed against you today by Reverend Fitzwater?"

Persistent SOBs. This was where it went bad.

"That's *Brother* Fitzwater; the man's not an ordained minister. And it's [*Bleep*]."

"Did he say 'bullshit'?" asked Svenson.

"He said 'bullshit,' " Hanratty confirmed.

"But surely the name 'Hit List' implies a homicidal intent," a reporter prodded him.

"Do you want all those men dead?" another asked.

"Isn't it hypocritical of you to oppose the death penalty when you're calling for their murder?"

"Do you approve of torture?"

That did it.

"[*Bleep*] you, and—"

The clip ended abruptly.

"More after this," said the newscaster with a contented smile.

"What did you say?" asked Svenson.

"Drop it," said Pete.

"Come on, what did you say?"

"I said, 'Fuck you and fuck your mother too.' Are you happy now?"

"Jesus, Pete, my mother watches this station," complained Svenson.

"Then you can fill in the fucking blanks for her," Pete replied much too loudly. It was turning into a belligerent drunk. He had broken bones before in this type of mood, including his own.

"You watch your fucking mouth when you're talking about my mother," said Svenson threateningly.

"What do you expect?" asked Hanratty. "Guy makes the news, he thinks he's too big to take a little grief from his pals."

"And I promised myself I would remember the little people," Pete said, damping his unwarranted anger. "Seamus, a round for the bar." He threw down a twenty. "I think I better grab some air."

There was plenty to grab outside. New York was gripped by a late-March chill that made it hard to believe it was technically spring. The streets at dusk were filled with the last rush-hour crowds, people in transit from business to home, and the first theatergoers beginning to converge on Broadway.

So why was Killharney upset over newsmen doing

their jobs? The questions were the same he would have asked, the same type that he himself had repeatedly posed to strangers deemed newsworthy. It was the confusion of roles that threw him. He wasn't used to being news, nor had he ever seen himself on TV before. Ten years ago, at least, winning the Pulitzer didn't rate air time. But now he was the celebrity Pomerantz had warned him about this morning, the target of the business of news.

It sucked.

Pete was surprised to find he had wandered downtown past the very building that was Fitzwater's nemesis. The Ramjet Theater's marquee advertised its current feature, *Soldiers of Fortune*, in discreet block letters, with none of the lurid posters out front that the straight porn houses used to hook patrons. And the stairwell leading down to the Speedway Lounge was brightly lit but unmarked. The only sign of its orientation was a man leaning in the doorway with a shaved skull, leather jacket, and tight jeans displaying a bulge the size of a grapefruit. He stared at Killharney, not speaking, not sending out any signals whatsoever, as far as Pete could tell.

Killharney pondered the signals that went unspoken, the secrets shared with no outward show. Here was a whole society whose rituals went unnoticed, certainly unremarked upon by the industry that Pete was part of.

Business and signals. How did these disjointed thoughts fit together? What truth was trying to find its expression in this unlikely locale?

A man and woman walking arm in arm nearly pushed Killharney off the sidewalk.

"I'm so in love," the woman said to her companion, both of them oblivious of their discourtesy.

That was part of it, certainly. Simple acts of love—or rudeness—were beneath the notice of news. Murder

49

and defilement, yes. But most of the truly important actions of life remained obscure, invisible. A vast, private universe surrounded the small circles of sensationalism. The world went unreported.

It was an old truth that periodically depressed him. News was a pandering business, and Pete was part of it—subject now, as well as gatherer and commentator. And it sucked. So he did what he usually did when the present seemed sordid or unpleasantly complex. He went to a basketball game.

Far below, the Knicks were getting stomped by the Celtics, a meaningless game at the end of the regular season, after which Boston would go to the playoffs and the Knicks would go home. There was none of the electricity that used to crackle in the Garden when Bradley would swish from the corner or the Pearl would create new moves in the middle of a layup.

Still, that wasn't why Pete was ignoring the game. Earlier he had been down courtside, studying the teams' power forwards, his old position. He had earned all-conference honors his senior year at St. Bonaventure's by playing an intimidating physical style. But every pro on the floor was taller, stronger, and quicker than he ever was. Even the third string subs would have danced up his spine.

So much for recapturing the happy past.

Pete chose instead to work. Chasing thirstily after a beer vendor, Killharney had been surprised to find how rapidly the vendor moved, and how quickly he sold off a tray of beer. So Pete introduced himself and asked if he could tag along. The beer vendor shrugged, the city equivalent of enthusiastic agreement, and the interview proceeded between sales.

"Basketball bites it," the vendor said. "Almost as bad as the Ice Capades. That crowd, the only items moving are ice cream, cotton candy, that crap."

"What about Cracker Jack?" Killharney asked, writing in his new notebook, whose cover wasn't yet scarred or bent by careless stuffing into pockets. The vendor passed three beers down a row, got back money, sent change back, and they kept climbing down the steep steps of the upper tier.

"Beah! Beah heah!"

The call cut through the arena noise with flat explosions of sound.

"The pits," the vendor finally answered. "Cracker Jack, peanuts, popcorn, you don't make squat on them. They start you on peanuts, you know. If you can push peanuts, you can push anything."

He sold two more beers.

"Basketball's a shit crowd anyway. Hopped-up jungle bunnies probably jumped the subway turnstile to even get down here. Hockey, you get a classier group, suburban, you know? Not afraid to spend a little money."

The vendor sold four beers to the same man, who had a stack of at least two dozen empties leaning next to his seat.

"What's the best?" Pete asked.

"Best what? Best item? Best crowd? Beah heah!"

"Both."

"Depends on the vendor. There was a guy at Wrigley Field, sold sausage links. Red hots. Walking death, you'd think. The guy couldn't make change quick enough. How many?"

Two more beers were passed to outstretched hands. Only one remained, and the vendor turned up the stairs to fetch a full tray.

"So it depends. Souvenirs are good because of the

high per unit. But beer's the best. Which is why I sell it. I got seniority, you know."

The vendor sold the last beer and picked up the pace going back for more.

"My personal best was a Sunday doubleheader out at Shea, the summer the Mets won it all. August '69 it was, the Dodgers were in town, and it was hot. I mean *hot*. Jesus, people were stacked up outside the beer room waiting for the blue laws to change. I sold four trays without moving ten feet from the door."

"How much did you make?" Pete asked.

"Figure it out. Jumbo beers went for a buck fifty back then. Twenty-four to a tray, twenty-percent commission, so that makes seven-twenty per tray."

Killharney wrote down the figure on faith.

"That day, which was the best, remember, hot, pennant race, doubleheader so your selling time's doubled, I sold fifty-eight trays."

"That's . . ."

"Around three hundred and sixty bucks, less dues and linen."

They reached the beer room and joined the line waiting to get restocked.

"Tell me something," Pete asked. "You ever watch the games?"

"What? A bunch of jigaboos running around in their underwear?"

"I mean ever," Killharney said.

"This is a job, for Chrissakes. Stand around like some geek, you never sell anything."

"But never?" Pete pressed.

"Once," the vendor admitted at last, and his voice shed some of its bite as he relaxed into memory. "Out at Shea also. The day Seaver struck out nineteen against San Diego. It was one incredible performance, let me tell you. He'd get a strike, two strikes, and everybody would start stomping and clapping in time, just waiting, you know? We all knew what was coming. The batter knew. Seaver knew. The whole damn stadium knew. And then strike three. Next batter. It was great."

"I bet."

"There's something about a streak, you know? When it's going on, when you're in the middle of it, it's irresistible. You can't take your damn eyes off it."

Killharney was staggering. A definite weave. Cops and lawyers, seven-figure lawsuits, bloodthirsty reporters. Jesus, a couple of them had spotted him in Toots Shor's after the game, and Pete was forced to duck into the ladies' room to escape further scrutiny. He also didn't recall drinking all that much at Toots, or the Garden, or the County Cork either. The weave, however, was undeniable, despite the obscurity of its origin. And that was a bad sign, the unobserved drunk. A definite bad sign.

Pete knocked into an overflowing trashcan, spilling garbage and filling the empty street with the screech of tin on concrete. What was that woman's name from this morning?

At least he had the vendor piece in place. And there was something earlier that the interview fit into, some thought or previous scene. Was it the hookers? He sifted through the remembered details, the bruised eyes of one of the girls, the second's tangerine hot pants and lime-green Cuban heels, the third's chapped lips and oversized ears. Maybe it was merchandising, the pimp's shopworn prostitutes and the vendor's complaint about pushing popcorn.

Sheila. Sheila McGrath was the woman's name.

No, it didn't have anything to do with selling, or hookers, or anything like that. But what, then?

Fucking Bisceglia. Killharney reminded himself that the bald little wop had once ghosted a Kennedy conspiracy book. Conspiracy junkies never kicked the habit. Would the pimp be a conspiracy buff? The pimp wouldn't give two shits. His life was business and pleasure. The business of pleasure.

That was it, the thought that had earlier drained off his anger. The business of life went unnoticed. With the vendor interview, Killharney had captured an important part of an unimportant man's life and declared it newsworthy.

He was drunk.

As Pete reached the stoop of his Hell's Kitchen walkup, he was suddenly inundated by a terrifying flood of light.

"Mr. Killharney!" a female voice called. "We're speaking with columnist Peter Killharney."

Pete's eyes cleared enough to make out a thin, wire-haired woman in pancake makeup, with high cheekbones and a sweater sized to sell her breasts. Behind her, a TV minicam protruded from the open back doors of an unmarked van.

"I'm Melissa Sanchez of 'Newsmakers,' and our viewers want to know how you feel about some crazed killer using your famous 'Hit List' for socially useful homicide?"

That was Bisceglia's phrase. What was going on here?

The woman shoved the microphone in his face.

"Suck my cock," Killharney said, and turned and took the steps two at a time, catching his foot on the top of the stoop and crashing stupidly into the doorjamb. He fumbled for his keys, took too long unlocking the door, and finally heaved himself inside, slamming the door shut behind him.

Jesus Christ.

A bead of blood slid down his face from a cut some-where above the hairline. Wiping away the blood, shaking from the shock, and still drunk, Pete dragged himself up the four flights to his apartment. At least his Hit List had gone from notorious to famous. He couldn't decide whether that was an improvement. Probably not.

There was a brown paper bag outside his apartment door.

Killharney looked around suspiciously, alert to more surprises. He appeared to be alone, although he was beginning to see double. He gingerly raised the bag, sniffed at it, hefted it carefully. It seemed to hold a single hard object. Pete reached in carefully and pulled out a Bible.

"What the fuck?"

He brought the offering into his apartment and snapped on the overhead light, which promptly burned out. So, bleeding and drunk, he stood in his dark studio that smelled of something gone bad, and felt his guts twist around the fact that he had made a total ass of himself on TV for the second time that day.

But they couldn't use that clip with its obscenity, he comforted himself as he barked a shin while groping for the kitchen light.

"Fuck."

Unless they bleeped it. Which they surely would do. His stumbling retreat was the stuff of slow-motion playbacks.

"Shit."

Pete turned on the light, opened a Rolling Rock, settled himself on his bed with a groan of deliverance, and opened the unlikely gift.

The Illustrated Holy Bible, the title page read. And underneath, CONTAINING THE OLD AND NEW TESTA-

MENTS. And below that, PRESENTED TO. The space was blank. The frontispiece was one of the illustrations, Noah and the Ark. Noah was on deck, reaching out to the dove returning with the olive branch, rainbow in the background. Gen. 8:18.

Intrigued, Killharney thumbed through the bizarre gift, looking, of course, for more of the cheap color plates. "Joseph Sold by His Brethren," Gen. 37:27,28. "The Spies and the Grapes of Eschol," Num. 13:25–27. "The Death of Absalom," 2 Sam. 18:1–15. "And Absalom was riding upon his mule, and the mule went under the thick boughs of a great oak, and he was taken up between heaven and earth." Sure enough, the illustration had the dumb fucker hanging in full armor from a tree while what looked like a palomino galloped off in the distance.

There was a loose plate in the middle of the book, which Pete took out. "The Law Given on Sinai," Exod. 19; 20:1–17. Moses held the tablets with his head reverently bent, a shaft of light buttering his sunburned, bearded face. And there was a smear of red at the bottom of the page inserted into the book of Jeremiah, where various verses had also been highlighted in the same dull red.

"We lie down in our shame, and our confusion covereth us," Pete read out loud in a sonorous, slurred voice. "For we have sinned against the LORD our God, and have not obeyed the voice of the LORD our God." Jer. 3:25.

"Destruction upon destruction is cried; for the whole land is spoiled." Jer. 4:20.

"The lion is come up from his thicket, and the destroyer of the Gentiles is on his way." Jer. 6:7.

Cheerful thoughts, Pete judged. Then his eyes focused, and his mind cleared. The red highlighting was dried blood.

The phone rang. The Bible flew from Killharney's frightened hands. The nut had gotten past the locked outside door. He could be in the apartment right now, waiting to carve up Killharney. Sweating with fear, he picked up the receiver.

"Hi, it's Sheila McGrath. Hope I didn't wake you up."

"Hi, no," Pete said, and his drunken heart thumped once before he remembered his panic. He stared through the bathroom door at the closed shower curtain. It was the only place to hide.

"I thought you would like to know. This just came in. Another of your Hit List just caught it. Bengelsdorf, the nursing-home Hitler."

"Murdered?" he asked. The phone turned slippery from sweat.

"He was found in a dumpster out in Astoria, his throat stuffed solid with dollar bills. Oh, and he was gutted."

Killharney felt anger mix with the fear. He wasn't going to let some Bible-spouting psycho gut him without one hell of a fight. Did the curtain move? He was terrified. What a terrible way for even a Bengelsdorf to die.

"Well, that's all," Sheila said, after a long pause that she'd obviously expected Killharney to fill with thanks. "Except while you're working on your first impressions, you should also work on your second. Remember me in your prayers."

Pete lowered the phone without saying good-bye, then thought better of it. The killer was probably waiting for him to hang up before striking.

"No kidding," Pete said into the dead phone. "Tell me all about it." He tiptoed to the kitchen utensil drawer and searched among the spatulas and can openers for a large knife.

"That's hard to believe. I'm surprised," he continued the sham conversation. He didn't own a large knife. A rusty Swiss Army knife represented the apartment's most potent offensive threat.

"No, I want to hear everything."

He sidled toward the bathroom. Crouching, he inched to the shower stall, then flung aside the curtain and stabbed up at nothing whatsoever.

"Merciful Mother of God," Killharney swore. And the awfulness of the day, the anger and embarrassment and alcohol and fear all caught up with him, and Pete let himself slide down the grimy tile stall. The faulty shower head dripped on his face. He tasted blood. His own. He had never felt worse.

Three

Killharney's desk was invisible under a pink drift of message slips. A bundled stack of mail five inches thick leaned against a seven-inch pile of loose letters and telegrams. The "In" tray held his disconnected phone. And a Western Union delivery boy stood waiting, eyes glowing with methadone patience.

"Sign," he said.

Pete signed and ripped open the telegram.

"MUST TALK," the telegram read. "DON'T SELL MOVIE RIGHTS. CDB."

"Movie rights?" Killharney asked.

"Warhol says we'll all be famous for fifteen minutes," said Sheila, breezing past. His eyes followed.

"Thanks for the call last night," he called after her. She didn't acknowledge the belated thanks.

"Sunday-section meeting at eleven," called Bisceglia from a safe distance.

"So what?" Pete asked, meaning drop dead.

"Be there."

"Why?"

"Ask Wilson, Hit Man." And Bisceglia slouched behind his typewriter, suddenly busy.

Why were all his enemies cowards? Smart selection. Killharney fetched his phone and plugged it back in. It rang immediately.

"You atheist!" an old woman screamed at him when he answered. "You, you Antichrist! You should crawl back into your snake hole and die!"

Pete hung up. The phone rang again right away. He reached for a handful of mail before picking it up.

"Thanks for getting back to me, peabrain," said his friend, *Newsday* reporter Bob Toohey. Killharney noticed several pink slips with Toohey's name littered about. There was also a windowed envelope with what looked like a check inside.

"What's up?" Pete asked, tearing open the envelope.

"Three out of ten snuffed, and he asks what's up. Jesus, Pete, you ride this one right and you got Pulitzer number two in a walkover."

Inside the envelope was a check for ten thousand dollars, signed by Cash D. Bayer.

"Jesus Christ," he said, feeling lightheaded with avarice.

"I know, he's risen," said Toohey. "Look, I got ten minutes to make the Suffolk edition. Give me a lead and I'm gone."

Pete realized he had to write up the Bible discovery.

"You suggesting I go into the charity business, Toohey? You ever give me a lead on Margiotta or the milk-pricing scandal?"

"Remember Camden."

"I remember Camden. And I also remember that dog show in Mount Kisco better than I bet your wife does."

There was silence on the other end as Toohey tried to come up with a topper.

"Fuck you," Pete's old friend decided, and hung up. The phone rang again, earning him scowls from everyone near his desk. Pete understood why it had been yanked.

"Which do you want first, good news or bad?" asked his agent, Shorty.

"Bad."

"Thirteen papers canceled your column."

"Jesus." This was real money. Margie would eat his beating heart.

"The good news is thirty-eight subscribed."

"Jesus. Jesus." What was thirty-eight minus thirteen? Whatever it was represented post-divorce dollars.

"Let me tell you, Pete boy, this is the tip, just the foreskin of that old iceberg. I took a flyer on some bioengineering stock courtesy your Hit List."

"Why doesn't that cheer me up more, Shorty?"

"One man's blood money is another's ten percent. You should explore tax avoidance with your accountant."

"I don't have an accountant."

"The IRS loves you, Pete. Gotta run."

Pete realized he should have asked about the ten-thousand-dollar check. It looked legitimate.

The phone rang yet again, and Killharney unplugged it to the ironic, grateful cheers of the workers around him. He opened a letter.

"Go back to hell where you came from," read the unsigned message. Terse. Pete scanned another, a ten-page, single-spaced indictment of his journalistic sins, complete with footnotes. He chucked them both. A third hate letter followed. He did not seem to be making new friends. What if he cashed the check?

"Pssst," someone hissed. Pete looked up and saw a short, unshaven man lurking by the elevator bank. Fiji. The tout was trying to look invisible as he caught Pete's attention, no small feat for someone wearing lavender houndstooth slacks and a Dallas Cowboys souvenir sweatshirt. Pete walked over to his furtive source.

"Pete, shit, I been calling you all fucking morning," Fiji whined as he darted nervous eyes at everyone.

"Hit the double recently, Fiji? You haven't touched me for over a month."

"Matter of fact, I turned a trifecta out at Aqueduct last week."

The closest the gambler ever got to a racetrack was a phone booth to call his bookie.

"So what do you have for me?"

"Christ, we can't talk here," the tout pleaded, scanning the newsroom with his usual, twitchy apprehension.

"Usual place, then. Say, noon."

"I got something for you, Pete."

"You always have something for me."

"No, really. It's about your Hit List."

"Noon, Fiji."

As Pete joined the queue of coffee addicts clustered by the constantly brewing machine, he regarded the city room that had frightened Fiji so. It looked more pathetic than terrifying. The face of the big clock over the elevator remained cracked, the desks too decrepit to give away, the high, once-beautiful windows almost opaque from exterior grime. The new publisher's only changes were to rename the paper the *New York Apple*—a title that still caused Killharney to wince—and to install wall-to-wall orange shag carpeting, Murchison's visual hint to reporters to spend as little time as possible there. It had worked.

Some things don't change, Pete thought as he brought the coffee back to his desk. Or was it the same? He looked over his mail and messages, recalled the constantly ringing phone, and hadn't he caught a new type of curiosity in the coffee drinkers' sidelong glances? He had. Killharney was no longer just a colleague, he was now news, a target, and his fellow reporters smelled copy. Was that why Sheila was doing him favors?

Paranoia was a strong tonic this early in the day.

He fed a sheet of paper into his typewriter and banged out the Bible piece, leaving out the specific verses cited, as Dombowski had requested. He polished the copy and gave it a final read before submission. Short, clear, good lead, all the facts up front and concise. He was a reporter, by Jesus.

"Killharney!"

Wilson's summons silenced the room. Pete looked up at the clock and couldn't see the minute hand through the crack, which meant it was five after some hour. Eleven. He grabbed his notebook, column, and Bible insert, dropped the last two off at the copy desk, and arrived at the meeting an inexcusable five minutes late.

"Ladies and gentlemen, let us rise. Mr. Killharney has deigned to grant us audience," announced Wilson, standing with exaggerated ceremony. No one else moved. Pete slumped into the nearest empty chair.

"What were you doing yesterday?" Wilson asked.

"I was—"

"I know you were at the police station, because I saw it on TV. And I know you were drunk because I also saw *that* on TV. It appears I've been reduced to keeping up with my reporters by watching television."

Wilson took a pencil and calmly snapped it in two. A woman yelped.

"Mr. Bisceglia, please acquaint Mr. Killharney with the Sunday section's main feature."

Bisceglia shuffled his notes. Killharney's eyes narrowed in suspicion. Wilson sat back contentedly.

"Uh, well, it's the Hit List story, that is, the murders. What else?"

"The gravediggers' strike," Pete suggested.

"Settled," said Sheila.

"Continue, Mr. Bisceglia," Wilson said.

"It'll be a standard mix of news, background, and commentary. A short bio for each of the deceased, with date of nomination and, uh, qualifications. Plus a time line of the killings and a sidebar on previous mass murders. I'll cover the media slant."

"What media slant?" Pete asked with threat in his voice.

"Concern yourself with your contribution," Wilson ordered. "By which I refer to your column, brimming with its typical pellucid prose. Now, Mr. Bisceglia, get together with the art department on the graphics suggestions and space availability. Mr. Rossetti, you handle the head piece. Let's see. Ms. McGrath. I trust everyone has introduced himself to our newest addition to the city staff and extended her every professional courtesy. She comes to us from the *Globe* with a Nieman Fellowship and a very solid ream of clips. Ms. McGrath, pull the biographies from the morgue and shoehorn them into however many lines Mr. Bisceglia comes up with. And work up a box on the history of mass murderers: Caryl Chessman, Son of Sam, the Hillside Strangler. I want roughs on my desk by tomorrow AM. Questions?"

Questions weren't welcome after marching papers from Wilson, and none were forthcoming.

"Fine. Permit me, therefore, to introduce the other topic for the day. The *Apple* is about to enter the electronic age. How many of you ladies and gentlemen are familiar with a VDT?"

"Is that a new social disease?" asked Sheila.

"Close," Wilson answered, smiling. "Close."

"It'll cost you fifty."

Across from Killharney, two black men dressed in rags nonchalantly dealt glasses of crack while a nearby policeman stared at some pretty secretaries. Business as usual in Bryant Park. Stockboys smoking dope, lunch-hour lovers rubbing thighs, and every type of illegal drug and desire bought and sold. Killharney once wrote a column about this modern agora that had resulted in a highly publicized police sweep of the area, moving the trade twenty blocks south to Madison Square for about a month. The operation had been hailed as an unqualified success.

"Fifty," Fiji repeated, agitated by Killharney's inattention. "It's worth fifty."

"It's worth nothing to me right now," Pete said, though he peeled off a tenner to indicate good faith.

"Bengelsdorf," the tout responded as the money quickly disappeared.

"Bengelsdorf."

"You interested?"

"Am I interested in a stiff? No. I'm calling back that pound note."

"Hold on. Jesus. I figured you might have a personal stake in his death, you know, your Hit List thing. So I figured you might be interested in why he was snuffed."

"Talk, Fiji. Or refund."

"Bengelsdorf didn't only stiff the droolers and cripples at his nursing homes, you know. He cheaped his employees too."

"Bad habits are hard to break."

"Don't I fucking know. But a bunch of his staff belonged to Local 109."

"One of Marchetti's cousins runs that one, doesn't he?"

"You got it. About a year ago, Bengelsdorf missed two payrolls. The shop steward talked to the cousin, who talked to Bengelsdorf, who blamed it on his accountant. A week later he got the poor slob's right hand in the mail."

The gambler leaned toward him, enveloping Killharney with stale cigar breath and palpable greed. "Last month, Bengelsdorf missed another payroll. A computer error, he said this time."

"Jesus, well, I guess there's no right hands on a computer," Pete said. "So you're telling me his death can be traced to machine breakdown?"

"Fill in the blanks."

"And this is your Hit List killer tie-in?" Killharney said, devaluing the information to keep the price low.

The tout snorted.

"Hit List killer." He spat over the park rail toward some scratching pigeons. "Jesus, you guys don't really believe the shit you write, do you?"

Pete passed over a twenty.

"What are you throwing this away on?" he asked casually, his mind sifting the inferences of Fiji's tip.

"Passion's Folly in the fourth. Out of the Blue in the feature. A and D on the double. Can't miss."

"Sucker's talk, Fiji."

"You're walking around thinking you're Mister Big Shot Hit Man and you're calling *me* a sucker. Make me fucking laugh." With a last snort and spit, the gambler legged off to find his bookie.

So there wasn't any Hit List killer? No rampage? Then there wouldn't be more Sunday features, or new papers subscribing to his column, or ten-thousand-dollar checks arriving from strangers. Pete wasn't relieved.

Why not?

Because he was greedy and hungry for fame?

Of course. But more than that. He didn't believe it. It wasn't over. It was, with all the certainty that bad news and nightmares contain, just beginning.

The Whitney at six. The uptown Whitney. Pete had promised Margie he would meet Peg at the Madison Avenue entrance, stay as long as his daughter desired, feed her, and get her safely on a train to Westchester. He had handled harder schedules.

Pete strode purposefully across the *Apple*'s immense art deco lobby, dominated by a heroic bronze sculpture of John Peter Zenger. Beneath the fabled printer's foot-long quill, forever poised in dot-the-*i* flexion, stood Bisceglia and that TV newswoman, Melissa Sanchez.

Interesting.

Vinnie reached for her, touching her shoulder in a gesture of hesitant affection, then turned and left.

Interesting.

Melissa saw Killharney and walked over, smiling knowingly.

"What was that?" he asked, deeply wary.

"That was Vincent Bisceglia."

"What did he want?"

"He wanted me to give him the time of day."

"And?"

"I told him"—and her glance fell to Pete's crotch— "four-seventeen. I'm ready."

"Ready for what?" he asked, a little surprised by his stab at flirtation. She held the pause long enough to acknowledge the sexual undercurrent.

"Ready to take you up on your offer," she said.

"What offer?"

"Why, Pete Killharney, don't tell me you make a habit of asking every girl to suck your cock."

He remembered the night her camera crew ambushed him. His eyes dropped to her deep cleavage, then down to where the bleached silk of her slacks outlined the outer lips of her vagina. As he watched, she slowly slid a long, blood-red fingernail down between them.

"Oh," he said.

"It's my lunchtime," she said, "and I'm hungry."

An hour later, in a suite at the Carlyle, Pete idly

toyed with the attachments to her mammoth vibrator. He couldn't even guess what some of them were for.

"You've just ruined a perfectly good obscenity for me," he said, twanging a ten-inch, rubber-spiked accessory. "I'll never be able to tell another Red Sox fan to suck my cock without thinking of you."

"Score one for women's lib," Melissa said. She lightly brushed her nails across his scrotum, then wrapped both hands around his cock.

"Aren't you supposed to be soft?"

"Slow learner," he said, stroking her perfectly round ass until he touched the cord to the electrified butt plug that was still inserted. Another sexual first for him.

"Well let's not let it go to waste."

Melissa swung her leg over and straddled him, stuffing Pete back into her.

"Oh," she said, catching her breath in renewed enjoyment. "Oh yes. Oh God. Oh God. Oh, hurt me!" And she began grinding herself against him. Her nails clawed and pierced his shoulders. Pete pulled her arms apart, and she struggled in a parody of bondage.

"Let me go! Let me go!" she screamed in pleasure.

He let go and licked at her puckered nipples to distract her from doing him further damage. She pushed his head away brusquely. He tried again and managed to get one into his mouth.

"Bite it," she ordered. "Hard. Harder! Oh my God. The switch! The switch!" Her hand blindly pawed the satin sheets. Killharney reached out and snapped on the anal stimulator, and Melissa catapulted into a string of orgasms that threw them both off the bed, still connected. Pete's head hit the carpeted floor with a dull crack. Melissa didn't appear to notice and continued to heave against him, and Killharney surprised himself by coming again.

This time the dull ache from his overtaxed gonads finally quieted him, and he slid smoothly out.

"Oh, that was lovely," Melissa sighed as she wiped herself on the sheets. "If all men were like you, a girl wouldn't need marital aids." She padded off to the bidet, leaving Pete on the floor, sticky and stunned. He gingerly touched his shoulders and came away with blood.

"You come here often?" he asked, glancing around the lavish bedroom from ground level.

"Not usually that often," she laughed, buffing her thin thighs with an oversized towel. "The network keeps it for me. They know I need to relax before going on the air at night."

"Night? Christ, what time is it?"

"Quarter of six."

Pete jumped up and began yanking on clothes. "I'm supposed to meet my daughter in fifteen minutes."

"Peter Killharney, you cad. You didn't tell me you had another date lined up."

She reached over to zip him, then bent down and swirled her tongue around the head of his prick, slowly slipping it between her wet lips and down her humming throat. The arousal hurt, and Pete gently lifted her up and into a more restful embrace. Their tongues played together a bit, and she bit his lower lip. It hurt.

"I've really got to run," Pete said, stooping to tie his shoes.

"Come and run," Melissa said dreamily as she extended herself in a feline, erotic stretch. "What was that verse, by the way?" she asked from somewhere within her cloud of sexual satiety.

"Verse?"

"In the Bible you found." She gave a cavernous yawn.

"Revelations," he instinctively lied. "Listen, you want to get together again sometime and, uh, have lunch?"

"Call me," she said, and gave him a last, tongue-filled kiss. "You really do something for me, Pete."

"Thanks," he said, and stumbled out the door.

Waiting for the elevator, Killharney felt enormous relief at having ended nearly eight months of sexual abstinence. He also felt like he had just barely escaped permanent injury. He sniffed himself. He stank of sex. Killharney felt ridiculously proud.

"What's going on, Daddy?"

Peg's concentration bunched three small, vertical lines on her forehead as she moved closer to the Rauschenberg collage. Silk-screened images of factory smokestacks, Martin Luther King, fast cars, stoplights, all overlapped each other in the greasy neon greens, Day-Glo oranges, and cotton-candy raspberries that made up the unnatural palette of modern, commercial America. Killharney had no idea what was going on. He was thinking of oral sex.

"I think the artist might be asking the same question," he hedged. His daughter looked back at him, eyes shining with admiration.

"Of course, you're right," she said and moved to the next painting, a de Kooning still smelling of linseed oil. "Oh, I know him. I saw some of this series when I visited Leslie in Sag Harbor last summer."

"Leslie?"

"Statler-Stevenson. You met her. Her dad's got a summer place out there. They're divorced too, her parents. How about the Oyster Bar?"

"The what?"

He wasn't keeping up with his motormouth very well this evening, though so far he had managed to avoid that particular endearment in conversation.

"Dinner. Mom said you promised."

"I'm good for it. Implied partnership with psychos has turned out to be financially rewarding."

"God, that's yukky."

"I'm glad someone else thinks so too."

He patted her shoulder. Then, with a slight hesitation that reminded him of Bisceglia with Sanchez, he took her arm in his. For the past three years, Peg had shunned all physical contact between father and daughter. Her acceptance now, he hoped, signaled the end of that stage of adolescence.

"I'm going to have oyster stew," she announced, and a couple next to them turned and stared. They were both wearing puce jumpsuits, zippers open to the navel. The man slowly regarded Peg up and down, while the woman was satisfied with a single, sustained, drop-dead look.

"God, people are so weird," his daughter whispered. "I mean, if looks could kill. No, I didn't mean . . ." She left off in embarrassment.

"Let's get that stew," Pete suggested.

Pete had bluefish and four beers. Peg ate six raw bluepoints, oyster stew reefed with goldfish crackers, a big glass of milk, apple pie à la mode, and coffee.

"When did you start drinking coffee?" he asked as she poured three packets of sugar into her cup.

"Last summer. Leslie's dad had a cappuccino maker, and we drank it every morning while reading the *Times*. And the *Apple*, the days your column ran."

"I'm touched by your loyalty."

"Don't make fun of me," Peg said, and he remembered how easily she bruised, how often he had hurt her with throwaway lines.

"Sorry," he mumbled.

"Have you ever been out to the Hamptons?"

"Once. An old basketball teammate was getting married, and his best man set up a bachelor party at some cathouse in Montauk."

"Spare me the details," she said, unconsciously imitating her mother's voice and diction.

"But not since it's become a fashionable place for writers to swap lies and avoid working. I don't need that."

"Oh, Daddy, you're so close-minded sometimes. I mean, you really cherish your prejudices, and it doesn't make you a better person. I think it's gross."

He cherished his prejudices? He cherished his prejudices.

"Muffy asked me to ask you something."

"Muffy's the—"

"Don't say it, the fat one. And I don't want to ask, but I promised, so I will." She caught her breath and batted her eyes at Pete, another unknowing imitation of her mother when Margie played the supplicant.

"Ready."

"Would you come speak to the journalism class at school?"

"No."

"Oh."

"That was easy, huh?"

"Why not? Muffy will ask."

"Because I don't know what to say."

"But—"

"Peg, I have Hollywood hustlers trying to buy me. My lawyer tells me to polish my image. Reporters, old friends some of them, are threatening blackmail if I don't make my innermost thoughts public. My editor is expecting a column to explain it all. Now, your request is the most disinterested I've gotten, but I'm sorry, I just have to plead confusion. I don't know what I'm doing. I don't really know what's happening. According to the

72

headlines, I'm in the middle of a mass murder spree."

"Muffy thinks it's a cop."

"What?"

"The killer. She thinks it's some cop who's soured on the system and has decided to become judge and jury too."

Dombowski would love that theory.

"Whoever it is, three men have been killed in a little over a month. I don't want to do anything that might conceivably trigger more murders, and that includes shooting off my mouth to a journalism class. I'm scared, Peg."

"Me too, Daddy. For you."

She gave him a comforting smile of support as she toyed with her hair, the girl and woman mixed together.

"Are you dating?" he asked. She began to blush.

"Sure. Of course. I'm fifteen."

"Anybody special?" The blush deepened.

"There's a boy I've been seeing some. Too much, Mom says."

"Can you see too much of this boy?"

Peg blushed deeper still. Pete guessed not. He compared this young crush to his afternoon's device-assisted fuck session. Hormones versus electrified latex. A glance at his daughter gave that match to hormones.

"Well, you be careful with that heart of yours, because it holds my own as well."

"Oh Daddy, you sap."

"Runs in the family."

"Oh, Uncle Brendan called. Mom invited him for Easter dinner. I think she did it so he could help me with advanced algebra."

"Don't disparage your mother in front of such a receptive audience. Inviting my brother was an act of Christian charity. He doesn't get out of that seminary enough." Pete checked his watch. "Come on, you have a train to catch. Let's do this again soon."

"I'd like that, Daddy," Peg said and, unsolicited, pecked his cheekbone.

After seeing his daughter onto her train, Killharney passed a newsstand and was shocked to see his own face staring at him from the cover of the *National Enquirer.* It was an old picture, taken when he was slack-faced drunk. The headline promised, HIT MAN TELLS ALL! EXCLUSIVE INTERVIEW WITH KILLER KILLHARNEY!

"What the fuck?" he said, slapping a dollar down and opening the paper to the exclusive interview he had never given.

It was a hatchet job, consisting of miscellaneous lines lifted from his columns sprinkled among exaggerated versions of his many public quarrels. The more sensational scandals he had uncovered were displayed in a way that made the wrongdoings of others seem somehow his fault. More unflattering photographs broke up the inside layout.

Pete wondered if he could sue. No, he was fair game now, and the designation made feel him tired and dirty. He had lost control. More and more people would judge him based on the lies they read instead of the truth he wrote.

Killharney looked at his reflection in the dirty glass doors leading out to Lexington Avenue. Clownishly sad eyes stared back. Then, in a reflexive change of focus, he was staring through the glass at something hurtling his way. He threw himself backwards as the door shattered, spraying great shards of glass over his curled, cowering body.

He was still alive. Something had been thrown at him. That was it. From a car. Yes.

Pete carefully lifted a large triangle of glass off his

head, moved a larger fragment from his crotch. As passersby gawked, he sloughed off the sharp debris, miraculously unscathed. An old brick rested in the center of the wreckage.

"Damn drunk," someone behind him said.

A woman, staring, tripped over the brick, fell, gashed her hand open, and passed out from the sight of her own blood. People rushed to her assistance, leaving Killharney to stew in his own excrement. He had been scared shitless and not even nicked.

Four

"It ate it."

"Excuse me?"

Sensing trouble, the computer consultant hired to bring the *Apple* into the post-industrial age hurried over to the model office work station.

"It ate it," Pete repeated. "The computer ate my column."

"Had you been storing by paragraph?" the consultant asked. "No, I suppose not. That's in tomorrow's lesson."

"It ate tomorrow's column," Pete said, more incredulous than mad.

"Perhaps it's a programming bug," the computer whiz said. He eased Pete away from the screen and sat down lovingly at the keyboard. "Let me troubleshoot this little glitch right now."

"Bug? Glitch?" Pete sputtered. "That electronic SOB just swallowed my column. What the hell are you going to troubleshoot into the blank space beneath my picture in tomorrow's paper?" He stormed away from the empty tube, unnoticed by the happily preoccupied consultant.

His own desk, however, was no refuge. Each day more mail and telegrams and hand-delivered notes had arrived, until the pile of uninspected correspondence had begun to inspire avalanche jokes. And the unceasing stream of phone calls made it impossible for Killharney to check his sources or follow up on leads or otherwise do his job right. It was great to be a celebrity.

What was he going to do about tomorrow's column? Pete had finally pulled the prostitute piece together, the pimp bantering with the booking sergeant while the shivering hookers swapped shoptalk about johns to avoid and places to keep warm between tricks. Now it was gone in a gulp of the new word-processing system, and Pete was left with notes and the shaky memory of a few felicitous phrases.

There were worse losses. He had tried to work a change on the beer-vendor interview, pushing against his still-forming concept of expanding what was considered newsworthy, but the column hadn't worked. Fuzzy thinking, perhaps, or just a poor choice of subject matter. Whatever the reason, the only truths revealed were trivial. And now the column was gone. Was it a sign? The phone rang.

"Yeah," Killharney barked into it.

"Use that tone of voice on me, and I'll peddle my beneficence elsewhere," Sheila McGrath barked back. "You're already 0-for-2 in the impressions department."

Was there another victim? Please no.

"Sorry. The computer just swallowed a column."

"It got one of my stories yesterday. Consider it an offering to the gods of electronic productivity. Listen, I'm down at Police Plaza. They've just pulled in the Hit List killer."

"Who says?"

"He says. True confession time. Apparently it was quite a show. I thought you might want to check it out."

"Jesus, sure. I'm on my way. I owe you a lunch."

"You owe me dinner for this one, you cheap mick."

"It's a deal. Thanks."

He hung up. So that was that.

It was over.

Done.

Pete was appalled to find himself saddened by the news. People would stop dying horribly, and he already mourned his lost celebrity. Why was it so difficult to align ego with ethics? The truth was, New York needed the killer in custody; it was Pete's problem to get his feelings in order. But there was something else, something other than shame that he felt.

"Damn, damn, damn," Wilson said, appearing at Killharney's desk. "That TV reporter Sanchez just scooped us on the Bible verses."

"What verses?"

"The ones in your note from the killer, for God's sake, the ones you declined to print. She just announced that they're from Revelations."

"They aren't," Pete said, now knowing why he had lied to Melissa. The editor turned benign.

"This is great," Wilson said. "Get right on the refutation. Tie her in knots."

"She would probably love it, but I'm busy. They've just pulled in the killer."

"The Hit List killer?"

"A confession."

"I don't believe it," Wilson said, voicing Killharney's other reaction.

"Don't believe it," said one of Dombowski's sergeants.

"What's the story?" Pete asked, hiding the unworthy relief he felt behind the front of the dutiful reporter.

"A guy bursts into the Twentieth Precinct this morning screaming he's the one, he's the Hit List killer. Waving his arms around, sweating, swearing, splashing the front desk with what he's calling holy water, right?"

"Cute," said Pete.

"It was a fucking zoo, let me tell you. A couple of cops were trying to pin him down, he's twitching and drooling, the desk sergeant bends over to read him the Miranda card and gets the bridgework kicked out of his mouth. And all the time the nut's blithering on about Revelations. Revelations this, Revelations fucking that."

"TV inspiration means a cop's going to eat through a straw for a month."

"Tell it. If you want Dombowski, he's at the press conference."

"Press conference?"

"Down at Criminal Court. DA's announcing the formation of the Combined Hit List Task Force. FBI's entering the act."

"That must thrill Dombowski," Pete said. A few years ago the Feds had granted immunity to a murderer Dombowski had nailed. Six months later, under a newly minted identity, the "invaluable informant" had killed a cop in Omaha.

"You can fucking guess. He told me to send you over. Wants to talk to you afterwards. Oh, and he said to tell you about the Stars of David the nut claims he carved in the victims' foreheads."

"Thanks a lot."

Pete phoned in the scoop, minus the Stars of David, then trudged dutifully over to the Criminal Court building to attend the press conference. The floodlights behind the gray TV barricades were already on, and photographers and sound men were running their final equipment checks. Reporters joked and gossiped and scanned the advance transcript of the mayor's remarks for the hook to hang their stories on.

Reporters made Killharney uncomfortable lately. They all seemed devoted to questions he didn't want to ask or answer. Already he had drawn editorial ink from the *Times, Post, Inquirer, Des Moines Register.* "Meet The Press" wanted him. "Sixty Minutes" had put out feelers. And to date his most cogent response had been "Suck my cock." Pete suspected this was not entirely adequate.

The mayor entered and read the prepared speech in his tough-on-crime voice, abstaining from his typical, mindless, entertaining ad libs. Pete passed the time by making a paper airplane of the press release and sailing it into Vinnie Bisceglia's bald skull.

"Hi, Pete," Bisceglia said, rubbing the impact point.

"I'm the mayor of all the citizens," the mayor was saying in response to a *Voice* reporter's question about subway crime, "and I'm confident our police can catch this killer and clean up the subways and keep order when the Yankees win another pennant. Or the Mets."

"Why is that guy bringing up subways?" muttered Pete.

"Because two hundred transit police have been cut from next year's budget," Vinnie answered, "and the *Voice* has been hyping it all spring."

"Hell, I can top that," Pete said. "Mr. Mayor," he called out, "since you're so confident our own police can solve these local murders, how come the FBI is being brought in?"

Hizzoner saw his cue for show time.

"Hey, a congressman was one of this nut's victims. There might be a conspiracy or something involved. I mean, we can't just assume the killer is from New York. He might have crossed state lines, right?"

"Are you suggesting the killer's from Jersey?" asked Killharney, which got a laugh.

"I'm saying we should be grateful for whatever assistance Mr. Flaubert and his fellow agents can provide our great city. I don't know about you, but I think it's outrageous that some psychopath is bumping off people right and left."

"Which one's Flaubert?" Killharney asked Bisceglia.

"Brown suit, third from the right."

Professionally serious, the FBI agent endured the limelight with stoic rigidity, immobile but for a rhythmic tightening of his already clenched fists. Pete noticed that a mousy little man at the end of the line was also regarding Flaubert with some private amusement. Killharney nudged Vinnie and pointed, but the reporter shrugged his ignorance.

"What about reports of a confession?" asked someone toward the front. There went that scoop.

The police commissioner quickly stepped in front of the suddenly worried mayor. "It's true that we have, that there is a man in custody at this time who has confessed to the, uh, the Hit List slayings."

The room buzzed at the news, and cameras clicked and whirred to catch the moment of pronouncement.

"But," the commissioner continued, and the room quickly quieted, "but it appears at this time that he is probably not the, uh, the killer in question. The Hit List killer, that is. That is, he isn't. He isn't the Hit List killer."

Killharney looked at his watch. The *Apple*'s early edition with the confession story and the Bible-verse denial should just now be hitting the stands. Time for some fun.

"Is it true he's quoting Revelations?" Pete demanded.

"That's, uh, true, Mr. Killharney," admitted the commissioner.

"And isn't it also true that, contrary to some rumors reported on TV, the Book of Revelations is not the scripture previously quoted by the killer?"

"It wasn't Revelations, no."

Pete felt the bright warmness of TV lights being turned his way. He looked around and saw Melissa Sanchez pushing toward him through the crowd. She looked furious.

"Maybe we could get back to the task force," said the mayor from the front.

"I'd like to ask Mr. Killharney," Melissa shouted indignantly, "I'd like to ask Mr. Killharney how he feels about having the blood of three innocent men on his hands."

People gasped.

"And I'd like to ask Ms. Sanchez," Pete countered, expecting he would regret it later, "how many men she's fucked to get in front of that camera."

The newswoman launched herself at Killharney's face, claws first. Bisceglia stepped hastily between them and had his cheek raked by the blood-red nails. Her audio man tried to intercede, and the trailing cord of his microphone toppled a row of lightstands, which smashed with many small pops of exploding glass. In the confusion, Killharney slid sideways, backpedaled, and escaped the room unnoticed.

"What's going on in there?" asked the policeman by the door.

"Epileptic fit," Pete said, and the cop ran in to add to the chaos.

"Goddamn it, Killharney!" shouted Dombowski,

emerging from the room. "The commissioner's going to put my ass in a sling for this." Then, unable to help himself, the detective began to laugh. "Christ, though, it was worth it. Did you see the look on her face?"

"Think she'll sue?" asked Pete, as they crossed back to Dombowski's office.

"For what, telling tales out of school? Everyone knows she tricks for stories. That call I got from the commissioner? One of his flunkies was getting his bones rolled by guess who. I wonder which fuck fed her that Revelations garbage."

"Some boys will say anything," Pete said as they entered the cop's office. Did Dombowski know? He opened his notebook to gather some news the old-fashioned way. "So what are New York's finest doing to soothe the mayor's orchestrated outrage?"

"Jesus, we have six detective teams working three shifts round the clock, and you ask me what we're doing. Checking out your hate letters alone keeps a couple of guys busy."

"The price of popularity."

"Fuck popularity. You can't believe some of the weirdos crawling out of the cracks over this one. There's a group on Staten Island claiming responsibility that's been strangling cats and leaving them strewn around the tomb of Cornelius Vanderbilt."

"Kinky," Pete said, wincing. Could he use that?

"Plus everybody's got a theory. We're averaging over two hundred letters and phone calls a day: killer's a Vietnam vet, defrocked priest, ex-cop, ex-con, JDL, the guy down the hall, fucking name it and we've looked into it."

So they had considered the ex-cop angle.

"Oh, we found the vehicle used for your brick assault."

"And?"

"Stolen. Forensics found nine marijuana roaches on the floor, an empty Mr. Boston blackberry brandy bottle, and some glassine envelopes whose residue is still being analyzed."

"Sounds professional."

"Shit, I'm surprised one of them wasn't passed out in the backseat. Hate to spoil your paranoia, but it looks like this one belongs in the random violence category."

The detective stood and walked over to a gleaming new coffee machine.

"You like my new toy?" he asked. "Discount place on Chambers donated it after we nailed a stickup team that had hit them five times."

"You're Homicide, Dombowski. You don't have anything to do with that nickel-and-dime shit."

"I said the guy was grateful, not bright."

The phone rang.

"Homicide, Dombowski. Yeah, he's here. It's for you," the cop said, passing the phone. As he removed the filter sieve, the plastic handle snapped in two, spilling soggy grounds down his suit pants.

"Goddamn it! Goddamn it, I'll kill that little Persian ratfucker!" the detective swore.

"Hello," said Pete.

"Killharney," hissed a whispering voice. "The word came to Jeremiah, 'And the carcasses of this people shall be meat for the fowls of the heaven, and for the beasts of the earth, and none shall fray them away.' Have faith. I won't let us down."

The line went dead. Killharney's face went ashen.

"What's the matter with you?" asked Dombowski as he dabbed at the mess on his trouser leg.

"It was him," Pete murmured, certain it was so. "It was the killer."

So far the notebook's only blemish was a water ring left
by his shot glass. Killharney stubbed out a Lucky next
to seven others. Deadline for his Sunday-section column
was tomorrow, and he still didn't know what to say. The
County Cork regulars, sensitive to the delicate act of
creation taking place in their midst, were having a shouting match over who was the worse manager, Yogi Berra
or Bob Lemon.

"Pitchers never make good managers," Svenson
damned Hall of Famer Lemon. "They don't got a quick
enough hook. Pitcher's dying out there, the other team's
teeing off on the poor slob, and fucking Lemon in the
dugout's dreaming of when he used to be able to pull
the chain in the same situation. Boom! Three-run shot
to the upper deck."

"Yeah, but you're just not remembering how bad
Yogi was," Hanratty rejoined. "A fucking terrible manager."

"Bullshit," Svenson said. "He won two pennants, in
different leagues yet."

"And blew both World Series."

"Didn't blow any fucking Series. L.A. had Koufax
and Drysdale, and that '73 Oakland team was one of the
great ones."

Should Pete work the publicity angle, Killharney as
media darling? Could a darling be surly and obscene?
Dubious. Should he search his soul, as Bisceglia suggested, or proclaim the lofty rights of the press, as his
lawyer wanted? No and no.

Who was the killer? Why had he chosen the Hit List
for his guide to serial murder? No, those were the wrong
questions, the types everyone else seemed fascinated by.
The fact was people were dying. And the truth? Kill-

harney turned to Seamus to order another scotch, and found himself staring into Hanratty's hat.

"Pick," he ordered.

"What?"

"We forgot to tell you earlier, Pete. We got a pool going, thought you might want to buy in. Pound a pop."

"What's the game?" Pete asked, reaching for his wallet.

"Guess the next Hit List victim."

"You're kidding."

"I already pulled the reverend. Svenson's got the judge."

"Sanderson's a shoo-in, you ask me," Svenson said. "He's got a squad car parked in front of his apartment building, so I figure His Honor's as good as naked."

"I got the limey, Todd," Seamus put in.

"A long shot," judged Hanratty. "He left the country last week."

Killharney looked at Hanratty, at Svenson, at Seamus.

"I don't believe what I'm hearing," he said. "Are you guys serious?"

"Talk about long shots, pray you don't draw the Mafia don," suggested Seamus.

"Or that corporate guy, Kreutzer," added Svenson. "He's hired a whole private fucking army to guard his Greenwich estate."

"Personally, I think I got a lock on it," said Hanratty, "but I don't want to discourage your contribution."

"You can't be . . . I don't believe . . . Do you realize what the hell you're betting on?"

Hanratty's mouth twitched, Svenson's jaw tightened, Seamus stared at the fly-specked ceiling, then, no longer able to contain themselves, they all burst out laughing.

"Jesus, Pete, the look on your face," Svenson was finally able to get out as he wiped away tears of laughter.

"I thought for a minute you didn't love us anymore," Seamus said.

"You jerks," he answered appreciatively. "You really had me going there."

"Easy target," Hanratty said modestly.

And the column came to Pete.

"Thanks, fellas," he said, turning eagerly to his notebook, "I'm going to steal this."

"Is that gratitude?" Hanratty demanded, hobbling away on his VA-issue crutches. "Guy's looking a little down, we cheer him up, and he rips off our great native wit."

"I didn't know you had any Indian blood," Seamus said, bringing Pete over a full shot of Dewar's. "Compliments of the house."

Pete raised the glass, saluted the bar, and began to write:

The patrons of Killharney's Bar are all good Americans. "I lost a leg in the war," the Doughboy tells people, in case they haven't noticed. "I work for a living," brags the Swede. Yes, these are good Americans, all moral men. They wait till noon on Sunday to drink. And they conduct the Hit List Lottery as a blind drawing.

"It's the only fair way," Hiram sums up the sentiment as he passes me the hat and takes my ten dollars. "If it was first come, first pick, no one would choose the mob goon or McCann, right? So take a chance, and if yours is the next to go, you're up seventy bucks."

I reach in, my hand closes on a slip, I pull it out and read the name I've chosen. It's

"Is Pete Killharney here?" Pete heard a woman ask.

"No, ma'am, you got the wrong bar. You want the County Cork on Broadway and 181st Street," said Seamus, his standard lie for those who occasionally pieced together the bar's location from the columns.

"Sheila?" asked Pete, turning around. She looked deathly pale and was hugging her down coat to herself with tight, trembling arms.

"I had to sign away my organs to get this address from Wilson," she said in shaky apology.

"Sit down. Sit down. What are you drinking?"

"Nothing. Scotch, I guess," she said, sagging into the booth. Killharney signaled for two.

"What is it?" he asked.

"Judge Sanderson."

"Jesus." So Swenson was right about the uselessness of police protection. And Killharney had another Hit List death to deal with.

Seamus brought over the drinks, and Sheila sipped at hers. Then a tear slipped from her brilliant green eyes, and another, and a stream started to flow. Pete handed her his handkerchief, which she pressed to her eyes as she silently wept, and Pete suffered the helpless ache of watching a woman's tears. He glanced self-consciously around the bar and caught some stranger who had been knocking back beers all night snickering at Sheila's distress. But all the regulars kept their backs scrupulously turned away, and their natural compassion ennobled the County Cork. His warm, shabby, chosen refuge. Killharney was a little drunk.

"I'm acting like an idiot," Sheila sniffed, then blew her nose in a wet honk. Regaining control, she downed the drink in a gulp. Killharney nodded for more.

"So Sanderson finally drew the maximum, did he?" Pete asked, to help her start talking. "Maximum" Sanderson earned his nickname from handing down the stiffest sentences allowable under law to everyone but certain friends of certain friends.

"Hanged. The killer hanged him from a manhole into a sewer underneath Sutton Place. The body was covered with slime and dried stripes of blood from dozens, hundreds of whip cuts," and she started trembling again. Sheila grabbed the second drink and downed it as quickly as the first.

"What about the police escort?"

"They were both murdered. Shot in the head as they sat in their squad car outside his house."

"Christ, the cops must be going crazy, with two of their own gunned down. When did this happen?"

"An hour or two ago." Sheila paused. "Pete, the killer called. Called you. I . . . I talked to him."

"You what?" A shock of anger and protective fear swept down his suddenly sweat-lined backbone.

"You weren't there, and he wanted to talk, so I let him."

"Sweet blood of our Savior, what did he say?"

"He rambled at first, Bible quotes about foulness and judgment. Then he whispered, 'Sanderson' "—Sheila imitated the hiss Killharney remembered too well from his own call—"and he told me where to find him, and I called the police and met them at Sutton Place, where they were just hauling up the corpse. Your friend Dombowski says Sanderson had been deliberately strangled. The neck wasn't broken like a typical hanging. Instead, the killer had tightened the noose until it crushed the windpipe. God, it's just so sadistic, so vicious."

Sheila started to shake. Pete fetched more scotch, which she drank off while twisting and untwisting the saturated handkerchief.

"I've probably seen a hundred stiffs during my career, but taking that call from the killer, then seeing what he had done right before talking to me, it's just too close, somehow. I can't distance myself. I can't . . ."

She began to cry again. Pete decided it was not the time to mention the distinct possibility that she had put herself in mortal danger by chatting with a psychopath.

"Don't cry," he said lamely, covering her hand with his own. You give lousy solace, Margie had once told him. "It's all right now," he said, over and over, stroking her cold, shaking hand. "It's all right. It's all right."

The drunk was beginning to fade into a hangover, turning his insomnia into a waking purgatory. His body felt like a bag of toxins, stomach uncertain, head ballooning painfully, mouth dry and tasting as if something furry had died in it.

Sheila had the right idea. He regarded her sleeping face buried deep in dreams—deeper, he prayed, than the nightmarish visions she had witnessed earlier.

Pete wondered what might have happened if she hadn't passed out in the taxi before giving him her address. He had taken her to his apartment, carried her up the three flights, undressed her to panties and bra, slipped her carefully between the dingy sheets.

Killharney the humanitarian. He wanted her desperately.

Why did he suddenly seem to be attracting beautiful women? Admittedly, Sanchez had a clear motive: She fucked for information. But what about Sheila, who had done nothing but help him since they met? What were her motives? Maybe she was also just cultivating a promising source. Maybe she liked him. Maybe there was no fool like an old one.

Sighing, Pete brought himself and a bottle of scotch to the waiting typewriter. He fed in paper, lit a Lucky, opened his notebook to the column in progress, and typed in what he had already written, up to where he had left off: ". . . the name I've chosen. It's . . ."

He ended the paragraph with ellipsis and started another.

How many readers want to know my pick? How many think my chance draw will determine the fate of one of the Hit List members? How many think it doesn't matter, that they all deserve whatever befalls them? ("Shoot them all!" shouts the Swede.) It all gets very ghoulish.

Six men have been murdered, yet almost everything surrounding these killings has had as much to do with morality as the Doughboy's random lottery. Good and evil disappear beneath the surface sensationalism. Well, I think that stinks.

The Killharney's Bar Hit List was created to censure men whose acts have wrought evil on the City of New York. They've been corrupt, cruel, venal, vainglorious. They thrive on their sins and it sickens me, so I proclaim their names and wrongs to a city that has permitted them to remain blameless.

Now six are dead. Murdered. Wrong on wrong. Evil on evil. And what has been the result?

Well, I've made money. Newspapers line up to subscribe to my column. I get unsolicited checks in the mail. I've also become a celebrity: phone calls, fan letters, speaking requests, surprise interviews, all of it.

Six men are dead.

I'm not alone in benefiting, of course. Others have likewise flourished during the bloodbath, selling papers, furthering careers. There's plenty of profit and prestige to go around.

Six men have been murdered.

But this is not a career break. This is not a media opportunity. This is murder, the first and worst sin that man can commit against man. Forget the juicy particulars. There is a killer dealing death, and I implore all moral men to join me in calling for the slaughter to stop. If anyone has a clue, any idea whatsoever that might hasten an end to this carnage, notify the police. If the killer is reading this, if my words do have some effect on your actions, I say, Stop! Stop killing. It's a crime and a sin and must cease. The killing must stop.

The clock below the Boss Tweed portrait strikes twelve, the Sunday signal to belly up to Killharney's Bar. Thirsty Doughboy demands to know my pick. I check my choice and shake my head. I've chosen "Not The" McCann, who's been dead thirty years.

Pete read over the column, crossing out phrases, marking others as "Awk" or "Lame" for morning revision. The bottle of scotch had been emptied during the writing, the cigarettes all smoked. He felt drained. As he reread the column a third time, he slumped closer and closer to the typewriter till his forehead rested against the cool, type-rutted platen.

"Water."

Pete awoke, face mashed against the typewriter, thirsty beyond hope. He lifted his head, and the skin came away with a dull, smacking sound. Joints frozen for hours in the ridiculous pose raised immediate and ferocious protest. What was he doing here? The column.

"Water," he heard again. Sheila. Carefully, painfully, he swiveled his throbbing head around. And there she was, in the underwear he had stripped her to, picking through his moss garden of a sink for a salvageable glass.

"Paper cups," he croaked. "Refrigerator. Top."

Sheila padded to the fridge, tidy breasts bouncing jauntily under the translucent bra. She excavated a cup and turned on the tap, as Killharney managed with considerable agony to heave himself onto the bed. Gulping sounds reminded him he was perishing from thirst, and he listened in helpless desperation as she drank cup after cup. Then—miraculous deliverance!—a dripping cup of the same was hovering above him. He downed it in a swallow.

"What happened to your face?" she asked, fetching a refill.

"I fell asleep on the typewriter."

"Does that work?"

Killharney looked over at the finished column.

"Apparently," he said. "Thanks for the water."

"I see my shoes and coat, but did you happen to notice a spare dress anywhere?"

"On a hanger in the shower. It got wrinkled in transit, so I steamed up the bathroom and hung it there."

"I'm impressed. The apartment doesn't look like its tenant regularly reads 'Hints from Heloise.' "

Sheila went into the bathroom and came out five minutes later, dressed and washed and looking ready for a full day's work. Pete wondered what the etiquette was in such situations. Should he offer to invite her back sometime when she was conscious?

"We new kids on the block have to clock in on time," Sheila said, bending over to give him a quick kiss. "Thank you for taking care of me last night, Pete. I'm glad that one of my longtime heroes turns out to be a gentleman in real life."

And she left. Killharney the hero? He had never been accused of that before.

The phone rang.

"How would you like a hundred thousand dollars?" a cheerful, determined voice asked.

"How would you like to suck my cock?" Killharney answered with the obscenity Melissa had supposedly spoiled for him.

Sheila! his heart called to the empty room. Come back!

Five

The Monday after the Hit List feature, Killharney left his Hell's Kitchen tenement to confront a steady drizzle and a gunmetal gray Bentley waiting at the bottom of the stoop. Murchison. Only a foreigner or a pimp would bring a Bentley west of Eighth Avenue. The chauffeur hopped out and held the door, and as Pete stepped in he noticed the Delahanty kid trotting off with the opposite side's hubcaps. Murchison was getting off easy.

"Peter, Peter, my lad," the *Apple*'s publisher said, his voice a blend of Jamaican lilt and Scottish burr, its pleasant, comforting cadence masking the most ruthless business mind Killharney had ever encountered in the newspaper industry.

"Early in the day to be slumming, isn't it, Angus?"

"It's been too long since we've swapped insults, eh?" Murchison smiled, showing teeth unmistakedly carnivorous. "A circuit around the park, Harrison."

"Yes, Sir Angus," the chauffeur replied, and the limousine headed toward Columbus Circle.

"*Sir* Angus?" Pete asked.

"You didn't hear? I finally got the slap of the sword from Queen Bess. Harrison's been applying the honorific religiously."

"Captain of industry, are you?"

"Given the caliber of my impoverished English competitors, I'm a bleeding admiral."

The Bentley powered past the oncoming cars into and around the circle, then smoothly cut across into Central Park.

"I'm sure you're as pleased as I over yesterday's Hit List spread," Murchison continued amiably. When Killharney didn't automatically assent, he chuckled. "Aye, lad, don't think I can't hear those dreadful thoughts of yours. It's the centerfold spread with the victims' before-and-after pics, isn't it?"

"I didn't know you had a man at the morgue."

"I doubt I do any longer. He's sure to be cashiered, don't you think? Greedy lad, but a weak sense of self-preservation. Not like us, Peter. The lottery hook was rather good, by the way. Have you seen this?"

The publisher passed over the *Star*, opened to a half-page picture of Killharney passed out in a corner of the Roosevelt Grill. The caption read, "Hit Man Killharney: Next to Go?" It was another smear masquerading as an exclusive interview in which Pete revealed that he dreamt about dying soon.

"Who reads this shit, anyway?" Pete said, depressing the electric window enough to eject the offensive rag.

"Millions," replied Murchison. "I particularly liked the bit about you returning from the loo with piss on your shoes."

"What do you want?"

"Pragmatic Americans. It's good to be stateside again."

"We're being followed, Sir Angus," Harrison announced. "Tan Chevrolet Citation. Two occupants."

"Well, lose them."

The chauffeur obediently swung the car sharply to the left, over the curb, across the sidewalk, and down a pedestrian path toward the Central Park band shell. The Chevy followed their detour.

"I'm just protecting my investments," Murchison blithely went on, oblivious of the old men and carriage-pushing mothers fleeing from the Bentley's charge. "A month ago you were an overpaid employee. You have since become, shall we say, bankable."

"You have me under contract."

"Aye, I do, lad," he purred, "which is why I want you happy. Wilson tells me the two of you have tiffs."

"We tiff, yes."

"A good editor, Wilson. Too ethical for my tastes, but a newspaperman to the marrow. He says he's unhappy with you. Are you unhappy with him?" Pete didn't answer. "Or with yourself?"

"Jesus, I'm being analyzed in the back of a Bentley."

The limousine squeezed between two hot dog carts and through the police barricade at the bottom of the park, drove a street mime into the gutter, cut off a hansom cab, and shot past the Plaza Hotel. The Chevy remained behind, blocked by the hansom's terrified horse.

"Well done," said Murchison. "Downtown."

"Yes, Sir Angus. And thank you."

"I'm no stranger to vituperation," the publisher said as they sped down Fifth Avenue. "When I expanded from Jamaica to Fleet Street, I took more than a little abuse from my peers: "bastard peddler of boobs and blasphemy,' 'wet nurse of the water closet.' I rather cherish that one, actually."

Ahead of them, a Cadillac with Texas plates bounced through a pothole and fishtailed into a cab. Harrison avoided the developing pileup with a deft flick of his steering wrist.

"Are your rides always this much fun?" Pete asked.

"You've got to keep life interesting. I don't mind the occasional scuffle or squeeze if I can get what I wish. Give them an inch and take the mile, I say. And I'll keep taking till fancy flees."

"And what then? What if the old satisfactions no longer inspire sufficient zeal?"

"Then your enemies will grind you to dust."

The Bentley pulled up in front of the *Apple* building, and passersby tried vainly to peer through the smoked glass. "Gangsters," one muttered authoritatively.

"Wilson's right, of course. You've been coasting for months," Murchison said. Killharney didn't bother to argue. "Take some advice, then, from a bastard son of a bastard. Play to your strengths. If you come up with a scoop, if you break this story, you'll be everyone's hero, including your own. Get a line on this killer and everything else will fall into place."

"I'll take it under advisement."

What did Murchison want? He didn't fly three thousand miles to give a pep talk. Killharney knew from experience that the publisher was usually a step or two in front of Pete's worst suspicions.

"I'm sure you will," he said as Harrison held the door. "I have your best interests at heart."

"And your own."

"Aye, my father might have sired bastards but he didn't spawn any fools. Trust me."

Never.

"Always," Pete said, climbing out. "By the way, you're down two hubcaps. Next time you want to chat, pick me up in a tank."

Murchison opened the other door. His face clouded with flouted Scottish parsimony. He slammed the door on Killharney's grin, and the limousine was gone in a flash of gunmetal gray. Its space was instantly taken by a tan Chevrolet Citation. Two men stepped out, official-looking, and familiar.

"Peter Killharney," one said. It wasn't a question. "Flaubert. FBI. Please come with us." It wasn't a request.

The room at 26 Federal Plaza was small, white, furnished in GSA-issue conference table and chairs, its only adornment framed photographs of the President and the FBI Director.

"That was some show you put on at the press conference, Hit Man," Flaubert said as Killharney inspected his credentials. The second man hadn't bothered to produce any on Pete's request, hadn't yet spoken, in fact. "The brawling reporter," the agent continued contemptuously. "You're a walking cliché, Killharney, a dinosaur. And don't think we've forgotten."

What Flaubert hadn't forgotten were the columns Pete wrote on the FBI's illegal wiretaps and break-ins of the Socialist Workers Party offices during the Vietnam War. Pete had insisted that anyone sworn to uphold the law could not break it for expediency's sake. The columns hadn't played well in law enforcement circles.

"You and Dumbo," Killharney retorted, "great memories both."

Flaubert placed his angry face an inch from Pete's.

"You come across with answers or we'll have your balls for breakfast," he threatened. The other man laid a hand on the agent's shoulder and gently drew him back.

"I think that Mr. Flaubert is, in his own fashion, asking for your assistance," he said in a soft, neutral voice.

"Who the hell are you?" Killharney asked to break

the good guy/bad guy role-playing. "And what the hell do you want?"

"Henry Baumann," he replied, passing Pete a card with his name and a Washington phone number on it. "And I want to find a killer. Any information you could give us would be greatly appreciated."

"Have you talked with the NYPD?"

"Yes, certainly."

"Then you have all the information I know."

Flaubert's face returned to its challenging proximity.

"You think we're that stupid? I'm warning you, we're an inch away from booking you on obstruction of justice. Any more horseshit and it's fingerprint and photo time."

Obstruction? What were they talking about? No, wrong question.

"What do you want?" Pete asked.

"General cooperation, keep the lines of communication open," Baumann said smoothly, as if no threat had just been issued. "Perhaps regular meetings. We'd also like to take a look at your notes on each of the Hit List members. Perhaps there's something a second set of eyes will notice."

Flaubert pulled out two envelopes.

"This is your obstruction indictment," he said with gleeful malice, "and this is a subpoena for all your Hit List notes."

"I burn my notes. It's public knowledge."

"Yes, I've read the columns about your annual Halloween bonfire," Baumann said. " 'The ghosts of forgotten phrases set free by flame to haunt the goblins that prey on the weak and silent of the city.' Of course we don't believe it."

"Believe it."

"I'm calling the marshals," Flaubert said.

"Call my lawyer while you're at it, and listen to him

laugh," Pete said, standing up. "Obstruction of justice. Did you really think I'd fall for that one?"

Flaubert handed him an envelope. It was a subpoena for all of Killharney's Hit List notes.

"And the other?" he asked, trying to appear unshaken.

"A bluff," Baumann admitted. "We need your cooperation. This murderer is an extremely dangerous man, a mad dog, and we've got to find a way to leash him. You do realize your colleague, Ms. McGrath, has placed herself in jeopardy by speaking with him."

They were pushing all the buttons. What was so important about his notes? What did he know?

"I know that," Pete said. "And I know that this subpoena is a quick court appearance from being quashed. So unless you let me in on whatever you're fishing for in my nonexistent notes, I believe we're finished with this particular line of communication." He headed for the door.

"You can reach me at the number on my card anytime, Mr. Killharney," Baumann called after him. "Please don't hesitate to call."

"Count on it," Pete said, and bounced off the still-truculent Flaubert blocking the door.

"I'm going to have your ass," he promised. "Your type makes me sick."

"So puke," Pete said and left.

After the morning's two interviews, Killharney's cluttered desk seemed a refuge. What did they want, Murchison and the FBI? And was there some connection between the two, Murchison setting him up for the interrogation? The publisher had lost the agents. Easily. But he would never collude with the government against one of his own reporters. Would he?

The more important question was why they wanted

his notes. Pete assumed they knew more than they were willing to tell him, but all the FBI could know for certain about his notes was that they contained information about Hit List members. So whatever they knew concerned someone on the Hit List. Who?

On his desk, a handwritten note sat on top of a pile of telegrams. It read, "You still owe me a dinner—how about Jams at seven? Sheila." Pete grinned like a fool and opened a telegram. It was an invitation from the ten-thousand-dollar producer for lunch at "21." A second telegram asked, DOES YOUR WIFE KNOW WHERE YOU EAT LATE LUNCHES? Killharney guffawed, and Vinnie Bisceglia stopped to stare at the outburst.

"The blackmailing bitch doesn't even know I'm divorced," Pete said, tossing the telegram to him.

"Killharney!"

Wilson's bark easily cleared the soft keyboard clicking and cooling-fan hum of the newsroom VDTs. The editor came out to meet Pete, as common as the mountain coming to Mohammed.

"You've got visitors," he announced, and sat himself with heavy dignity at the now-obsolete copy desk. Pete peered toward Wilson's doorless office and saw Dombowski and two other men, one a stranger and the other— oh Jesus, Scherer.

Host of a late-night radio talk show, Art Scherer was an abrasive cretin with an ego and intellect to match the morons who called him to rant about welfare cheats, UFOs, and whether DiMaggio was a better fielder than Mays. Be sure with Scherer. Pete turned to escape.

"Get your Irish ass in here, Killharney," Dombowski bellowed. "We've been waiting over an hour for you to show. They really pay you for working these hours?"

Pete put on his happy idiot grin and went to face the day's third unwanted confrontation.

"This is Detective Ho, the police psychologist assigned to the task force," Dombowski introduced Pete to the nearsighted, nervous Asian. "And you know Artie Scherer."

"How's it hanging?" greeted Scherer. The idiot grin held.

"Sit down, for Chrissakes," Dombowski said. "And listen. We got a plan."

"No," Pete said.

"We're going to trap the killer."

"No."

"We're going to put you on Art's show, you say some provocative shit—Ho will script it out for you—and then we open the lines, the killer calls up to chat, we run a trace, and two minutes later he's in custody."

"No."

"You know how fast those electronic tracers are nowadays, practically simultaneous."

"Like the orgasm," Scherer said.

"Mr. Killharney, may I call you Pete?" the psychologist asked with that unctuous professional calm Pete despised. "Pete, I've worked up a psycho-forensic profile of the client. Would you care to comment on my construction?"

"No."

Scherer worked a sigh long enough to show he knew it was futile. Dombowski, however, was undeterred.

"Shut your fucking mouth and hear Ho out," he said.

"I suppose I don't need to point out that we're dealing with a very seriously disturbed individual," the psychologist pointed out.

That out-idioted Killharney.

"You're describing someone who's shot, strangled, throttled, flogged, castrated, buggered, and gutted six men as seriously disturbed?"

"Very," Ho said. "Morphologically, I would categorize it as an overcompensated superego, a gross perversion of the inner policeman, the, ah, ethical sense. It's not unlike certain religious fanatics who are willing to wage war to further supposedly pacific theologies."

"Kill for Christ," Scherer explained.

"Just so," said Ho. "And from the underlined parts of the Bible you received, I infer a strong religious upbringing or training. An ex-seminarian, perhaps, or a fundamentalist minister's son."

"We're following up on it," Dombowski told Pete with a straight face.

"Whatever the causative factors, his psychosis appears ineluctably fixated on you. He regards your relationship as that of prophet and follower, of messiah and avenging angel, of father and son."

"I don't have a son," Pete said, but the shrink was immune to irony.

"He may not have a father either," Ho said, excited by the idea. "Paternity notwithstanding, my profile concludes the killer should be enormously sensitive to your opinion. I'm sure he was confused by your column Sunday. He must want to talk with you, to explain himself, to find out why you don't approve. Now is the time to give him that opportunity."

"Then put the murdering fuck away," Dombowski said.

Through the doorway, Pete saw Sheila get off the elevator, and he gave her an affirmative nod about the dinner. She grinned.

"If you go on Mr. Scherer's show and express your disapprobation, much like a father scolding his wayward son, well, we're hoping to get feedback."

"Feedback?" Pete sputtered, thinking of Bengelsdorf stuffed to death with dollars. He turned angrily to Dombowski. "That's great. That's just fucking great. You want me to go on this jerk's show and put my life on the line for some pinhead's textbook theories. So tell me, what happens if I get the homicidal psycho pissed at me and you don't happen to nail him?"

"Pete," Ho answered, "it's only a matter of time before disenchantment sets in. If it hasn't already. A line from your column, a chance remark quoted or misquoted in other media, and suddenly you're going to be the enemy."

"Enemy?" Pete didn't like that.

"It's unavoidable. For now, he sees you as a messiah, perforce a perfect, omniscient being. Do you think you can continue to meet that expectation?"

Dombowski snorted derisively.

"Just as he's transferred onto you his craving for moral superiority, he'll eventually transfer his rage. He may already be gunning for you."

Pete didn't like that either.

"I'm not going to bullshit you that the plan's safe as Sunday school," Dombowski said. "Actually, Inspector Herlihy was going to come today to ask you himself, except the commissioner needed handholding. I'm not a salesman, but Christ, Pete, we got to get this guy, and legwork and blind luck aren't doing it. If we don't put the nut away, you know he'll kill again."

"It's a high statistical probability," Ho said. Both men ignored him as they tried to find a common ground.

"I'll have the whole watch on alert," Dombowski promised. "Every available cruiser, SWAT teams on mobile ready. The TA cops will have the subways covered, Port Authority the terminals, tunnels, and bridges. Even the Staties are in on the action. I'm telling you, thirty seconds into the call, we'll have ten squad cars converging on the killer. Keep him on the line three minutes and he's ours."

"Does Wilson know about this?"

Scherer looked at Dombowski.

"Your publisher has cleared it," Dombowski said.

Was Murchison in on this also? Pete felt like a puppet being jerked through some *danse macabre* whose purpose remained opaque to him. Which way would he twitch to this pull of the string?

"There's a killer to catch," Pete said.

"We'll get him," Dombowski said.

"You do that. If that psycho-fucking-forensic profile of yours is accurate, it's him or me."

The men's silence assented to this truth. Pete recalled Lopiccolo's bloody bull's-eye, imagined Sanderson's whipped, shit-daubed corpse. The danger of unpredictable violence quivered in the suddenly close office and turned them all stern and wary. And behind it, whispering through the danger, fear.

Pete didn't even see the first punch.

It caught him on the cheekbone and bounced his head against the marble toilet stall in the newsroom's lavatory.

"You fucker! You fucker! You fucker!" Vinnie Bisceglia screamed as he launched another fist at Pete's face. This one caught the ducking Killharney on the forehead and was followed by the rest of the enraged reporter. Together they grappled foolishly on the disinfectant-drenched tile floor.

"You had no right! You fucker! Missy was, she was, me and Missy . . ."

Killharney ended the tirade and fight with a solid knee to the groin. Vinnie deflated into a fetal ball as he clawed for breath, and Pete rolled away and stood up unsteadily. He inspected his face. No blood, but a bruise was beginning to rise along the cheekbone, plus three knuckle marks just below the hairline.

"Shit," he said, and pressed a paper towel soaked in cold water against the damage. Bisceglia remained on the floor, his gasps gradually turning to sobbing. "You mind telling me what the hell's going on?" Pete asked his prostrate co-worker.

"Ma, ma, ma," the reporter explained.

"Illuminating, Vinnie," Pete said. He wondered what chance he would have against a singleminded psychopath when a wimp like Bisceglia could ambush him so easily. A glance in the mirror answered that one. None.

"Get up, for Chrissakes," he said, holding out a hand. "And stop blubbering, the ten-timing bitch isn't worth it."

"Don't you dare," Vinnie said halfheartedly, struggling to his feet with Pete's help.

"Blow your nose." Pete passed him his handkerchief. "And wise up. You're not the first or only fool she fucked for a lead." He noticed the crumpled telegram on the floor. "Not to mention that little piece of blackmail there."

"You don't understand her," Bisceglia said, sniffling.

"I know, she's just a nice girl trying to get ahead in a tough world. Let's face it, Vinnie, there's no free lunch or easy pussy for the likes of us. Oh hell!"

Pete looked at his battered reflection again. There was no way he would be let past the door at the "21" Club.

"How would you like to be taken to lunch at '21' by a Hollywood producer?"

"What?"

"Yeah, tell him you're my agent and order everything on the menu. Some panderer who calls himself Cash D. Bayer finds great filmic values in mass murder. Maybe you can pull a story from it, the selling of slaughter or something."

"I've never eaten at '21,' " Vinnie said, then eyed

Pete with suspicion. "What's the catch? Why are you offering me this?"

"Because I look like I just stepped out of Gleason's Gym. And because for me it wouldn't be a free lunch. I don't need even the appearance of profiting from the killings. And hell, call it a peace offering. I didn't know you and Melissa were such a tight item."

"No one did. It was our secret."

"I bet that woman has more secrets up her snatch than a parish priest working the box before Easter." Pete wondered if he should go to confession before the radio show. He hadn't been since Peg's first Communion.

"Don't they all," Bisceglia said bitterly.

Including Sheila? his unworthy, black Irish heart asked.

"You ever talk to a killer before?" Pete asked. Sheila stopped sucking in a forkful of fettuccini.

"Didn't your mother teach you never to chat up murder when you take a gal out for a well-deserved meal?"

"She died before getting around to those subtle points of dining etiquette."

"I'm sorry. I shouldn't have blamed her for your manners anyway. And she certainly had nothing to do with you showing up looking like a prelim punchy."

The swollen bruise from Bisceglia's sucker punch had turned several shades of purple. It probably clashed with the dark green dress Sheila was wearing. With the soft, simple wool setting off her red hair, she looked both stylish and colorful, and a thin strand of buttery parmesan streaking her chin only added to Pete's attraction. He had tried to drink only enough to dampen the fluttering he felt in his chest whenever he looked at her. It hadn't worked. Worse, he couldn't stop thinking of her in her underwear. Killharney the romantic.

"Bisceglia was trying to uphold the virtue of a fallen woman."

"From what I've heard, Melissa Sanchez has a reputation that's immune to improvement," Sheila said, frowning at her plate. Had she heard about them? Ah, guilt and lust, what a good Catholic boy he was.

"Well, the answer to your killer question is once," she said. "Twice, if you count my Uncle George."

"Uncle George?"

"A Boston cop. He blew away two stickup men outside a liquor store. Oh, and there's also Brian."

"Brian?"

"My cousin. Another cop. He was walking with his fiancé when a snatcher grabbed her gold necklace. Brian pulled his service thirty-eight, the punk went for a pearl-handled forty-five, and Brian fired three times. One hit the heart, one the pulmonary artery, one the liver. By courtesy, they listed the heart shot as cause of death, but any would have done the trick. He was quite the family hero after that.

"But before last week, the worst murderer I ever talked with was a guy who raped and strangled a Boston College coed," Sheila continued. "I was nineteen and working for the campus weekly, and he was a big black mother, six-six, six-eight, two hundred fifty pounds. And bald, with a scar running from his left eyebrow halfway back his skull, like someone had hit him with an ax. Which someone had, as it turned out.

"So I asked him, 'Why did you do it?' Incisive probing. 'Do what?' he asked. 'Rape and strangle that woman,' and I should add he was found fucking the corpse, his hands still wrapped around her throat. 'Did you know her?' 'We got to be friends real quick,' he said. 'Did her looks turn you on?' 'How the fuck I know, it was dark.' 'Then why did you do it?' I asked again. And he smiled and said, 'Feels good. You get a taste of dead meat, you want more.' "

" 'You want more'?"

"He got life. I got a recurring nightmare and became editor my junior year, which helped me land a job with the *Globe* upon graduation, which led to getting this job on the *Apple*, which brings us up to tonight."

"Are you saying I owe the pleasure of your company to an ax-scarred rapist?"

"And murderer, residing to this day at Walpole. Get me coffee and that chocolate mousse cake I saw on the menu, and we'll wax philosophical about it."

Pete signaled the waiter and also ordered another scotch for himself. What came after dessert were propositions Pete hadn't had to deal with, or offer, for almost twenty years.

"You know something that's been bothering me," Sheila said between mouthfuls, "is how did the murderer know you were down at Dombowski's office, that day I phoned you about the confession?"

"I've wondered that myself, and I don't like the implications, such as he knows my habits, or has been following me, or something along those lines."

"Well, what did your murderer say to you?" she asked.

Which reminded him of Melissa Sanchez. Pete hesitated, angry at his own suspicion. Was he being used? Or was she just finishing the other half of the conversation? This is what my murderer said, what about yours? Pete answered on trust.

"He said, 'Have faith, I won't let us down.' "

"Mother Mary," Sheila whispered. "Mine was in chains and behind bars. Yours might be following you."

"Maybe it will end soon," Pete said without conviction, part of him sure the radio trap would fail. He finished his scotch and switched the subject. "Listen, about that night we sort of spent together."

"I can still barely think about it, I'm so mortified. And after giving you all that grief about first impressions."

"Shock hits people in unpredictable ways. You didn't puke or cause a scene. You did just fine." Mentioning puke was sort of getting off the romantic rails. "No, you scored high in the first-impressions category with me. In fact . . ."

"That's kind of you to say so, but—"

"What I mean to say is that you're welcome to a return visit anytime."

There. A proposition has been tendered. It hadn't been much harder than chewing ground glass. Sheila played with her coffee cup. Killharney was suddenly very thirsty.

"I told you I've admired your column for a long time," she answered, and Pete felt his stomach drop with disappointment. "And now I like the person who writes them. You seem like a sweet man despite your sarcasm."

But.

"But I just broke up with someone I was going with a long time—living with, actually. Up in Boston. And I'm trying to establish a new life here, and do well at work." She shook her head. "No, that's not it. The truth is I'm scared. I'm scared of being hurt right now. I just can't face it." She stood hastily. "Thank you for the dinner, Pete. We're square now. I have to leave."

"I'll call," he said to her departing back.

"No. Don't. Please." The monosyllables trailed after her like bitter crumbs he could follow to nowhere.

"Scherer says a one-eyed man in the land of the blind still couldn't hit the outside shot. Isn't that right, Pete?

"Scherer says never bet on fading the five point. Joy Springer from Smoot, West Virginia, called in last week to spread the word that five is the Devil's number.

"Scherer says, if you can't stick it out, stick it in. Good evening, aloha, and welcome. For sure, be sure, it's Scherer."

With sickening fascination, Killharney watched Scherer's pencil mustache twitch and roll as the radio jockey spat out inanities in a confident, confidential baritone. Pete was fearful, semi-drunk, and deeply suspicious of his host.

"Late-night radio freaks, you are in for a treat all reet tonight. A real tenement-burner. Speaking of which, do you know they have professional building strippers, I'm talking box ad in the Yellow Pages, guys who specialize in salvaging slum plumbing, windows, doors, fixtures, everything, before the owner orders a dose of Jewish lightning for the future parking lots of the Bronx and Brownsville."

Pete gaped at the utter fabrication.

"Well, I think it's a crime," Scherer said, "and Scherer's sure you do too. Sound off."

The phone in the studio rang instantly.

"Save it, save it for later, phone-in fanatics. For on my show tonight is none other than Mr. Hit Man himself, columnist and ex–hoop star Peter Killharney. Hey, Pete, your fans still remember you," Scherer said as the phone kept ringing. He sliced his finger across his throat, and the ringing ceased. "Say hi to the public, Pete."

"Hello, it's good to be here."

"And joining the Hit Man this evening is police psychologist Dr. Billy Ho, who's going to tell us what makes a madman tick. But first, do you itch and burn where the sun don't shine? Then listen to this."

The studio engineer inserted the hemorrhoid-salve cassette, and Scherer fell back in his chair, taking deep

112

breaths like a ballet dancer catching his wind backstage between entrances. Pete lit a cigarette, and the talk-show host turned to him with an injured scowl.

"Smoke hurts my throat," he said. Which explained the tiny studio's two dozen No Smoking signs. "And I don't want my throat feeling as bad as your face looks."

Killharney's face looked a mess, Bisceglia's bruises having faded to a mottled yellow and brown. Pete hadn't made it to confession. He stubbed his cigarette out, and Scherer turned back to his microphone.

"You hear that, all you truckers and cabbies out there? Two shifts on the road and you're going to need a diaper tonight. So, Ho, get it? Soho? So, Ho, tell me, who is this maniac, anyway? I mean, what's he eat for breakfast, what makes him kill? Is this some sort of warped Robin Hood complex or what?"

The task force's psychologist proceeded to stumble through his laundry list of pathologies, touching on unresolved Oedipals, socioreligious matrices, the anal-retentive need for approbation.

". . . So, just as child is father to the man, this very disturbed individual's craving for a strong father figure is itself father to his acts of righteous—that is, ah, *perceived* righteous—vengeance."

"Hey, leave it to an expert to take ten minutes to say something simple: The creep's an orphan. Okay. We've heard from the egghead. Now let's hear from the Hit Man, then let's hear from you. But first, let's hear from our sponsor."

An aspirin ad played over the studio monitor as Scherer congratulated the psychologist.

"Hey, you did good, Ho. A natural. And you say you've never done live radio before?"

"No, no, this is my first," Ho said, pleased by the patently insincere praise.

"How do you like it?"

"It's great. Exciting."

"I know what you mean, Doc. Take my advice and get laid after the show."

The ad ended, and Scherer spoke into the microphone again.

"So Pete Killharney, one of the best white basketball players to come out of New York City, syndicated columnist, winner of the Pulitzer Prize, renowned drinker, self-appointed conscience of the city, and inspiration for a lunatic killer, just answer me one question, would you? How the hell do you sleep nights, huh?"

Killharney, looking over the list of pointers Ho had pressed on him, was caught unawares by the question. He should have known Scherer would be out for blood on his home turf. Pete had no intention of playing patsy.

"Well, Art, during the break you were telling Detective Ho that sex helps." Pete covered the mike and grabbed Scherer by the throat. "One more cheap shot and I'll vivisect you." Art nodded his understanding.

"Ha-ha," the jockey said over the air, "but seriously, Pete. The shrink says the Hit List killer's doing all this for you. What do you say to that?"

"I say it's garbage. My reaction to being linked with the Hit List killer in any way—legal, psychological, or spiritual—is anger. I'm mad as hell that some screwloose punk pretends he's doing me a favor by butchering people. He's not doing it for me. He's not doing it because of me. He's murdering for himself, for his own selfish and criminal ends."

"Pour it on," urged Scherer.

"All this psychobabble about arrested development, and all the recent noise about journalistic culpability, it's all missing the main point."

"Which is?" asked Scherer.

"Murder One. Six gruesome, premeditated homicides. This is a police matter."

"But—" said Ho.

"No, I'm tired of buts. The truth is, crimes have been committed. What difference does it make if a criminal decides to see himself as an avenging prophet? The man is a murderer, and no one should forget it. The police aren't. They're trying to apprehend a killer, not a case history or a symbol of First Amendment abuse. And as I said in my column last Sunday, if my words carry any force, any weight whatsoever, I plead with the killer: Give yourself up! Stop! The killing must stop!"

Pete found himself trembling from the prescribed outburst. He had tapped a core of fury that must have been building within him for weeks.

"There you have it, radio lovers," Scherer said, "the expert and the Hit Man. Have they said it all? You tell me."

The phone rang.

"Scherer says, you're on the air. Hello."

"Yeah, uh . . ."

"Right. Next."

Scherer's engineer punched the cut-off button, and the next caller immediately came on the air.

"Scherer, old buddy. E.J. here."

"How's it hanging, E.J.?"

"Can't complain. Had me a twosome last week, identical twins except for—"

"Save the bragging for the Elks Club cookout, E.J. What's your beef?"

"I want to nominate someone to this Hit List thing here. With a little luck the bleep will get wasted."

The mute button responded expertly under the engineer's intuitive sense of the diction of Scherer's typical callers.

"Keep it clean, E.J.," Scherer warned.

"Sorry. So okay, it's this girl's father. A real jerkola. Won't let her see me, won't let her talk to me. How the fuck does he think the fucking world got populated?"

"Storks. Next?"

"Hi. Listen, I want to say, I want to, like the other guy, like nominate? I want to nominate this Killharney character to his own damn list. I mean, who the hell does he think he is, telling people to go out and kill people? I think he should be at the top of the list, that's what I think."

"Pete, you want to respond to that?"

"Well, for those of you who, like this caller, are obvious illiterates, let me explain that nowhere in my writing or my life have I ever advocated murder." He told himself to settle down. He was still fuming. "To take the life of any man, even the SOBs who make up the Killharney's Bar Hit List, is, like the song goes, a crime and a sin, and I condemn it."

"An eloquent defense. Or excuse. You're on the air, hello."

"By the lost planet of Vulcan, along the astral highways of light by which the immortal Ra surfs in everlasting grace—"

"Next."

"I, hi, Art, I got a great idea. Killharney should ought to nominate the Hit List killer to the Hit List, you know? That way, the nut can turn around and kill himself, and the whole thing will be over."

"Sounds like a pretty good idea to me. What do you think, Pete? What do you think, radio land? Aloha."

"Pete." The voice hissed over the studio monitor.

The hair on Pete's head stood at attention. So that really happens, he thought foolishly. He glanced toward the glass-fronted engineering booth. Why weren't they going crazy tracing the call? He pointed frantically at the monitor. The telephone technician nodded that he knew, and made motions for Pete to keep talking.

"This is Pete Killharney. What do you want?"

"Pete, I haven't let you down. You can count on me."

"I've counted to six already," Pete said, sounding cocky and disapproving despite his terror. "Why don't you cut it out? Give yourself up. There are people who can help you, who *will* help you. I'm sure Detective Ho can—"

"Why were you with that slit Thursday, Pete? Why did you take her home the night we punished Sanderson?"

Pete froze. Sheila.

"Forget the gash. We've got each other, and we've got so much work to do. I'll pray for you, Pete."

The line went dead. The call hadn't taken a minute. The radio engineer cued a public service spot, and over the monitor came the voice of a concerned celebrity pitching for some gruesome, fatal disease. The phone rang again.

"It's Dombowski," Scherer said, passing Pete the phone.

"Yeah," he said in a deceptively calm voice.

"We traced it. The SWAT teams are converging on the location right now. Maybe we got him."

Pete heard something in Dombowski's voice.

"What's wrong?"

"It— the call came from your apartment, Pete."

"What!"

"We're waiting to . . . What's that?"

A hand muffled the conversation on the other end, and Killharney began to tremble again. Dancing spots blurred his vision as he fought to keep control.

"We cordoned off the area and gained ingress into your apartment," Dombowski said in a quiet voice.

"And?"

"And he had been there, all right."

"How could you . . . ?"

"Your whole place is covered with blood, Pete. Bed, bathroom, everything. I got to go."

Blood.

Bed.

Slit.

Gash.

And the anger erupted. Pete kicked his chair clear across the room on the fly, its impact shattering the engineering room's picture window into ten thousand pellets of safety glass. He snatched the chair from the wreckage and pounded it against the floor again and again until a splintered leg was all that remained recognizable. His foot, he was sure, was broken.

He looked up. Everyone was staring at him, and in their eyes was registered the intensity of his rage. For the first time in two years he was possessed of a furious purpose. He felt free and clear and directed.

"Gentlemen, excuse me," Killharney said, limping to the door. "I've got work to do."

Part Two

Six

The sunlight sparkled off the Hudson, but the steep hills rising up either side remained in shadow, darkness bracketing the cheery spring light within the river's edge. Before him was the Bear Mountain Bridge, as slender as a thread at that distance. Behind him were the cooling towers of the nuclear power plant at Indian Point. It was strange country, closed and gloomy, so unlike the two-mile-wide lower Hudson. Here the river still fought for passage through hills holding obstinate dominion.

Close by, near Carmel, New York, Killharney had spent an intensely unhappy adolescent exile, torn from his city, orphaned, his world hemmed in by the dark, rolling hills and provincial tedium of rural Putnam County. Basketball and brains had been his escape. And rage. So now, basketball the stuff of record books and lies, and rage sustained only by the danger of an angered psychopath, he returned at last to the area of his early misery.

Notwithstanding, Killharney was in a ridiculously good mood. The warm spring afternoon, the fresh river breeze, the rented car humming briskly past a lumbering freight train, all sang to him of freedom and limitless possibility. Other than for court-mandated visits to Peg, Pete hadn't been out of New York City in over two years. Here, on the road, like a true American, he felt in control of his destiny, running in front of danger. This exhilarating delusion of unfettered scope was compounded by the irony that the destination for this leap into freedom was a Catholic seminary.

"The prodigal returns," said his brother, Brendan, eyes twinkling with benign mischief. He had put on weight and lost hair in the last two years, and to Pete his little brother resembled all the middle-aged priests who had populated their early life together.

"Don't tell me," he replied, "you're the fatted calf. The cloistered life appears to agree with you."

"The grace of God," Brendan said, patting his sizable paunch. "Let's walk. I want to show off my handiwork."

He guided them away from the immense granite seminary, with its useless turrets and decorative battlements, past immaculate beds of spring flowers, and down a crushed-clay path that curled into the woods. Pete tried not to limp from his broken toe. No need for a cast, the doctor had told him. Just stay off it as much as possible.

"Nice day," Pete said. "Nice air. Nice trees."

"Ever the nature-lover," Brendan laughed. "Remember that time you shit in your pants when we spooked the groundhog behind the Connollys' outhouse?"

"It was a bear."

"Yeah, and how many Hail Marys did Father Joseph give you for telling that one?"

"Ten. He liked round numbers."

The path grew gradually wilder, the upkeep lagging behind nature's constant scattering and dissolution. The mansion was no longer visible through the budding forest. Pete's foot throbbed with every step, and he wondered how far his brother intended to hike.

"You ever go back?" he asked.

"To Carmel? Sure, a couple of times a year. I know the priest at Saint Luke's, and I visit the graves. It was better for me, remember."

Pete remembered. After his father died, and his mother got sick and then died, and after six months at that hellhole orphanage on 115th Street, the two boys had been sent upstate to foster parents, Ma and Pa Connolly. They had been decent enough guardians, though distant and penurious. But they were guilty of the inexcusable offense of not being his parents, and Pete had hated them with all the fury of impotent grief.

Moreover, something in Pete had frightened them. His quickness, his temper, his eagerness to fight, all the skills he'd needed to survive in Hell's Kitchen threatened the Connollys' quiet world. Their response was to work him till he hadn't the energy for any possible wickedness. Gentle Brendan got the love, and Pete the hard labor and the occasional beating. Fifteen years had passed before Pete forgave his blameless little brother. And the Connollys? Had he ever forgiven them? Probably not, no.

"They've gone to a more perfect judgment than mine," Pete said.

"You can't still be mad at them."

"I have better candidates closer to home."

The trail ended, and the trees, and everything else but air, and Pete stood shocked at the precipice of a hundred-foot cliff. The view, overlooking the lighted blue strip of the Hudson twisting through the dark hills, was unexpected and strangely calming.

"You like my view?" asked Brendan.

"Did it yourself, did you?"

"With some help from On High. But the path's mine."

"Therapy for the thinker?"

"For the doubter. Oh, I've got the notebooks for you," he said, quickly changing the subject. "I sent Brother Finney over to Amenia with the safe-deposit key to fetch them. He was quite excited by it all. Swears he wasn't followed."

"Followed?"

"Too many spy flicks in his formative years."

They admired the view.

"You know," Pete said cautiously, "I can understand your wanting to leave the priesthood, cynical hellbait that I am. But not why you came back to that." Pete jerked a thumb toward the invisible castle that was his brother's home and vocation. "Especially with that math appointment at Villanova set up."

"A mystery to you, is it?"

"You could say that."

"I suppose I became reconciled to doubt," Brendan said. "When I was younger, doubt was as vague and insubstantial a concept to me, personally, as the Virgin Birth must be to you."

Pete carefully didn't respond.

"We discussed the inevitability of doubt in seminary, of course. But I was spared that particular test. I was blessed, chosen, called. I carried Christ in my heart. He was just there, always."

"What happened?" Pete asked.

"What happened? I got ordained. I was assigned a nice little parish in Pennsylvania. I spread the Gospel and administered the sacraments." His brother paused, his eyes staring into the past. "People came closer to Christ through my ministry.

"And what happened? A standard tragedy, involving one of the first couples I ever married. He was captain of the football team and she the head cheerleader, if you can believe such clichés really happen. I gave them instruction, and married them, and baptized their baby, a beautiful, beautiful child. And we all flourished in Christ's loving bosom.

"Then their little girl got leukemia. And four months later she was dead. And a month after that the mother committed suicide. And the father just vanished. Left his whole life behind without a word to anyone. Boom, boom, boom. A common story."

The priest kicked a stray piece of clay over the cliff, and it tumbled soundlessly through the air downward, downward, until it vanished from view.

"Except without warning I found myself without faith. I prayed to God, asking why. Why? All I heard were the hollow reverberations of the tragedy, boom, boom, boom. And for the first time I tasted the dust of doubt. It nearly strangled me."

Pete knew. He had found out about the halfhearted suicide attempt from a contact in the Cardinal's office, but he had left it to Brendan to bring it up himself, and Brendan never had.

"So you left," Pete said.

The priest nodded.

"But you came back."

"I came back. I became, as I said, reconciled to doubt."

"How?"

"Sleight of hand. I swapped the word *uncertainty* for *doubt*. And one thing slum orphans know about is uncertainty."

The sun began to slide below the hills on the other side of the Hudson. It had been too recently winter for the air to retain any warmth, and the woods were fast turning chilly and somber.

"It's not the same, of course, though occasionally I

125

feel Christ as strongly as I ever did. For a while. And I sometimes administer the sacraments, but I no longer pretend they'll ward off the bitterness and horror that are every man's measure in life. So that's my secret. I've broadened my faith to encompass uncertainty. And life goes on, and good acts can continue to be accomplished. But it's getting cold, and I'm sure you're hungry."

The brothers turned away from the precipice and headed back down the carefully cultivated path.

"How do you keep going?" Pete had to ask, for himself as much as for his brother. "How do you keep on in the face of such a bleak, ambiguous vision of life?"

"Sometimes habit is all I have to get me through. But vision's a good word, for I do have a vision to sustain me, faith or no. I believe the teachings of Christ represent the best that man can strive for, can hope and pray for. The more uncertain our lives, the more essential it is that we cherish and champion our vision of the Good. What else is there?" he asked his dissolute, disillusioned brother.

"Truth," said Pete, "and dinner."

"You always were metaphysical," his brother said.

After eating, Brendan led Pete from the seminary's cavernous main dining hall, down tapestry-lined corridors, to the classroom where he taught ethics and parish finance.

"You said you needed a place to think and a sympathetic ear, so I made preparations for you." The priest unlocked the door and snapped on the lights, old-fashioned frosted globes. The classroom's chairs had been pushed to the perimeter to make space, and the front desk had been set with legal pads, a variety of pens and pencils, and a two-foot stack of notebooks that represented fifteen years' worth of investigative reporting.

Pete sniffed appreciatively. The standard chalky classroom smells were overpowered by the aroma of a thirty-cup coffee urn. His eyes, however, were drawn to the blackboards covering two sides of the room. One board was labeled MURDERS, and underneath:

Name	Cause	Weapon	Symbolism
Lopiccolo	Strangled	Piano Wire	Castrated
Murry	Shot	.44	Buggered
Bengelsdorf	Choked	Dollars	Money-stuffed
Sanderson	Hanged	Noose	Shit-dipped

A second chalkboard said ENTRY/EXIT:

Name	Hit List Entry	Date of Death
Lopiccolo	12/14/81	3/3
Murry	12/22/84	3/17
Bengelsdorf	12/06/79	3/29
Sanderson	12/12/80	4/20

A third was titled CONTACTS:

Bible
Police station call
McGrath call
Radio station call / Apartment destruction

The last board contained the current Killharney's Bar Hit List:

Name	Recommendation
Marchetti	Mafia don
Hazelton	Investment banker
Kreutzer	Industrialist
Todd	Takeover specialist

Hall	UN representative
McCann	"Not The"
Fitzwater	TV evangelist

Two blackboards remained blank.

"I'm impressed," Pete said, pouring himself a cup of coffee while he studied the information surrounding him. "Recommendation, I like that."

"Thought you would. Give me your first impression."

"A lot of facts," he said, swiveling his gaze from board to board.

"Indeed. What else?"

Pete studied the second chalkboard.

"It's been less than two months since it all began. Six murders in just over six weeks, counting the ambushed cops."

"The corpses have piled up quickly, and there are a lot of them," his brother agreed. "And a lot of murder weapons, and modus operandi, and when you review your notes you'll undoubtedly turn up a multitude of suspects."

"Help," Pete pleaded.

"What you need is a way to organize all this information, to sort it in such a way as to converge on some tenable theory or course of action." The priest walked over to one of the blank blackboards. "Let's say this slate represents the universe of suspects."

"Sounds like mathematics," Pete said suspiciously.

Brendan drew a line down the middle.

"We state the hypothesis: the killer is a male. A safe guess, given the strength needed to commit some of these murders. Yet right away you've eliminated half the suspects."

"Let me make a second," Pete said. "Let's reject what everyone else accepts without question, namely that the killer is an unknown psychopath, a Son of Sam."

"Why do that?"

"It's useless. The Hit List killer may turn out to be some pudgy post office employee who's being told to kill by a neighbor's dog. But if so, I personally can't do anything about it. And besides, I don't want to believe it."

"All right, we discard the null hypothesis," Brendan said, then drew a big circle in the male half of the board and labeled it SANE KILLER. "That leads straight to the organizing principle I'm proposing for you. Do you remember Boolean algebra from Mr. Sonberg's senior math class?"

"You're kidding."

"Boolean algebra's a simple visual system for discovering logical connections. Each circle stands for a possibility, a working assumption. You assume the killer is sane, for example. All right, let's make another. Let's assume there is some personal link between you and the killer."

He drew a circle inside the first and wrote in it KILLER KNOWS YOU.

"Why?"

"Just an assumption. Here's another." He drew another circle intersecting the second and called it RELIGION. "Now where the circles overlap represents those suspects with a religious bent who also know you."

The priest tapped his chalk against the small, football-shaped wedge and drew a third circle for MOTIVE cutting into the others, forming what looked like the Ballantine Beer logo. He darkened the tiny area where all three met.

"If we pick a motive," and he wrote ENVY in the unlabeled circle, "and look at where all three assumptions concur, we're left with a manageable pool of culprits compared to what we started with, maybe even with one prime suspect. Here, for instance, we might start with a brother"—he pointed to the first circle—"who was a washout as a priest," he made the sign of the cross over the second, "and who envied his big brother's worldly success."

"You!" Pete said.

Father Brendan tried to look criminally insane.

"I sense a point being made," Pete said. "This system doesn't help much if your assumptions stink."

"A tool, not a cure," conceded Brendan. "While writing out all this, however, I noticed a few assumptions that can't be made, the most striking of which is the lack of regularity."

"You mean mass murderers usually don't switch weapons for each killing," Pete said.

"That's one. Also, the victims weren't murdered according to their chronological age or date of entry onto the Hit List. They weren't killed following any discernible scale of venality or evil. In fact, I found only two links binding the murders together."

"My Hit List."

"And Bisceglia's observation that the punishments fit the sinners' peculiar failings."

"It had crossed my mind that Murry's desecration might just as well be explained by the fact that he was a big Irish asshole," Pete said. "Which leaves my Hit List. Let me ask your professional opinion. Is this guy really a religious fanatic?"

"Jeremiah is not a prophet for the faint of heart," the priest said. "Someone seeking the role of scourge could pick worse scripture to pervert. Fitzwater bothers me, though."

"Fitzwater?"

"He's your newest addition, I know, but the other murders haven't followed chronology. If the killer truly sees himself as helping you and God usher in the Millennium, then the casting down of false prophets like Fitzwater should have been a priority for a religious avenger. Instead, three others have died."

Brendan turned back to the board thoughtfully, then drew an arrow between the circle for motive and the one labeled KILLER KNOWS YOU.

"I didn't explain my first assumption when you asked, but I can't help but think there must be a reason you've been singled out. Whatever his motives, and whoever else he's after, the killer definitely means to wreck you in the process. He's also after you, Pete. Why? Why you?"

Killharney leaned his caffeine-charged head against the cool stone that framed his unlit bedroom's leaded-glass windows. Outside, a nearly full moon highlighted the surreal topiary that the original owner had cultivated. A whole menagerie of sculpted shrubbery pranced motionlessly on the back lawn: privet pachyderms, cypress giraffes, boxwood giant tortoises, wisteria teased into the shape of a pouncing hawk. The seminary had maintained the topiary when it was bequeathed the estate, so now Pete could look down upon the travesty mating of flora and fauna and see an eerily lit reflection of his own confusion of roles as both reporter and story.

Pete had studied his notebooks for most of the night, seeking the connections the FBI seemed confident were there. Enemies had been easy to find for the Hit List members still living. Todd had ruined men and companies, Marchetti murdered by profession, Hazelton was despised by the investment community and city government, and Sissy Hall was similarly loathed for her political grandstanding. Fitzwater was a pious fraud, and the rumors about Kreutzer's Nazi collaboration had reportedly placed him on another hit list, prepared by the Jewish Defense League.

A rough count also gave Killharney a list of fifty vindictive bastards who would gladly cheer and perhaps hasten his own ruin. And that was only going back a decade.

But no comprehensive pattern had yet emerged connecting the four murders or predicting who the fifth might be. There were, however, some curious connections between individuals, living and dead, stray links that might be random but were almost certainly less than the key the FBI thought Pete held.

Item: Hazelton and Sanderson belonged to the same church, the east side Trinity Episcopal, whose congregation had divided over whether to sell the air rights above their parish church. Sanderson had been pro-development, but Hazelton, the man who had taken out full-page ads demanding that New York City declare bankruptcy, had railed against the lucrative scheme. Eternal solvency carried the day, and Hazelton had quit the church, which now squatted like some Gothic toadstool beneath a fifty-story condominium.

Item: Todd, the asset bleeder and takeover pirate, had gone to the same English public school as the *Apple*'s publisher, Angus Murchison. They were supposed to hate one another.

Item: Nicaragua. The late Congressman Murry had been a close friend of Somoza's, that country's deposed dictator who had suffered the fatal misfortune of having his car collide with a bazooka shell. Murry had served on the Congressional oversight committee for intelligence activities. Kreutzer Industries was supposed to provide cover for CIA operatives overseas and had lost its Nicaraguan factory to nationalization by Nicaragua's revolutionary government.

Item: Murchison had been a British MI agent during World War II, specializing in the Caribbean because of his Jamaican birth.

What did it all add up to?

To paranoia, to vast conspiracies having nothing to do with a homicidal psychopath murdering prominent slime. This time of night, Pete's brain would willingly seize on the simple solution that everyone was out to get him, that there was a vast, interlocking web of intrigue behind the grisly deaths. The probable truth was too hard to face right now, that most likely the killer was some pimply stockboy on angel dust, and all of Pete's effort was a waste of energy, a joke.

He closed his eyes and let the fatigue wash over him. A joke. It was all a useless joke, like the stupid bushy animals outside. Pete opened his eyes and gazed at the topiary. His drooping eyes made the elephant's trunk sway in the moonlight, then separate from the body and migrate to the giraffe.

What?

Pete blinked. Someone was threading through the topiary with the quick, furtive movements usually seen in bad spy movies. What had looked like the elephant's trunk shifted position again, this time ending up in a crouch behind the tortoise. Invisible in his unlit room, Pete watched as the form glided across the lawn and disappeared from view behind an ivy-draped turret.

The Hit List killer.

Killharney realized he had been expecting this since the killer first announced his intentions. Whatever logic sustained these murders, Pete could see only one conclusion: his own death. The killer was coming for him.

Pete looked around in the darkness for a weapon to defend himself with, and his eyes fell on the wrought-iron hearth tools leaning against the bedroom's fireplace.

He hefted the ash shovel, but its blade wasn't right for bashing. The tongs didn't have enough mass. The poker's sharp point looked murderous, but— But what? Pete grasped its handle and positioned himself in ambush behind the door, and waited.

And waited.

What was taking the killer so long?

What if his intuition was wrong? What if it wasn't the killer? What would someone else be looking for?

The notebooks.

Pete opened the bedroom door a crack and peered down the hall, which was dark, silent, and empty. He tiptoed down the corridor, thankful for the frayed carpets that deadened his inexpert stalking, then knelt at the top of the massive front staircase and surveyed the entrance hall. It looked deserted, which was what Custer said about the Little Big Horn.

The coward dies a thousand deaths, Pete reminded himself as he expired a few dozen times at the top of the stairs. The hell with it. He cautiously descended and headed for the classroom where he had left the unguarded notebooks. The door was closed, causing a moment of wild doubt, then he noticed the strip of tape on the door, keeping the lock from springing shut. He gave the door a nudge, and it swung open enough to reveal a man dressed in black bending over the notebooks, busily photographing.

Click, click, flip the page. Click, Click.

With little thought and less caution, Pete pulled the fire alarm and brought the iron poker crashing down on the interloper's head. The spy dropped soundlessly to the floor. Pete wondered if he had killed him.

"What's the matter? What happened?" asked a breathless Brother Finney, the first to arrive.

"Caught a burglar," Pete said.

Finney snapped on the lights, and Killharney, still gripping the poker, worriedly turned over the unconscious body. The face beneath black camouflage was nondescript, and unfamiliar. There wasn't any bleeding.

Brendan bustled into the room, followed by what seemed like the rest of the seminary.

"What happened? Are you all right?" his brother asked.

"Fine. There wasn't any fight. I conked him from behind and he went down. He was photographing the notebooks."

Pete looked at the open notebook. 1984, the year Hazelton and Murry made the Hit List. Were they the key?

"Saints watch over us, how did he know they were here?"

"He probably didn't," Pete said, inspecting the palm-sized camera the man had dropped. Of course, the 1984 notebook could merely have been on top of the stack. "He must have been following me and got lucky."

"He doesn't look very lucky," Brendan observed. "Brother Finney, would you be kind enough to see if our uninvited guest needs medical attention?"

Finney leaned over to help, but the supposedly concussed spy leaped up, performed a series of blindingly fast short jabs that left the seminarian grabbing his throat in agony, and before anyone could stop him, he was out the door and gone. A half-dozen sedentary priests gave hopeless chase.

"Finney, Finney, are you all right?" Brendan asked in horror. Finney replied with choking sounds and collapsed, Pete just catching his head before it cracked against the floor. The seminarian gasped for breath and turned a bright, bright red.

"Relax," Pete said in a calming voice. "Breathe

135

through your nose. Slowly now, regular breaths. That's better. Relax now. Relax."

Finney gradually regained control, and the desperate crimson faded. Winded priests filtered back into the room, their failure evident on their flushed cheeks. In the distance, a fire truck's siren broke the country stillness.

"Don't . . . touch . . . camera . . . finger . . . prints," Brother Finney croaked.

"He was wearing gloves," Brendan said. "Did you know him, Pete?"

"Never saw him before."

"Who is he?" wondered Brendan, then thought more. "Or should I say, who hired him?"

My God, thought Pete, a conspiracy!

The processsion rode the elevator in silence to the sixth floor, then marched on orange-striped carpet down the patterned mustard corridor to a forest-green door. The fashionable Upper East Side.

"I think I'm going to puke," said Svenson.

"I've seen better during the DTs," Hanratty agreed, shifting uneasily on his crutches. Pete rang the bell.

"Come in," Sheila said, sighing as she opened the door for them. Hanratty hobbled past her to the studio's single picture window. "I don't really think . . ."

"No ledges or balconies within rappelling distance," he called out. "Window secure."

Svenson opened a toolbox and took out an electric drill and a set of metal bits.

"Where's an outlet?" he asked.

"The closest is in the kitchen, but I don't have an extension cord."

"I do," he said, stringing a grounded yellow line into

the minuscule kitchenette. Ten seconds later the drill was grinding through the apartment's metal front door.

"You have any ice?" Pete asked her.

"I heard you were on the wagon."

"It's for my foot."

He had paid the price for Brendan's nature walk; his broken toe was twice its normal size. Sheila put together an icepack, and he cooled down his foot while his friends installed the steel latchplate and second deadbolt lock on her front door.

"How's sobriety?" she asked, sitting next to him. She was dressed in jeans and a Boston College sweatshirt and looked more beautiful than ever to Killharney.

"As a matter of fact, I looked the word up in Bartlett's yesterday. Spinoza termed it a species of courage, but I found a Berryman quote that sounds closer to the truth: 'Something can be said for sobriety, but very little.' "

"All done," announced Svenson, smoothly clicking the Medeco deadbolt in and out.

"You boys do good work," Killharney said to them, "and housecalls yet. Better not let your union hear about this, Svenson, they'll pull your card for sure. Let me buy you both a duck."

"What?" asked Svenson, looking up from repacking his tools. Hanratty had found a broom and was sweeping up the filings from the door.

"One of those duck dinners that Czechoslovakian place up the avenue specializes in."

"Let me raincheck it," Svenson said. "Wife's aunt is coming over, and I promised to tape her muffler."

"I got tickets for wrestling at the Garden," Hanratty also excused himself. "But don't worry, you'll pay."

"Thank you both," Sheila said as she saw them to the door.

"Nothing," said Svenson.

"Any time," said Hanratty, and they left Sheila and Pete alone together for the first time since their dinner. They stared silently at each other for a disquieting amount of time, then Sheila turned away and walked to the window.

"Rappelling distance," she muttered. "You know, I grew up with cops watching over me, guarding me, keeping me away from life for what they knew was my own good. I've fought to get away from that mentality, so this security business sets off some very old resentments."

"I was followed yesterday," he told her. "Someone assaulted a priest and tried to photograph my notebooks."

"So you don't burn them."

"No. And Sheila, you talked with the killer. You heard what he said about you during the radio call. Neither of us can afford to pretend you're not at risk."

"No, I know. I'm not saying it's right, what I'm feeling. I'm sorry about the priest. I'm . . . oh hell," and she turned her back to him. Was she crying? What was going on?

Pete took a step toward her, then went and hugged her from behind. Sheila turned into his arms and wept.

"This is not how it's supposed to be," she said.

"No," Pete agreed, and kept holding her. Her head fit on his chest as if she had been matched to him. He felt himself stir, and she felt it also. Pete quickly released her. They stood a foot apart, looking into each other's eyes, uncertain what was happening.

"I think it's dangerous for us to be seen together until this killer's caught," he finally said.

She nodded, and they continued to stare. Her green eyes glistened with the tears. The edges of his vision began to quiver and blur. Sheila slowly drew off her sweatshirt, and Pete reached for her.

It had not started well. Pete had handed Wilson his notice of leave of absence, and after scrutinizing it carefully, the editor had dropped it in his wastebasket.

"That wasn't a request, Chief," Pete pointed out.

"I would appreciate hearing your reasons," Wilson said.

"I want to stop the killing. I want to find out who the Hit List killer is and make sure he doesn't kill again."

"Son of Sam went on a year, the Atlanta child killings two. They never caught Jack the Ripper. Are you prepared to pursue this indefinitely?"

"What's my choice? Nowadays, whenever I cover a news story, I become the story myself. I haven't gotten a good investigative tip from my sources for weeks, and who can blame them? People think twice about blowing the whistle when it could lead to someone's death. No, I've got to follow this through. I've got to find the killer to regain my profession, not to mention my self-respect."

"A recent concern of yours, though I'm pleased by its manifestation," Wilson said. "I still see no need for a leave of absence."

"I don't think four columns a week recounting my obsession is especially interesting or appropriate, and it would be grotesque to churn out human-interest columns in the middle of a murder spree.

"But it's not just my effectiveness as a reporter. The police psychologist says I'll eventually become a target. The killer's already made threatening noises about people close to me," Pete said, thinking of Sheila. "I'm a danger."

"Rather melodramatic."

139

"Six men have been melodramatically murdered, for Chrissakes, and I'm going to do whatever I can to end the horror without exposing anyone else to harm."

Wilson applauded, belying his scowl of exasperation. "Bravo, Mr. Killharney, you're out to play Sam Spade. And what exactly do you imagine you'll do? No, let me tell you. You'll look up information, take notes, dig up fresh sources, follow up on leads, doublecheck rumors, in short all the actions you as a reporter would have taken to break the story."

"I'm not breaking any story, damn it."

"You're not listening. This leave won't magically make you something you're not. You're a reporter, not a detective. What you see, and why, and how and when and where you work, are all the determining traits of a trained newspaperman. Why turn your back on them?"

Killharney didn't answer. Wilson saw the hesitation and pressed his argument home.

"Don't give up the best in you, Pete. It's true I want you on my paper. For all the aggravation, you can be one hell of a reporter. But I honestly believe you should stay in touch with the tools of your trade if you want to help catch this killer. Let me propose a compromise. Cut back to two columns a week. On the open days I'll run your old columns nominating each Hit List member. Readers will get some good background, and your current columns will play off and build on them."

"And what happens when they run out?"

"We renegotiate."

Pete wavered fatefully. It wasn't a bad idea. And Wilson was right. He was a reporter.

"I work alone on this," he countered.

"Your choice, though you're throwing away resources. I know Bisceglia has someone at the SEC who can provide financial background on the Hit List members. My advice is to use anything you can, but whatever

140

you do, do it outside my office. I've got a paper to run, so get the hell out and good luck to you. If you break this story, you deserve respect from both of us."

He lay alone on his brand-new sheets, on his brand-new mattress, staring across his relentlessly scoured floor at the boxes filled with blood-caked personal effects. The apartment smelled of paint, coat after coat applied until the splatters stopped bleeding through. Except for the boxes, no trace but memory remained of the desecration.

Pete was glad he had kept the boxes. He needed their obscene evidence as a touchstone for his anger and resolve. Movie heroes made decisions, and their lives were awesomely changed. They made Pete's commitment to find the killer seem suspect, provisional, dependent on a level of urgency that daily habits inevitably sapped. All that remained to sustain his rage through sober, sleepless nights was a broken toe, a box of dried hate, and Sheila.

Do your best at what you're best at, Murchison had said. Don't give up the best in you, Wilson had seconded. Well, Pete had once been great at anger, but he had changed, lost his need for it, and hadn't found an adequate replacement to fuel his drive for truth. Sighing, he lit a Lucky and dragged one of the boxes over to the bed. Tonight he needed his hate hands-on.

The first thing Pete pulled out was his Cambridge *Shakespeare*, so encased in blood it appeared to have been dipped in a bucket of it. Yes, double-dipped even; fingers of the first immersion stuck out from the hardened veneer of the second. He opened the book, and the coagulated shell cracked with a sound both brittle and sticky. The inner pages were unstained, however, and he read a sonnet at random:

Where art thou, Muse, that thou forget'st so long
To speak of that which gives thee all thy might?
Spend'st thou thy fury on some worthless song,
Dark'ning thy pow'r to lend base subjects light?

Good fucking question, Pete thought, dropping the volume back in the box with a shiver of revulsion.

He burrowed deeper and brought up his Bible, which had been dappled with stray drops of dried blood but not specifically fouled. Why would a religious fanatic take the time to ruin a secular book Killharney had written about as his personal favorite, but not bother to exclude—or single out—the Bible from the general vandalism?

Intrigued, Pete emptied the rest of the contents onto the floor. Books, papers, a photograph of Peg with her smile cut in half by a translucent red glaze, his Pulitzer certificate that Margie had framed for him one good Christmas long ago, now smeared with a cross of blood.

Why did a killer who supposedly saw Pete as a partner in righteous vengeance spend time committing such small gestures of obvious spite? The answer flew in the face of the current assumptions about sanity or religion and fit in well with his own. The killer despised Killharney, just as Brendan had said. Yet such viciousness not only ran counter to religious fervor, it seemed also to conflict with the cleverness that lay behind the planning and execution of the four killings to date.

Then he saw the pencil, an unlabeled number 4 fattened with blood. Pete carefully wrapped it in a new handkerchief and called Dombowski.

"You work too late," Pete told him.

"Fucking tell me about it," the detective said. "I've been entertaining G-men. Top-level coordinating session, with Steptoe sitting in."

"Steptoe? *The* Steptoe?"

Ex-Captain Stephen Steptoe had run a precinct with a police-brutality complaint rate over twice the city average. A tight precinct was how he explained it. No coddling. Criminals shouldn't expect a bed of legalistic roses on his beat. Of course, the record showed the non-coddled criminals to be almost exclusively black, though Puerto Ricans were also permitted to be beaten and framed. Or lost. Pete had managed to uncover what was left of one of these "lost" suspects, had gotten three columns from it, and a week later Captain Steptoe had resigned to take a position in private industry.

"The same," Dombowski said. "He's head of Kreutzer's security, you know."

"Christ, you mean that army up in Greenwich?"

"Twice right. So I'm working late tonight, and in waltz Flaubert and Steptoe and that Baumann joker. To discuss mutual security considerations, if you can believe that shit. And I'm not telling you any of this."

"I'm not listening," Pete agreed. "I got something for you."

"What?"

"A pencil. Not mine. Looks like the killer might have used it to stir blood with. Want me to bring it down?"

"A pencil can wait till tomorrow. Besides, off the record it sounds like another convenient slipup."

"Another?"

"Forensics swears the killer's been planting clues. A bootprint placed at the Sanderson scene, blood pushed under Bengelsdorf's fingernails. I don't know what the fuck to make of it, but bring down the pencil. Maybe we'll get lucky."

Pete hung up and asked himself what type of homicidal maniac left clues and showed sadistic attention to minutiae. In his mind, the murderer began to take on a

143

confusing, frightening human shape. No longer some anonymous killing machine, the Hit List killer was mean, smart, habitually savage, and hated Killharney. Hell, except for the smart part, that sounded like Steptoe.

Pete stopped his assumptions from galloping too far from plausibility. Perhaps the killer wasn't a nut, perhaps he wasn't religious, perhaps he had a personal grudge against Pete, but these shaky perhapses didn't add up to an ex-cop as the murderer of a United States congressman. Time to get back to facts.

Killharney fetched another, heavier box, its weight due to his Royal typewriter, his oldest friend and inanimate nemesis. What looked like a whole gallon of blood had been poured into its guts. He hit a key, and it slapped against the caked platen and stuck there. Junk. It was so much bloody junk. Pete shoved the worthless machine back and carried the boxes down to the garbage cans in front of his tenement.

A gruesome sight greeted him. Someone had used the chain binding the garbage cans to the stoop railing to hang a stray cat. Was the stiffened, mangy corpse another message from the killer? Pete looked up and down the block. The winos outside the SRO hotel were arguing incoherently. Old man Petronelli was walking his Chihuahua. No one else was out.

No, Pete decided, my messages haven't been as subtle as a strangled cat. This little abomination was just part of the social wallpaper of the neighborhood; random violence was the rule in Hell's Kitchen.

What was he doing here? Why had he moved back after the divorce? And what would he be like if he hadn't left, if he had grown up here instead of being banished upstate? Worse, worse than he was, for sure. He wanted a drink desperately.

The phone was ringing when he returned to his now totally impersonal apartment.

"It's me," said Margie.

"To what do I owe the honor?"

"Two things. First, I want you to speak with Peg. We've been fighting all night. She wants to visit you, and I absolutely forbid it. I will not have my daughter exposed to—"

"I agree."

"What?"

"Absolutely."

"Oh. Well." She hadn't anticipated such easy acquiescence. "Then I guess we can move on to reason number two."

"Ready."

"Pete, I'm getting married. Again."

"Oh," he said. He hadn't been ready for that.

"I thought you would be ecstatic. It lets you off the alimony hook."

"Who's the intended?"

"His name is Bob Granger, and we've been seeing each other for about six months now, and, well, we both think it's a good time to formalize things. It's his second, too."

"Ah," Pete said, swallowing back the cheap shots that were clawing their way up his jealous throat. "What does Bob do?"

"He owns a lawn-care business. You may have seen the ads."

"You mean Granger Grooming, 'Where the Grass Is Always Greener'?"

"He's very successful," Margie said defensively.

"Well, gee . . . congratulations."

"Thank you, Pete."

"You tell him for me he's the luckiest groom in the world."

She hesitated, trying to decide whether the pun was intentional.

"I mean it," Pete lied.

"That's sweet of you, darling. Here's Peg."

"Hi Daddy, what do you think, some news, huh?"

"Yeah, super."

"His son's a moron. Plays football."

"Intelligence is found in unlikely places, Peg. Athletes have their own window on reality," he said, sounding pompous and false. He had known a lot of athletes, and most of them had been morons.

"I want to talk with you," she said.

"So talk."

"No, not like this. When can I see you?"

"We'll have to put off a visit for a while, motormouth," he said, deliberately using the aggravating nickname. "I've declared myself officially off limits till this psycho is caught. Hazardous material."

"I'm not afraid."

"I am."

"I'm coming in tomorrow," she persisted, her father's daughter.

"I won't be here," he came to the sudden conclusion. "This apartment's obviously not safe. I'll be flopping around in different places, and don't ask where because I don't even know yet myself."

"Please, Daddy."

"Peggy, I know I haven't been there when you needed me sometimes. And I can understand why you want to talk to me about what's happening, what with the marriage and all. But—"

"You don't understand anything!" she screamed. "I hate you! I hate you!" And she hung up.

Hung up on by his daughter, replaced by his ex-wife, self-exiled from his new sweetheart, cut off from the easy routine of his professional life, and soon homeless, Pete felt untethered, whirling helplessly in a maelstrom of unbridled hatred and sudden death. And if he did nothing, his instincts told him that he would soon be dead.

"Hell, no!" he shouted, his declaration echoing hollowly around the characterless studio.

Pete packed a bag and left his home and heart and past behind, and went looking for the story that would save his life.

Seven

There was a killer, who would kill again.

The only lead Pete had was his Hit List. The FBI and whoever broke into the seminary (if he represented another player) weren't the only ones who saw it as central. A deep intuition had begun to operate on Killharney that the Hit List held the key to the killings. The truth was to be deciphered by some combination, some knot of interlocking motive and victim and opportunity, that he hadn't yet glimpsed.

Why do men kill? Greed, love, power, fear. Pete decided to explore the first and accepted Vinnie Bisceglia's SEC contact. Unfortunately, a Wall Street deli at noon was not the ideal place to carry out introductions.

"Jimmy," Bisceglia tried.

"Ham and cheese on, ham and, fuck, missed him," Jimmy Whoever said. Someone sprayed Pepsi over Pete's left ear.

"Jesus Christ," he said.

"Jimmy Gruin," the SEC lawyer responded. "Pleased to meet you. Hey, Vinnie, you're keeping better company nowadays. A savior yet. Killharney, right? Ham and cheese," he bellowed. "Right, no, no mayo, mustard. On rye. And a Tab. Got to watch the waistline now I've rounded the big three-0."

An old fraternity brother of Bisceglia's, Jimmy Gruin had the ex-jock's beefy athleticism that would fall to fat in another five years. Pete surreptitiously poked a finger into the inch of flab that had collected around his middle and ordered a yogurt.

They took their lunches to Battery Park, where a bench opened up for them when a Japanese family, cameras outnumbering children three to one, scurried off toward the Staten Island Ferry Terminal to watch the commuter ferry dock.

"I love to watch the stockbrokers score their noontime joints," Jimmy mumbled through his ham and cheese. "I mean, Jesus, who would trust the shit that's pawned off in a park? There's only one explanation: marijuana addiction. You've read about it, now see the gruesome reality for yourself."

This guy was an asshole, Pete thought.

"So tell me," he said, "were any of the Hit List members in securities trouble, or any other financial hot water?"

Gruin began to adopt the judicious glaze of lawyerly deliberation. "Rumors, smears, and innuendo welcomed," Killharney encouraged him. "Take Judge Sanderson."

"He sure as hell never worried about money. Two years with the Brooklyn DA taught me which judges were for sale. Sanderson was. And often."

Pete remembered the CEO's son who got a suspended sentence from Sanderson for clawhammering his girlfriend into a vegetable. The courthouse regulars swore the price covered the cost of a chauffeur-driven tour

149

through the Lake Country that Sanderson and his wife took a month later. So the asshole did know something. "Let's see, Lopiccolo was set," Jimmy continued, warming to the subject. "His welfare SROs were money machines, city-guaranteed income and practically no maintenance. Whoever's taken them over has tapped into a golden flow."

Pete wrote a note to himself to find out who.

"Bengelsdorf, now Bengelsdorf liked to play the futures. Got burned badly a few times too, if I remember."

"Cute, a high-risk dabbler bankrolled by geriatrics," Vinnie Bisceglia said.

"What about the late John Michael Murry?" Pete asked. "The congressman was known for his accessibility, wasn't he?"

"Hard call. The Interior Committee that Murry sat on has oversight into almost every aspect of business in America. Unless you blind-trust your assets, there's no way to avoid the appearance of occasional conflict of interest. So without a smoking gun, there was practically no way we could have mounted a successful prosecution."

"The only smoking gun Murry ever got near was the one shoved down his throat," Pete said. "That leaves the living. Hazelton served on the SEC for a term, didn't he?"

"That nut? He doesn't have all the baggage strapped down tight upstairs, let me tell you. You know he wanted to abolish the SEC? Every damned meeting he would stand up and give this speech about creeping statism and how the governors should all resign as a matter of conscience."

"I never heard Todd accused of a conscience."

"We'd love to nail the douchebag. So would the IRS. FBI wants him too."

"What are you looking for?" Pete asked.

"Stock tampering. He's been jerking around the price of Camden Fabricators, softening them up for a take-over. They have some patents that American Wrapper covets. So with Todd's help, Wrapper will swallow the company, grab the patents, and dump what's left for the write-off. A London bank is handling the arbitrage."

That was just the activity that had earned Todd his Hit List nomination: Steal a company, then plunder it until all that remained was a stripped shell and the permanent loss of blue-collar jobs.

"Did you say London?" Vinnie asked. "Do you suppose that's why he left the country when he did? He might be using the Hit List killings to hide behind while he plays pirate."

"You know he started out as a smuggler. You should ask Murchison about him. He got Todd interned during the Second World War because he didn't trust him not to play both sides of the fence."

"Speaking of smuggling, Kreutzer might do some shady shipping himself," Pete suggested.

"I don't know what you mean," snapped Gruin, nervously looking around as if he suddenly feared they were being watched. Curious reaction.

"I mean the CIA is in the business of clandestine arms transfers, among others," Pete said, "and Kreutzer's Latin American plants provide a perfect cover for moving armaments."

"As far as the SEC is concerned, Helmut Kreutzer is a law-abiding American businessman. There's no story there, take my word for it."

The lawyer stood up to leave.

"What about Marchetti?" Pete asked.

"No comment. *Nada*. Zip. I got to go. You owe me for this one, Vince. Field boxes the next Yankee home stand, right?"

"Right," Bisceglia agreed quietly, and Gruin steamed off, still searching for spies. Killharney half expected to see Baumann feeding the seagulls nearby.

"Why do you suppose he got so bent when I mentioned Kreutzer?" Pete asked.

"If you work for the government, you're told hands off domestic companies fronting for the CIA overseas. I also heard that the Feds finally have something on Marchetti."

"You're doing some legwork on this one, aren't you, Vinnie?"

"Christ, I never liked Jimmy Gruin," he said, changing the subject. Bisceglia looked as if he had been caught torturing puppies. "He always treated me like dirt."

Which sounded exactly how Pete had always treated him.

"Thanks for setting this up," Pete said in partial atonement. "The guy's an asshole, but he filled in some blanks."

"Yeah?" Vinnie seemed nonplussed by the thanks, probably the first he had ever gotten from Pete. "So what did you learn?"

"For one thing, I learned that if greed was the motive for the killings, the payoff's taking place on a personal level."

"Psychos don't kill for money."

"Psychos can be killers. Killers can kill for money. Therefore, psychos can kill for money."

"That's a bullshit syllogism, Pete."

"There's a lot of bullshit in general surrounding these killings," Killharney said, thinking of the purposely sensational deaths, the many murder weapons and possible motives, the planted clues, the vast supply of suspects. "I have this picture in my mind of layer after layer of diverting lies that the murderer has hidden himself behind."

"You don't believe he's crazy?"

" 'Though this be madness, yet there is method in it,' as the Dane said. And what I believe is that if we don't cut through the bullshit, more men will die."

Killharney decided to visit a law-abiding American businessman.

The road to Helmut Kreutzer's Greenwich, Connecticut, estate wound with unnecessary curves around the rocky hills that signaled the beginning of New England. Occasional homes could be glimpsed behind the running stone walls: Tudor mansions, glass-sheeted moderns, oversized Georgian Colonials. It was all very private, very exclusive, very, very pricey. Just the place for the head of a corporation to live.

But not for the corporation itself. Kreutzer had made the Hit List for relocating his corporate headquarters in the suburbs, a move that had cost New York City a thousand jobs and millions in taxes. In his nominating column, Killharney had insisted the move's justification rested as much on its proximity to the chairman's residence as on the ballyhooed reasons of tax relief and quality of life.

From the road, nothing of the Kreutzer manor was visible except a driveway barred by heavy metal gates, and an adjoining gatehouse manned by armed sentries. He drove by without slowing, and noticed in his rearview window one of the sentries methodically copying down his license number. A half-mile farther on, Killharney pulled over and thrashed his way back through the woods, shredding his clothes and bloodying himself on the brambles and barbed locust saplings, eventually coming up against a ten-foot-high fence topped with razor concertina.

Through the chain-link fence, Pete looked past the

last fringe of greening woods, down a sloping lawn, and back up a hill carpeted with daffodils. At the top of the rise rested the largest wooden house he had ever seen, wing upon wing of clapboard, a monstrous multiplication of shutters and multipaned windows, terraces, and balconies. Pete couldn't believe one man inhabited all of it. Maybe Kreutzer changed bedrooms weekly.

"Don't move!" a voice behind him ordered. "Put your hands against the fence and spread your legs. Now!"

A rifle barrel stabbed painfully into the base of his spine to hasten compliance. Pete was expertly patted down for weapons, then handcuffs were slapped on one wrist, his arm jerked back to hook the other, and Pete was spun around to meet his two uniformed captors, faces devoid of expression, their automatic rifles trained at his heart, which was thumping with fright.

"Hi, guys," Pete said, surprised his voice was steady. "Where's the war?"

After a half-hour of boring terror in the gatehouse, a car pulled up outside, braking a spray of gravel that sputtered against the window. Then the doorway was filled with ex-Captain Stephen Steptoe, looking as vicious and disdainful of humanity as ever. Pete had forgotten how physically intimidating the man was in person. The crispness of Steptoe's starched, perfectly tailored uniform didn't dampen the radiating waves of hostility, and small tics of fury periodically jolted his frame, twitching his fingers into fists as he restrained his obvious eagerness to crush whatever got in the way.

"Well, well, fucking well," he said, "look who was apprehended trespassing on posted property."

Steptoe swiftly closed the distance between them and boxed Killharney's ear so hard his vision crossed. Through the ringing, whose effects Pete knew would disappear without physical trace, he heard Steptoe's caustic chuckle.

"How's my number-one cocksucker doing these days? You're a big star now. I even saw your picture on the *Enquirer*."

He boxed Killharney's other ear, setting up stereo inside Pete's skull.

"So how do you like it, Hit Man? How do you like being the one getting butt-fucked in public? Me, I love it. I watch Missy Sanchez eating you alive with those interviews of hers and I feel all warm and tingly inside."

What interviews?

"You want this to make tomorrow's column, keep it up. I'm sure Kreutzer would love reading about how his hired help beats up reporters. Great publicity for a chairman of the board."

The security chief raised his fist again, and Killharney reflexively flinched. Steptoe laughed, then punched him in the kidney, another untraceable blow that almost made Pete vomit.

"Yeah, it's real good to see you again, Peewee." The ex-cop's voice turned hard. "What are you doing here?"

"I want to see Kreutzer," Pete gasped. Steptoe laughed again.

"You dumb fuck. That Hunkie's scared shitless by your Hit List. I bring you to him, he'll die of shock and I'll blow my bonus. I got contract incentives for keeping the old fart breathing, and if you and your killer stay clear of him for a year, I'll be a wealthy man."

"What's going on?"

A pretty young woman wearing a designer jogging suit had entered noiselessly and was staring at Killharney's handcuffs.

"Caught a trespasser, Mrs. K.," explained the gatehouse guard, who caught a withering Steptoe scowl. Pete seized the opportunity.

"Mrs. Kreutzer, I'm Pete Killharney, from the *New*

York Apple. I'd like a chance to speak with your husband, if I may. It won't take long, I promise."

"All right," she easily agreed.

"I don't think that's a very good idea, Mrs. Kreutzer," said Steptoe, fists twitching rhythmically at his sides.

"You can leave the handcuffs on if you think I might be a menace," Pete offered.

"Oh no, certainly not," the wife said. "Somebody take those things off, please. They look like they must hurt terribly."

At a reluctant sign from Steptoe, the guard unlocked the cuffs.

"And we'll take your car, if you don't mind, Stephen. Ready, Mr. Killharney?" She pivoted and skipped out of the gatehouse with a dancer's exaggerated turnout.

"Thanks for everything," Pete said to Steptoe, who had literally turned purple with suppressed fury.

Kreutzer's wife got her security chief's Camaro up to seventy in the half-mile of curving drive that led to the main house. They sped through rows of cultivated rhododendron hedge and manicured evergreen plantings, past a pruned apple orchard, a tennis court, a putting green, stables, a gazebo, and bed after bed of spring flowers.

"I hope I won't be putting Mr. Kreutzer out too much, arriving unannounced like this," Pete said, thinking of Steptoe's description of his fearful employer.

"You obviously haven't met my husband before."

"I'm looking forward to it."

"Well, I doubt Helmut Kreutzer's been put out of anything since Hungary in 1956. Here we are."

They pulled up underneath the mansion's porte cochere, and the butler opened the door for them.

"Would you tell Mr. Kreutzer he has a guest, Bernhard. Mr. Killharney from the *Apple*."

"Very well, madam," the butler said, and left trailing a faint effluvium of disapproval. Mrs. Kreutzer led Pete through rooms filled with the furnishings only the very rich could favor: Williamsburg walls, Aubusson rugs, Waterford chandeliers, Regency furniture, incidental pieces of sterling and porcelain, and oil paintings everywhere, including a very familiar-looking Impressionist.

"Manet?" Pete asked.

"An early Matisse," she said, pausing so he could admire the painting of a young girl in a blue dress, shyly smiling at something to her right. "Helmut says he only picked it up because the dress color matched the Pompeii tiles around the fireplace, but that's his way of joking."

"Funny," Pete said, transferring his attention from the painting to the cobalt-colored ceramic that didn't look particularly worse for 1,500 years of wear.

They moved on through another living room, a sitting room with attached greenhouse, a library, and a sun room whose French doors looked out over the hill of daffodils. A glass walkway led from the sun room to a glassed-in pool, where the butler, towel in hand, stood waiting for a lone swimmer doing laps.

"I'll take that, Bernhard," Mrs. Kreutzer said, relieving the manservant of the thick towel. The butler performed an almost imperceptible bow and disappeared.

"Bernhard's invaluable," Mrs. Kreutzer said.

"Did you say 'vile'?" Pete asked.

"No, but that's what I meant."

They watched the swimmer do five laps, ten, fifteen; then, without warning, Kreutzer launched himself from the pool and stood before them, gasping for breath, water streaming off his wide, knotted shoulders and overdeveloped chest. There were dozens of small, ragged scars stitched across his heaving back. As his wife draped the

157

towel around him, the industrialist held out his right hand to shake. It was missing the pinky and half the ring finger.

"Helmut Kreutzer. So finally we meet, after years of distant adversary. You like my scars?" he asked in a jovial, mid-European accent.

Killharney had in fact been staring.

"A souvenir of the Revolt. I tell people it's how the Russians stamp their exit visas."

"I have class now, Helmut," his wife said. "Is it all right to leave Mr. Killharney to you?"

"I promise I'll behave," he said to her questioning look. "Stephanie knows my temper. Come, have coffee."

He strode off, and Pete followed dutifully behind. If Kreutzer was scared of him, this was one hell of an act.

"I swim one mile every day," Kreutzer said. "Weight training, sparring, one-mile swim. No jogging. No. Bad for the bones. Swimming is the perfect exercise."

"If you're a shark," Killharney said. Kreutzer beamed at him.

"Precisely," he said, and smiled, showing a mouth missing all its front teeth.

In the sun room was a tea cart loaded with toast, croissants, jellies and jams, and the industrialist's dentures, which he slipped into place without a trace of self-consciousness.

"And of course ballet," Kreutzer continued, swallowing half a croissant with barely a chew. "That's Stephanie's doing. 'You are too tight, Helmut,' she tells me. 'You must keep the body flexible to keep it young.' So I work at the barre right along with her. I'm ridiculous, this lumpy old man in tights. Stephanie, she is so good, so terribly good."

"A fine woman," Pete agreed, disoriented. A country gentleman chatting about exercise and praising his talented wife wasn't what Pete had expected from the stories about this supposedly pitiless businessman, this ex-Nazi.

"But you haven't come to hear me brag about Stephanie," Kreutzer said. "You're unexpected, but your intentions are not. You wish to ask me questions, yes? So ask."

"Who wants you dead?"

"Your Hit List killer."

"Who else?"

"That would take weeks to list," Kreutzer laughed, delighted at the idea. As he contemplated candidates, he folded three pieces of toast together and bit into the mass with casual ferocity.

"Well, my business rivals wish me no long life, but we fight our fights with lawyers and tender offers. The Russians, of course." He paused, and his steel-gray eyes momentarily clouded. "But it would be too much to blame these murders on Russians, no?"

"Perhaps something Agency-related," said Pete. "You've been called the CIA's Nicaragua connection. Before the revolution, that is."

The industrialist gave Killharney a thorough, assessing stare before becoming the happy millionaire again.

"Under every bed, the CIA," he joked. "Reporters see always the CIA. And Nazis. Aren't you going to ask me about the Nazis?"

"One at a time."

"No, the lies are related. You see, I'm a patriot. I love America, because I love freedom. All my life I fight for freedom, for freedom is life. Those who call me Nazi, well, they don't know Helmut Kreutzer."

"So you still provide cover for the Agency?"

"So many wars," Kreutzer said vaguely. "Too many.

159

I think I'm too old to play these young men's games anymore. I think now it's time to let others fight. Me, I'll keep myself flexible and love my lovely wife."

"Tell me something. With all these murders, and you a potential target, are you afraid for your life?"

"Honestly? I am afraid to die. I admit it. But all my life I'm a target. The Nazis, the Russians, the Jew bankers. I live today because I take precautions."

"I've met your precautions. Steptoe tells me you've given him incentives to keep you safe."

"Incentives?" Kreutzer chuckled. "So he calls them incentives. Let me ask you a question, Mr. Killharney. How are you keeping safe from this madman you've inspired? After all, we all must take precautions against our enemies."

Pete had the distinct impression he had just been threatened by this benign, devoted husband.

" 'When clad in the armor of a righteous cause, the humblest citizen is stronger than all the hosts of error,' " he quoted.

"You believe that?"

"William Jennings Bryan did. He also believed in the silver standard."

"I enjoyed our talk," Kreutzer said, signaling its end. "Perhaps we meet again—that is, if your armor proves sufficiently righteous."

Pete's car had been recovered and was waiting for him out front. Next to it, Steptoe and Stephanie Kreutzer were locked in a whispered conversation, Steptoe doing most of the talking. He reached out and put his hand on her shoulder, a gesture that reminded Pete a little of Bisceglia reaching out for Melissa Sanchez. They quickly broke off when Killharney came out, and the security chief turned angrily to Pete.

"You keep the fuck out of my way," he ordered with

refreshingly candid menace. "I see you anywhere near here again, and you're lost. Understand?"

Pete understood. Steptoe lacked his employer's subtlety, but they both managed to get their point across. Killharney drove away from the beautiful house, through the beautiful grounds, and he couldn't shake the feeling that it was all just window dressing over a core of viciousness, perhaps even evil, way out of his league. It scared him. He wanted a drink.

"My dear, this is such a rare treat. Imagine, actually having tea at the Russian Tea Room. Restores a sense of order to the cosmos, doesn't it?"

Lilly Han, the *Apple*'s diminutive gossip columnist, chattered away as they were led through the Romanoff excess of the restaurant made famous by its neighbor, Carnegie Hall. She steered them past the main tables ("Wrong time of day, and definitely wrong company; you may be notorious, Pete, but you're hardly chic") to an unobtrusive corner that afforded a clear view of all arrivals. The waiter held her chair, and she alit with the delicacy and care of a thirsty mosquito. Lilly, intimate with the rarified dream world of the see-and-be-seen, was known to bite.

"So," she said, "tea?" and proceeded to sample a gooey delight from the restaurant's pastry cart.

"I'll never get over you," Pete said as she claimed a last buttery flake with an expert flick of her tongue. "You're so tiny—tiny hands, tiny ankles, tiny waist, tiny ears—but with the ten-gallon stomach of a starved stevedore."

"You think I have tiny ears?" she asked sweetly, touching one with an inch-long fingernail painted green to match her jade necklace and earrings. "So do I. And

161

I was kidding about the wrong company. The truth is, by sitting away from the good tables, and at an off-hour yet, we generate more gossip than if we tore off our clothes and dallied in the Plaza fountain."

"I didn't know you were into water sports."

"You bad boy, teasing me when you have no intention of following through. But if I can't frolic with you, at least I can keep other people wondering. After all, for me gossip is almost as good as sex. Frequently better, now that I think about it. So what's your pleasure?"

"I'm looking for a motive, a thread connecting the slaughter," Pete said. He had no intention of telling the gossip columnist that he wanted the dirt, if any, on Kreutzer and his wife. "Everyone assumes it's religion. But just to be contrary, I find myself searching for some other reason. I ask myself, why do people murder? And the answer is often greed, or love, or power, in other words your very stock-in-trade."

"You're so wicked," she murmured, but her eyes began to sort through the possibilities.

"So what's the word on my Hit List members? Why might they be killed? Or kill?" he added.

Lilly gave him a long look of speculation. "You're a perverse man, but that's one of the reasons I find you so attractive. Where do you want to start? Shall we disparage the dead or execrate the living?"

"The dead, by all means."

"I was afraid you'd say that, because I know frightfully little about the departed. Your Bengelsdorfs and Lopiccolos were scarcely the right sort of people, were they?"

"Scarcely," Pete agreed. "What about the congressman?"

"Everyone said he fucked around, but everyone says that about all politicians. Then again, he did have that five-year affair with Hazelton's wife."

"Did Hazelton know?"

"I should hope not, my dear. A man like that, God knows what he would have done if he had found out. You saw his performance on that detestable Melissa Sanchez's TV show."

"Actually, I didn't. Tell me about it."

"Oh, that woman," Lilly groaned, "she always looks like she just swallowed a bucket of warm come."

"Now Lilly."

"Well, she gives all of us working girls a bad name," Lilly complained. "I bet she would fuck anything for a story."

"I was asking about Hazelton," Pete reminded her. Did Lilly know about Sanchez and himself? Of course not. Pete hoped.

"He went over the edge while on the slut's show. She asked why he had demanded that New York declare bankruptcy, and he started quoting whole articles of the United States Constitution to her. Then he moved on to the Bible and his voice got louder and began to crack, and by the time he got around to you and your Hit List, he was screaming and every third word was edited out. I wouldn't get too close to that man if I were you. Remember what he did to Sanderson over that church business."

"What's that?"

"Nothing except practically strangle him during a vestry meeting over those air rights. He picked the late judge up by his throat and shook him like a baby rattle. Sanderson was in a brace for weeks with a sprained neck."

"Why didn't I hear about this?"

"Darling, the church is like a family, with the same disinclination to air its dirty linen."

"But Lilly's job is dirty linen."

"Peering up the assholes of the soon-to-be-has-been, if I recall the line rightly," she said. Pete winced.

"Who told you?"

"Who said it?" she answered, then leaned forward and creased his cheek with the flat side of her long, sharp nails. "Don't fret so, Pete. I've been called worse by worse people, and most of the simps who take me on couldn't turn a phrase with a spatula. What else do you want to know?"

"How about the Englishman, Todd?"

"Young girls, they say. Very discreet about it."

"No kidding," Pete said. "But not useful, unless blackmail of some sort is behind the killings."

"Too Byzantine, if you ask me," said Lilly. "Your killer seems quite a bit too unhinged for blackmail. And besides, Sissy Hall would be a more likely target for blackmail, what with her lesbian appointments secretary."

"But she's married," Pete protested, "and a mother," he added lamely, sounding naïve even to himself.

"It's a good thing her husband's gay, then, isn't it? We've all wondered how they managed to beget issue."

"But how could the Senate confirm a lesbian for UN ambassador?"

"Because they relied on the FBI for their dirt instead of Lilly. Who else?"

"Marchetti?"

"Good family man, no vices. Most Mafia are like that, I'm told. They get off in other invigorating ways."

"And Kreutzer?"

"A dream."

"A dream?"

"If you dream about dominating men, which I don't suppose you do."

"Not on a recurring basis."

"Well, take Lilly's word for it, then. Helmut Kreutzer was born in the wrong century. He's the classic robber baron. Oh, what I could have done with such delicious raw material!"

"Someone beat you to it."

"Do you know the story? The wealthy tycoon, dead wife in the distant past, goes to the ballet, spots a girl in the corps, and falls in love on the spot. He attends all her performances. He sends her flowers. He sends her notes. Finally he introduces himself. They go to dinner. Soon it's dinner after every show—death to a dancer, I might add, but this story has a happy ending. One night after dinner, he produces a six-carat rock, he proposes everlasting love and devotion and, not incidentally, marriage. She accepts, it's off to Nicaragua on a transcontinental elopement, then back to his Greenwich estate and happily-ever-after."

"You're sure about the happily-ever-after part?"

"It's a fairy tale, Pete, don't be a scrooge."

"That means you don't know."

"That means no one knows. Helmut Kreutzer guards his privacy, and he's another one I wouldn't cross if I cared about my personal health. If only you chose your friends with as good an eye."

He looked at her questioningly.

"Oh, don't pay any attention to me, it's pure envy talking." The gossip columnist sighed. "Why are Irish girls so pretty?"

"What are you talking about?"

Lilly reached across the table and kissed each of his hands. "You're still criminally handsome, but we're only allowed so many mistakes in love or life before we run out of chances. Listen to Lilly. Love not used is love lost, and Sheila McGrath's worth killing for. So don't be stupid, Pete, darling. And do be careful. You're one of the stars of my fantasy life, and I just know it wouldn't be the same if you were dead."

The Hit List had been narrowed to seven: Kreutzer, the industrialist; Hall, the UN ambassador; Todd, the take-over specialist; Marchetti, the Mafia don; Hazelton, the investment banker; Fitzwater, the demagogue; and "Not The" McCann, a man dead thirty years. Of them all, only the corpse didn't have to worry about being the killer's next target.

As for the victims, they were yesterday's news. True, the congressman had had some conference room in the Rayburn House office building dedicated in his honor, and a lecture series had been started in Sanderson's name at his old law school. But they were already as good as forgotten by the public. And the slumlord and the nursing home operator had vanished without further mention from anyone anywhere.

Which meant someone was quietly making the money they used to. Who?

Fiji might know. But the word was Fiji had hit a quinella and hopped a casino bus for Atlantic City. Leave it to a gambler to celebrate winning by switching to a new way to lose.

Red Ethel did know.

"Bea Bengelsdorf," Ethel said without hesitation, when he visited the doyenne of the Municipal Research Center.

"The bereaved spouse?"

"You've never met the widow Bengelsdorf? She makes her late husband look like Albert Schweitzer, that one."

"And Lopiccolo?"

"I'm an old woman," Ethel complained. "I don't know everything anymore."

"But you can find out," Pete said, tendering the box of chocolate-covered cherries with exaggerated furtiveness.

"Bribes, yet," she muttered, summoning over an assistant and whispering instructions, which the slim young man flew away to fulfill.

"I get so worried for you, Peter. Every morning I read the paper, I look first to see if that madman has done you in."

"But I'm the safest guy in the city. Without me, he wouldn't know who to kill next."

"Some funny joke."

"Laughter's my only armor. I don't have a private army to protect me like Kreutzer."

"That Nazi," she hissed. "If he's next to go, I shed no tears."

"Are you sure about the Nazi business?"

"Sure? What's sure? A whole town in Hungary was transported to the camps. Over three hundred Jews. No survivors. They say Kreutzer was the local SS liaison."

"But if there were no survivors, how do you know Kreutzer's responsible?"

"Never Again," Ethel muttered, the Jewish Defense League slogan. The assistant returned and passed her a piece of lavender notepaper.

"Interesting," Ethel said, scanning the information. "Three of Lopiccolo's properties on the Lower East Side were bought the day after clearing probate."

"By whom?"

"Sal Daniele."

"The garbage czar?"

"He just married a niece of Marchetti's."

"Jesus Christ, I wonder if the slums were part of the dowry."

"Wonder all you want, but none of your altar-boy obscenities in my office. You're as bad as that girl just in here."

"Girl?" Sheila?

"Pretty thing, but such language! She hit her hip on

an open file cabinet—of course you can't move in this junkyard without banging into something—but still what she said an old woman shouldn't have to hear. And won't repeat."

"When was she in here?"

"When? She's here now. Third floor, Articles of Incorporation. But where are you going?"

"To see a reporter about a story."

Killharney hurried through the inner court that had frightened him two months before, and up the Surrogate Court's wide marble stairs, then slowed his stride so he wouldn't appear anxious. He pushed open the door to the records room, and there stood Melissa Sanchez, neckline plunging to the breasts adored by Nielson Heads of Households throughout the Greater Metropolitan Area. Both loosely haltered globes quivered as she filed her blood-red nails. Around her, six subordinates searched busily through dozens of open record books. Melissa, aloof from the effort, finished her nails and arched her back into a broad, feline yawn.

"Hard at work?" Pete greeted her.

"That's what the secretary asked her boss," she said, dropping her gaze to his crotch. "So which lucky girl's getting the benefit of the best tongue in the tabloids?"

"I don't kiss and tell, Missy," Pete said, deliberately using Bisceglia's endearment. It registered no effect. "A quality I could suggest to others."

"You got me into some very hot water with that Revelations lie. And talk about telling, the network still wants to file slander charges for those terrible things you said about me at the press conference. Appear on my Hit List interview series and I'll tell them to drop it."

"I don't think my publisher would approve."

"Come with me." Melissa dragged him out to the hallway, leaned him against one of the pillars ringing the open courtyard, and gave him a full minute of tongue-fencing kiss, pushing on him with breasts and thighs until he was bent backwards over the low railing. Pete looked down at the floor thirty feet below, where Miss Jergens the librarian was looking up with a furious scowl.

"Let's do it," Sanchez gasped. "Let's fuck all afternoon, then do the interview. We'll be so hot."

"I heard Hazelton got pretty hot on your show."

Three men in pinstripes came toward them and Melissa disengaged herself. They all checked out her stiffened nipples.

"I swear he made those accusations on his own, Pete. No prompting. Christ, we had to bleep half of them, though I couldn't bring myself to cut 'offal-eating bogtrotter.'"

"Catchy."

"It's what makes TV such a vibrant medium, that marvelous spontaneity. Come on my show. It'll give you the chance to finally tell your side of the story. People just don't know you the way I do."

"That's certainly true," he said.

"And, Pete, if this interview goes well, there might be a real opportunity for you. My producer's been talking about adding a guest commentator spot to round out 'Newsmakers.' You could be just what we're looking for. Don't worry about your publisher. I'm sure our lawyers can find you an out if it's contracts you're worried about."

"It's not at the top of my list right now. I think I'll pass, but I'll sleep on it."

"If you need help, call me. I have just the thing." And she goosed him before returning to her minions.

This was a woman who knew how to get what she wanted. If sex didn't hook him, maybe ambition would. Killharney wondered whether the cast of her sexual net might snare some vital clue, whether he should string her along in the hope she would provide him with information. No, given how horny he felt right now, he would probably tell her his life story in return for an autographed picture.

Why do men kill? Greed, love, power, fear. Pete doubted he would find out much about love through Melissa Sanchez.

Pete sat at his office desk and wove late-night fantasies.

Suppose a Puerto Rican nationalist who blamed Congress for not granting the island independence lived in a Lopiccolo slum and had a mother in a Bengelsdorf nursing home and was once sentenced by Sanderson to a long stretch in Attica. The killings really had nothing to do with Killharney or his Hit List. It was all coincidence.

Fiji wanted him to believe as much. Tapped out from his junket to Atlantic City, the tipster had tried to sell Killharney the story that Lopiccolo had really been murdered by a tenant, an unstable ex-Trappist who had since committed suicide by strapping himself into a machine of his own manufacture that had slowly bled him to death from the pressure of a hundred spring-loaded needles.

"What more do you want?" Fiji had pleaded. "I give you a nut, violent, religious, a Lopiccolo slum-dweller, and my sources swear his fellow tenants swear he did it."

"But, Fiji," Pete had pointed out, "the religious part didn't start until after your hot suspect played personal pincushion. And if he didn't kill the other victims, who did?"

Who indeed? Killharney's digging into greed and gossip hadn't yielded much. Kreutzer was happily married, though his wife might not be. Todd liked little girls, Murry had fucked around with Hazelton's wife for years, Bengelsdorf had lost big in the futures market, Marchetti had distributed Lopiccolo's assets. There were plenty of small connections, but so far no unifying theory had emerged, linking killer and motive and victims. Assuming there was some hidden link, that the killer wasn't the solitary psychopath of Killharney's worst dread.

The mail on Pete's desk assumed no such thing. New variations on the ex-cop, ex-con, and ex-priest possibilities continued to arrive, plus more personal suggestions: You should look into that crazy dago Alonzo, the man with the raccoon, and so on. Sun signs and the Tibetan Book of the Dead were in vogue this week, and the hate letters had kept coming too, from political conservatives who adored Sissy Hall, from cabdrivers and steamfitters and old ladies with poison pens, and from fundamentalists rallying to their sullied leader, Brother Atwood Fitzwater.

That was one bit of bright news. The preacher had dropped his reckless-endangerment suit against Killharney. Pete didn't know how Fitzwater had pulled it off, but somehow the evangelist was back in the good graces of his fellow Bible-thumpers. What's more, Fitzwater had scheduled a big revival at the Coliseum, during which he was going to invite the killer to strike him down or else come forward and be saved. Pete noted the date on his calendar under the heading, "Hallelujah for Hypocrisy!"

Other news wasn't as cheery as the lifting of a five-million-dollar lawsuit. There was a memo on his desk from Sheila McGrath that read:

> I heard a rumor that the police found a fingerprint at the Sanderson crime scene, which they sent to Washington to match, and which Washington has lost. All copies have also disappeared. You might want to check it out.
>
> P.S. Your buddy Dombowski is livid.

As if that weren't enough, McCann wanted a meeting. James McCann, great-grandson of "The" McCann and grandson of "Not The" McCann, charter member of the Killharney's Bar Hit List. Pete didn't want to meet McCann. He didn't want to think about meeting any McCann. Instead, he continued his fantasizing.

Killharney took a legal pad and began to draw circles, his brother's organizing algebra. Suppose, as everyone did, the killer was a religious nut. He wrote RELIGION in one circle and INSANE in another. Under RELIGION he wrote the names Fitzwater, Sanderson, Hazelton. Under INSANE he wrote Hazelton. What about Marchetti? No, the Mafia don inhabited a world of rational violence. Who else?

But no, that was crazy, assuming it was one of the Hit List members who was killing off the others.

Then why did Hazelton fit both criteria? Hazelton, who had several screws loose, who was prone to violent rages, who hated Sanderson, who had a possible motive for murdering Murry? Suppose two of the murders were camouflage, useless scum who should die anyway. Dispatch them while getting rid of your wife's lover and the evil presence in your church, and use Killharney's columns as the coverup. Who would suspect an upstanding citizen like Hazelton, himself a potential victim, when everyone knew it was some religious fanatic doing the killings? Sound plausible?

No.

Pete sighed disgustedly and discarded the scrap paper covered with senseless circles. On a new sheet he drew a circle and labeled it KILLER KNOWS YOU, then crossed it out and replaced it with KILLER HATES YOU. That sounded right. In a second circle he wrote MOTIVE, and outside it he wrote RELIGION. It still stirred nothing in him. He tried ENVY, listening for the resonances that

172

gave off. Who would envy Killharney? A fellow reporter? Bisceglia?

Or was he looking at motive the wrong way? Perhaps the impetus for the killings didn't come from some inner trait, some warped personality flaw, but rather was a response to an outside force, a threat or other pressure. What circumstances would drive someone to murder a half-dozen men? Something, someone was hiding among the welter of bodies and motives.

Where are you? Why are you killing? Who's next?

Pete looked up wearily. At the other end of the city room, through the open doorway of Wilson's office, one of the wall-mounted televisions was filled with a head shot of Melissa Sanchez, wet lips twitching and pouting as she mouthed her copy to the empty room.

Eight

The burly patrolman emerging from Dombowski's office appeared close to tears.

"You got to be out of your fucking mind to go in there," the cop said, still pale. Discretion was obviously called for. Pete rapped gently on the open door.

"Go fuck yourself!" barked Dombowski. So much for discretion.

"Is this Lost and Found?" Pete asked. "Or just Lost? I heard some fingerprints have disappeared on you."

"They'll find them," Dombowski said without conviction.

"Yeah, in Jimmy Hoffa's hip pocket they'll find them. So what's the story?" Pete sat uninvited in the rickety visitor's chair whose padded armrests were blackened from the grime of a thousand nervous forearms. In a corner stood a stainless-steel, forty-cup, industrial coffee urn. Dombowski had gotten serious.

"There's no fucking story. Off the record, the lab managed to lift most of a thumbprint off the rope that strangled Sanderson and matched it to one of the dollar bills stuffed down Bengelsdorf's throat. The FBI's running a check."

"Rumor has it they sent them to Mars for verification."

"I said they'll find them," Dombowski growled. "These guys are professionals, goddamn it. They don't lose evidence."

"Unless they want to."

"What the hell do you mean by that?"

"What if someone down there buried them? What if something funny's going on and you're not being kept informed? You're local, Dombowski. There's a lot you don't need to know."

The hint cut too close to the lieutenant's own worst misgivings to tolerate.

"Why don't you fucking ask Flaubert yourself?" he shouted, throwing a mimeographed sheet at Killharney. "Here's his schedule. He's the FBI nursemaid for Sissy Hall this week. Why don't you go ask him if the Federal government's deliberately suppressing information about a mass murderer? Jesus Christ, you're turning as nutty as your killer."

"*My* killer?"

"And don't think I don't know where you got this, either. Your squeeze McGrath's been pumping her cousin on the force for tips. You can tell the little bitch I've put a stop to that."

"You watch your fucking mouth!"

"And you watch your fucking step. Haven't you noticed that woman's near every break that's happened in this case? She and that Sanchez slit both always know more than they rightfully should."

"I don't have to listen to this crap," Pete said, standing. "If those prints don't turn up today, you'll read about it tomorrow."

"That was off the record, goddamn it! And you think I fucking care if you expose those clowns? You'd be doing me a favor. Now do me another and get the fuck out of my sight."

Flaubert's schedule said "Women in Power Speech—TR Home," and gave an unlikely address in the middle of the Chelsea warehouse district. When he got to the block of seedy factories, Pete was surprised to find a well-maintained brownstone with a historic landmark plaque identifying it as the birthplace of Teddy Roosevelt. A National Park Service ranger in a crisp green uniform greeted him at the door and gave him directions to the room where the UN ambassador was speaking.

"Just up the stairs and turn right at the statue," the ranger said.

The stairs were a vast monument of carved oak rising from the perfectly preserved nineteenth-century entrance hall, beyond which sitting rooms and a formal dining room set for dinner could be glimpsed. The statue turned out to be the famous Remington portrayal of Roosevelt as Rough Rider, rearing up from his horse and grinning that wide fool's grin that must have frozen the blood of his enemies. The room where Sissy Hall was speaking was filled with silver-haired matrons all giving the speaker their rapt, approving attention.

"Those bra-less pinheads who have certainly liberated themselves from common sense—not to mention the moral foundation on which this country is based—pretend to speak for the rest of us. Let me ask you ladies, on what authority? What have they ever done except jiggle their sweatshirts and sputter swear words for the TV cameras? Have they run companies or built a professional practice? They certainly have not. So who has a better right to speak for American women than women who have delivered the goods? Gals, I'm talking about you."

The whole room became a sea of bobbing blue-rinses, with the exception of Flaubert standing watch up front, and a man directly in front of Killharney.

"Contemplating a sex change?" Pete whispered in his ear. Baumann flinched but immediately recovered, then someone grabbed Pete's arm and bent it backwards painfully.

"Give me a reason to break it," hissed Flaubert.

Pete kicked the agent's shin hard and tore his arm free. Baumann stepped between them.

"Neither the time nor the place, gentlemen. Why don't we go somewhere quiet?" He ushered them out of the room.

"Killharney, Pete Killharney," Sissy Hall's voice called to him. Pete turned around and found the whole audience staring at him. "I want you to know I don't consider you my enemy. I might be one of yours, but that's your problem. Myself, I have too many duties to waste time nursing childish grudges."

The women vigorously applauded the ambassador.

"Tell that to Hack Janacek," Pete said, and left the room.

"Refresh my memory," requested Baumann.

"Janacek was the ambassador summarily recalled after a remark he made about Sissy Hall's office decor made the *Washington Post*."

"That's right, the one about Laura Ashley receiving more State Department funds than ninety percent of the developing countries. This looks cozy enough," said Baumann, unhooking a velvet rope across the door to the master bedroom. He sat on the antique bed and gave Killharney a smile devoid of emotion. "Now, what can Mrs. Hall do for you?"

"Retire from public life. But she's not why I'm here. I came to see you."

"Us?" Flaubert asked. Baumann's eyebrows fluttered.

"Yeah, Mutt and Jeff from Washington. What happened to the fingerprints the NYPD sent you to match?"

"A bookkeeping problem," Baumann said smoothly. "It happens all the time, believe me. We have them. We'll find them. Everything's under control."

"Tell that to the killer's next victim. And speaking of bookkeeping, the day after you asked for my notebooks, someone apparently convinced of their existence broke into the seminary where I was visiting my brother."

"Have you changed your mind about giving us access?" Baumann asked.

"They still don't exist. For Chrissakes, a priest was assaulted! Dombowski's investigation is being sabotaged, and you clowns are playing coy. Something smells rotten."

"I don't like your tone of voice or your implications," Flaubert said, "and I don't know what the hell you're talking about, seminary break-ins and priests being assaulted. I think you're nuts. Just keep away from Mrs. Hall, do you hear me? You've harmed her enough with your damned Hit List crap."

"Gentlemen, I think we can reach an understanding," Baumann said, calming his associate. "We're all working on the same side, after all. Mr. Killharney, if you uncover any information that may help find this killer, I'm sure you'll pass it along to us. In turn, we could provide you exclusivity on certain aspects of our investigation as it proceeds."

"Such as?"

"Such as we're seriously exploring motives other than religion."

"You don't think he's a nut either," Pete said, searching Baumann's face for reaction.

"I think if we both do our jobs and get a little luck going our way, this whole unpleasant affair can be tidied up," he replied, his eyes devoid of the passion that fires most men on a quest. Catching a killer, or whatever he was up to, was a day at the office for Baumann.

"Who are you?" Killharney asked.

"One of the good guys," he assured him.

Pete hoped it was true. He had no idea what to do if it wasn't.

From across the hall came the thunder of applause and the scraping of chairs as the audience of self-satisfied, powerful women stood in ovation.

"More!" they cried. "More!"

The only indication that it was a bar was the small, faded "Piels on Tap" sign tucked into the single barred window facing the Brooklyn docks. Across the harbor and surprisingly close, the Statue of Liberty shone her torch in vain on the dark, crumbling wharves. It was an area dripping with failure and corruption; it even took a twenty-dollar bribe to get a taxi to bring Pete here. As he tugged on the heavy iron door, Killharney wondered how the hell he was going to get home.

Hostile eyes flickered across the entering stranger. To be expected, for it was a neighborhood bar, a workingman's hangout. Everyone in it knew everyone else, and if they didn't they didn't want to. But Pete knew the etiquette necessary to enter such small, guarded worlds as local taverns, ballpark bleachers, boccie leagues, poker games. He moved deliberately to the bar and waited to be served. Haste and anxiety were to be avoided as sure signs of vulnerability, as were boisterousness and too-easy familiarity. The rule was drink your drink and mind your own fucking business.

The bartender eventually detached himself from the Yankees game on the TV over the bar and approached Killharney.

"What can I get you?" he asked.

"Coke," Pete said, continuing his abstinence.

"No Coke, Pepsi," said the bartender, the tag line from an old comedy routine. The other patrons along the rail chuckled at the wit.

Pete smiled enough to acknowledge the joke and his ability to be the butt with no hard feelings. He was an okay guy, the others quickly assessed, and they all turned their attention back to the TV.

It was good to be back in a world he knew, a world where the sense of right and wrong, no matter how warped by bigotry or chauvinism, still obtained. Baumann's calm amorality unsettled Pete. He had said he was one of the good guys. Yet the man reminded Killharney of a snake lying in the shadows, waiting for vermin to come close enough to consume in a single reflexive swallow.

This was a clearer world, this bar filled with blue-collar friends, this anonymous refuge from the unmeet-able demands of job, family, life. Pete remembered the beer-vendor column, in which he had tried to portray the reality of an unremarkable life. Maybe the effort to capture the truth within these unnoticed lives could replace his now-intermittent anger as the wellspring for writing. He hoped so. Pete couldn't count on enemies to do the job anymore.

"I'm looking for McCann," Pete told the bartender. "The name's Killharney."

Heads turned. So this was the Hit Man. Some showed only enough interest to indicate they weren't impressed. Others glared in open hostility. No one spoke. On TV, the Yankee pitcher Ron Guidry recorded what the announcer said was his third strikeout of the game. Pete began to feel uncomfortable. This wasn't the place to attract silence.

"Over here, Killharney," someone called from the corner. Pete looked in the direction where the voice came from and saw a modestly overweight, middle-aged man in a rumpled business suit with a plain, boyish face and weary eyes. Nearly the last of the Irish clubhouse leaders, McCann didn't look the part of sworn enemy. He looked, in fact, a lot like Pete's brother, Brendan.

"Glad you could make it," McCann said as Pete sat down across the table from him. Neither man offered to shake hands. "Hell of a night."

He took out a pack of cigarettes and shook two free. They were Luckies, by coincidence or design. Pete took one to indicate that negotiations were open. The two Irishmen lit up and smoked through another Guidry strikeout, a hard slider that the batter missed by three inches.

"A shame about Murry," McCann said finally.

"He was a corrupt hack," Pete replied.

"Yes, but he was *our* corrupt hack. Ireland will miss him, rest his sullied soul. He read your column religiously."

"I'm not flattered."

"And hated your guts."

"Now I am."

They both smiled at the setup. Pete's worst fear about meeting the current head of the McCann clan was coming true. He liked him. Pete struggled to maintain some of the momentum of his ancient grudge.

"No doubt you wept for Sanderson too. He was your corrupt judge, wasn't he?"

"We haven't owned judges for two generations," McCann answered, refusing to be baited.

"What do you want?"

"The same thing you do."

"Which is?"

"I want my name back."

Pete felt the tendons of his neck tighten. Never.

"Every year I have to open the paper to see my family's name next to slumlords and mafiosi, every goddamned year since you started your Hit List. And for what? For a sin committed by a long-dead and never-mourned great-uncle." McCann's voice rose as he vented the anger of calumny too long endured. "He didn't make your father drop dead, Killharney."

"Just my mother," Pete said. "And my little baby sister. And I'm never going to forget."

"No, of course not," McCann said, more quietly. "My great-uncle was a weak, even a despicable man. He gambled and drank and whored away all the good his brother and father had struggled two lifetimes to achieve. He ruined many families, like yours, who thought they could rely on us. Both my father before me and I have put in two more lifetimes trying to undo the curse he made of our name.

"Once lost, a name is almost impossible to retrieve. Someone is stealing yours, and if he isn't stopped soon, the name Killharney will be as infamous as an old man's dog called Sam."

"So what's the deal?" Pete asked. "What are you selling?"

"Information. I'm told you want to know about Murry, about Sanderson, about mob connections, about Teamster tie-ins. You want to know what the street knows, what the police know. We may not own judges, but we still have access across the board. If you're serious about finding this nut, we can help."

"And the price?"

"Lay off my family. Yours was a terrible loss, but

there must be other ways to honor your mother and sister than by dishonoring mine. I'm not asking you to forsake their memory, but is their only remembrance to be a yearly cheap shot at a disgraced dead man?"

Pete didn't trust himself to answer, didn't want to give in to the reasonableness, wanted to keep the easy hate. But he needed information, and the need showed.

"I'll add a sweetener," McCann said, sensing it. "I don't really have to be talking to you now. If I had done nothing, you would have ceased to be a problem."

"What do you mean?"

Someone opened the front door to leave, and the damp cold rushed through the bar.

"There's an ex-member of the Arsenal Gang, name of Mulhady. Ever heard of him?"

"Mulhady? No," Pete said. The Arsenal Gang was one of the last in the long and inglorious line of Hell's Kitchen's Irish youth gangs.

"Nice kid. Till he went to 'Nam. He came back minus three toes and his humanity."

The name registered. Crazy Mulhady. Pete remembered a story about someone who'd said something about Mulhady's sister and had been found a week later, shot thirty-six times. Rumor had it Mulhady also made beer money doing grudge jobs for the mob.

"So?" Pete said, trying to sound unconcerned.

"So he took a positive dislike to you. Thought you gave the neighborhood a bad name. The sweetener is he's been taken care of."

"Taken care of?"

"If he hadn't, I wouldn't be worrying about next year's Hit List."

Where was McCann coming from? Was this man with the weary eyes, who didn't own judges anymore, who ran voter registration drives for new immigrants

183

and pretended to fix parking tickets by paying them himself, who only wanted to clear his family's name, was he truly at ease with the businesslike murder of irritants?

"I'm not sure thanks are appropriate," Pete said.

"A crazy. Uncontrollable. He reminded me of the type of lunatic your murderer must be. So what do you say? Do we have a deal?"

McCann held out his hand. Pete regarded it as fear, anger, present need and past wrongs, unspoken threats and vague promises all churned within him. He needed a drink. He needed McCann. Pete shook the outstretched hand.

"First installment," McCann said, no trace of triumph showing. "Whoever is killing the others didn't kill Lopiccolo. A wacko tenant pulled that one."

"Yeah, and has since conveniently killed himself. I had a tout try to sell me that a week ago," Pete said scornfully, already regretting the deal.

McCann shrugged.

"I'm not asking you to believe it. I'm telling you it's true. What you do with it's your own business."

What if it was true? What did it mean when a murder spree was started by one man but perpetuated by another? It might mean the cleverness that permitted him to successfully murder the Hit List victims not only accompanied but instigated the other killings. Moreover, it was cleverness of a very particular, professional type. Whoever the Hit List killer was, he knew what he was doing. The possibility frightened Pete in a way he wasn't sure he wanted to explore.

"More to follow," McCann said. "You need a ride home?"

"If it's not out of your way."

As both men knew, they lived three blocks from each other. Before tonight they had never said hello.

Christ and Saint Peter's Church was so tasteful it had to be Episcopalian. Shaded by mature sycamores in the middle of a quiet side street on the Upper West Side, the tidy brick church had a red tile roof and small stained-glass windows protected by vandal-proof Plexiglas. A bulletin board out front advertised a meditation group every Wednesday, day-care in the undercroft, and a spring movie series, this week featuring Fellini's *Satyricon*. It hardly seemed the place to be looking for fanaticism, religious or otherwise.

Nor did Robert Law Hazelton show any outward sign of fervor. An hour ago, Killharney had watched the investment banker arrive at the church he had adopted after losing the air-rights battle at his previous parish, and the dessicated old man looked nothing at all like a hate-crazed mass murderer.

But Hazelton as perpetrator might explain the two-killer possibility. Congressman Murry, the lover of Hazelton's wife, was the first victim of the second killer, and Hazelton had a history of uncontrollable rage. While not a professionally violent man, he was the most plausible suspect directly connected with the Hit List that Pete had yet constructed from his brother's circles of inference.

Across the street, the organ swelled into the recessional. Early-bolting worshipers began to filter out, followed by the less hurried faithful. Almost the last to leave was Hazelton, who stood at the curb blinking into the sun as he raised an arm to signal nonexistent taxis. Was he blind as well? Pete crossed over to him.

"Mr. Hazelton, Pete Killharney of the *Apple*. I'd like to ask—"

Before the introductions could be completed, Hazelton had wrapped his liver-spotted hands around Pete's throat with what the police would term homicidal intent.

"Let me alone! Let me alone!" Hazelton screamed, and tightened his grip on Pete's throat.

"Stop," Pete gurgled. He was being murdered by an old man in front of a church. He short-punched Hazelton in the Adam's apple, and the banker collapsed. Horrified parishioners hastened to his side, except for one man on the corner whose smirk seemed vaguely familiar. A Hazelton-hater, no doubt.

Pete walked away from the church rubbing his bruised and throbbing throat. Whatever Hazelton lacked in professional experience, he more than compensated for with fury. That old man could easily have decapitated Sanderson barehanded. Where had he seen that smirk before?

A long black Cadillac pulled up in front of him, and two impeccably dressed giants climbed out.

"Good morning, Mr. Killharney," the Hercules on the left greeted him politely. Gesturing toward the limo's open door with a fight-scarred hand, he asked, "Would you care to accompany us?"

"Not particularly," Pete said. "Does it make any difference?"

"Not particularly," the other gorilla replied, and they tossed him into the limo. Ten minutes later he was brunching with a Mafia don.

"Glad you could join me. You probably won't believe this, but I like your columns. That Doughboy cracks me up."

Sal Marchetti showed no sign of humor as he stared out the café windows at the Rockefeller Center skating rink. Keeping his eyes locked on something outside, he methodically worked a soft, plump, perfectly manicured pinky around his hairy ear. The sun reflecting off the ice outside made his diamond pinky ring twinkle cheerfully throughout the task. Waiters hovered. Bodyguards leaned against strategic pillars that commanded a view of all the restaurant's exits.

"What will it be? Bloody Mary? Mimosa? No, I forgot, you're on the wagon."

"Just coffee," Pete said. How did Marchetti know about his temperance?

"Coffee for my guest, and cappuccino for me. I got a confession to make," the Mafia don said sheepishly. "I had what the DA loves to call an ulterior motive when I picked this place for our little chat."

Outside, a chubby little girl dressed entirely in pink, her plain face dominated by an enormous Roman nose, waved as she skated uncertainly past. Marchetti gave a big wave back.

"Maria, my first granddaughter," the multiple killer said with bashful pride.

"A beautiful child," Pete ventured, knowing when to keep a lie short.

"I spoil her rotten, of course, but what else are grandfathers good for?"

"Brunch, and maybe a little chat."

The coffee and cappuccino appeared, and Marchetti motioned the waiters away. Food would wait.

"You got good manners, Pete, I like that. Now my son, Fredo. Fredo's got no patience."

For the first time Pete noticed Freddy Marchetti lounging with one of the bodyguards. Ready Freddy, the nickname derived from his reputed willingness to pull the trigger with little or no provocation, glared at Pete with an intent less polite than mere impatience.

"I tell him, you can't have manners without patience, and without manners, you're nothing but another rich slob. He don't listen, though. He should be here with us now, chatting it up, but I tell him, no, Fredo, you'll start with the threats and spoil everyone's appetite. Sons. Daughters, they listen to you. Hey, Pete, how come you haven't seen your daughter in so long?"

"I don't consider myself safe company at the moment. And I'm a little surprised by the thoroughness of your concern."

"I'm concerned. You're a great writer, I mean that. An asset to New York. Your Hit List I don't appreciate, but hell, the good with the bad, right? These killings, though"—and Marchetti shook his head again—"it's bad business, these killings. Very bad business."

"They're that," Pete agreed, thinking most people didn't associate murder with business.

"And a disgrace to our city. I mean, a United States congressman murdered, and a judge. Just terrible."

"An expensive loss. I don't suppose you lit any candles for Bengelsdorf, however."

"We had no quarrel with the man."

"The street says otherwise."

The don sipped cappuccino, brushing whipped cream from his mouth with meticulous care. "Whenever someone is killed, the street says 'Mafia, Mafia,' like a parrot that only knows one word. Get serious, Pete. We got a crazy man out there. These murders weren't only wasteful, they were sloppy, overdone."

Pete thought of the shoe box containing the accountant's hand and wondered what "overdone" meant in such a context.

"I trust you're taking precautions," Pete said, the same words Kreutzer had used.

The don grinned broadly as his granddaughter wavered by once again, her face damp and blotchy from exercise.

"There are a dozen men within a mile of here who

are more of a danger to me than this piece of shit," Marchetti said with no sign of worry. "It's you who needs the security. Did you know someone's been tailing you for over a month now?"

"You mean Mulhady?"

The don looked puzzled.

"I'm told a trigger man from the Arsenal Gang didn't like my looks. I was also told he had been taken care of."

With a jerk of his head, Marchetti fetched his son over and whispered to him in Italian. Freddy laughed, a mirthless bark, and answered in Italian with appropriate gestures. Marchetti smiled and turned to Pete.

"This Mulhady? The shooter? He was stabbed in the back by his girlfriend while in bed with another woman. My son says he died in the saddle." The don's eyes twinkled with sad amusement. "May we all have such bliss when it's our time."

So much for McCann's sweetener. But he hadn't been lied to, Pete realized. Mulhady had been taken care of. Pete admired the skillful use of half-truth and found himself glad that McCann didn't really deal in murder. But then who was following him?

"Thanks for the tip about the tail. I'll keep a look over my shoulder from now on."

"You do that. The guy's good. What were you and that SEC lawyer talking about last week?"

The payoff. The don didn't waste any time collecting. He must be in some serious trouble to risk pumping a reporter for information. Bisceglia would love to know, Pete thought, surprised at himself for considering his colleague.

"Financial gossip, mostly." He felt Marchetti's eyes boring into him, demanding more, so Pete followed another of his rules: tell the truth if it helps. "Nothing about you. I asked, but he refused to say a word."

"They're up to something down there," Marchetti muttered. "They're sniffing around like dogs in heat. But there's nothing to find. I might be a bastard, but I ain't no bitch."

They both laughed briefly, then Marchetti stood up. Brunch was apparently over. At the door, one of the bodyguards appeared and engaged Freddy in urgent conversation. Ready Freddy hurried over and conveyed the information to his father in quick bursts of Italian. Marchetti turned somber.

"I have sad news," he said. "Hazelton's dead."

"I was just with him," Pete said, shaken by the news. The killings were coming closer. Death on death, wrong on wrong. He had lowered himself to talking with mobsters and mortal enemies in his effort to stop the killings, and the blood continued to flow.

"How did it happen?" he asked, suppressing a macabre vision of Hazelton as a ticker-tape mummy.

"Suicide," Marchetti said. "He jumped from the steeple of his old church and splattered himself all over Park Avenue."

"The Antichrist is in Afghanistan," said a young man wearing army fatigues and toting a huge wooden cross on his shoulder. "The Russian invasion was a CIA cover to install the Rockefellers as regents for Satan on earth. Read all about it," he suggested, and passed Pete a mimeographed sheet.

"Thanks," said Killharney, and moved quickly away. Too quickly. He backed into another young man dressed only in a G-string. Instead of a cross, this one held a placard that proclaimed CHRIST LOVES GAYS TOO.

"Better watch who you back into," the protester warned with a wink.

The "Salvation or Doom" revival had finally arrived, when the Hit List killer was supposed to strike down Brother Atwood Fitzwater as a false prophet, or else confess and be saved. Church buses ringed Columbus Circle. Antiseptic teenaged guides praised Jesus and directed the faithful inside. Amplified organ music swelled above crisscrossing floodlights like those usually found at Hollywood openings, and every hallelujah and howl of protest was being recorded by newspapers, radio, and TV.

The revival had also drawn crackpots by the hundreds and engendered a gay rights demonstration led by Mr. Rod Long himself. Behind him, about three dozen gays danced a rhumba chain around a bus identified as the property of Christ and the Pleasant Hills Baptist Church. The scrubbed congregation within gaped at the writhing circle.

"Why don't you boys play chorus line someplace else," directed a mounted patrolman, his half-ton of horseflesh easily scattering the chain. The cop spotted Killharney. "Hey, Pete, did you see the schlong on that faggot? Christ, it was bigger than a fungo bat. I'm glad my wife ain't here. I mean, the guy might be a fruitcake, but that's some banana he's got."

Pete could see the headline: TOP BANANA RHUMBAS AT REVIVAL. There were a week's worth of columns here, if this were another time, if Pete weren't himself saddled with a half-ton of guilt. After Hazelton's death, Killharney had again been tempted to take confession. Instead, he sought out Herlihy.

"I have to take the stage at exactly seven minutes after seven," a frighteningly obese woman was imploring the police inspector when Pete located the command post. She turned to Killharney. "It's a holy number," she said, and went into a fit.

"Another prophet," Herlihy explained as they watched five cops heave her onto a stretcher and haul her away. "That's the seventh so far this evening."

"A holy number, I'm told."

"Sure. Mickey Mantle wore it. What can I do for you?"

"Not a thing. No body counts tonight. I just dropped by to say hello."

I killed Hazelton, he wanted to blurt out in irrational admission. I might as well have given him the shove.

"Well, it's a comfort to see someone sane in the midst of this madness."

"Heard anything new about the lost fingerprints?"

"Nothing yet." The inspector's sad eyes flickered with what might have been momentary anger.

"It's a fucking outrage!" screamed a familiar voice. "Who ordered those storm troopers to stop my camera crew?"

Melissa Sanchez descended on Herlihy with a fury spawned of good footage missed. The lights of her mini-cam came up, and she upgraded her language to network neutrality.

" 'Newsmakers' is having its constitutional right to free speech denied, and I demand to know who's responsible!"

"Certainly, ma'am," agreed Herlihy with ratings-dimming courtesy. "The Beatific Broadcast Network, as sponsor, has exercised its copyright to prohibit cameras or other recording equipment inside the building this evening."

"But—"

"As I'm sure you know, article 33b of the 1978 copyright law states quite clearly that—"

"Oh fuck, shut this yawner off," Sanchez ordered. The lights went off. "We'll do a voice-over of the initial encounter and splice in the fairy footage. Jesus, Pete Killharney!" she exclaimed, seeing him for the first time.

"Hi, Melissa. I was stirred by your courageous stand for the rights of the press."

"Yeah, I bet that's what stirred you," she said. She dragged Killharney away from the command post, pushed him between two parked vans, and gave him a deep, tongue-first kiss. This was getting to be a habit. Her hand dropped to his crotch. "I've missed you terribly."

A Fitzwater guide popped into sight.

"Can I be of any assistance?" she asked.

"Sounds kinky enough to be fun," Sanchez said without removing her hand, "but I don't feel like sharing tonight, honey."

"Oh," said the guide. "Oh," and disappeared.

"So what's up besides this?" Sanchez asked as she stroked him with slow provocation.

"I'm looking to be saved," Pete said, and held her hand still.

"Look no further. No, seriously, when are you coming in for a screen test? I talked to my producer, and she's really excited about lining you up as a guest commentator."

"I'll call you."

"Look for me later. I've got to get back to my crew or they'll think the best about me."

She blew Killharney a kiss, and he returned to Herlihy. The inspector was getting good mileage out of discreet silence.

"What was that crap about the copyright law?" Pete asked, to dispel the unspoken smirk that hovered around them.

"I confess I've ruined miles of footage by quoting bogus legalese," Herlihy said with no trace of repentance. "Any confessions of your own to make, Peter?"

193

A man in full evening clothes presented himself to the inspector and snapped out a crisp, military salute.

"I carry a message to all mankind," he announced.

Made obsolete by the new Convention Center and scheduled for demolition to make room for twin skyscrapers, the Coliseum held a morbid pall that was emphasized by the huge banners suspended from its flaking ceiling. THE END IS AT HAND, read one, and Pete thought of Hazelton. YE MUST BE BORN AGAIN, read another, tardy advice for suicides. REPENT OR BE DAMNED, a third proclaimed. This wasn't the place to be hanging out with a bad conscience.

Ironically, no one had linked him with the one Hit List death in which Pete felt complicity. The coroner had found a walnut-sized brain tumor during the autopsy, and everyone seemed to accept that as the cause for the fatal leap. But Pete remembered Hazelton's resentment-fed power during their confrontation, and he knew he had hardened the old man's resolve to seek final escape.

Contrition was cut short by a brass band blaring its way down the center aisle. Behind it, a hundred-member chorus dressed in red, white, and blue processed while singing an inspirational anthem:

"Oh, you can tell . . ."

"You can tell . . ." echoed the baritones.

"When you meet me, Jesus . . ."

"Jesus Christ . . ."

"By the holes in his hands and feet . . ."

"Feet, feet . . ."

Still singing, the band and chorus filled bleachers on either side of the stage. A group of intent, nervous children shuffled down the aisle carrying lit candles, followed by about a dozen second-string preachers, all looking properly reverential, though a few did glance back up the aisle with what a sinner like Pete might think of as envy.

For bringing up the rear of the large procession, separated from the rest by a good thirty feet, was Brother Atwood Fitzwater, dressed in white but for a black cross centered over his heart like the crosshairs on a rifle sight. Fitzwater eventually reached the stage and mounted a pulpit that placed him above everyone else. The hall quickly hushed. He looked to his left, to his right, then his voice boomed over the public address system through the benefit of a concealed body microphone.

"Do you believe Jesus Christ is Lord?" he asked.

"Yes!" the congregation screamed back.

"Do you believe Christ died for your sins?"

"Hallelujah!"

"Are you a sinner?" he asked them, lowering his voice confidentially.

"Yes," they eagerly answered.

"Are you ready to be saved?"

"Oh yes!"

"Are you ready to be born again?"

"Yes!"

"Praise Jesus," Fitzwater said, and another hymn started up at the cue. When it finished, he slowly descended from the pulpit and threw himself on his knees at stage level.

"You see before you," he said, "the most miserable man on God's great earth. I have walked away from Christ's saving grace not once, friends, but twice! Pray for my soul." And he hung his head, and not a whisper broke the silence. Fitzwater lifted his face back into the spotlight.

"You know my story. You know I was a derelict, a drunk, a disgrace in the eyes of man. You know God spoke to me, even as I lay drunk in my own vomit and excrement, that Christ told me to be born again, praise Jesus! That he raised me up and gave me the power to preach the Word, Amen!"

"Amen!" came several responses.

Fitzwater stood and started to pace. "Oh yes, He raised me up, and I became so high and mighty that I thought maybe Jesus should shove over and make a little room for me there on the right-hand side of the Lord, have mercy on me! But I'm here to tell you," he bellowed, "I'm here to tell you that our God is an angry God, Amen! I'm here to tell you that he who God raises up, so can He cast down! I'm here to tell you, friends, that God Almighty turned His grace from me, and I was chastised, and mortified, and cast into the wilderness."

Face dripping sweat, Fitzwater stopped pacing and faced his audience.

"I went and got me out my gun. Yes, I did. For I still couldn't look a good Christian in the eye and call him brother. Even after this revival was scheduled, even after I had been welcomed back into the fold, some satanic part of me held me back from begging Christ's forgiveness. It would have me burn in hell forever, rather than confess my sin and be saved, Lord have mercy!"

Fitzwater bowed his head in histrionic shame. Then, from beneath the snarl of sweaty hair obscuring his face came a low chuckle.

"But sometimes Satan outfoxes himself. Because the very day I was going to pull the trigger, that poor diseased man Hazelton succumbed to the same black temptation."

Fitzwater threw his head back and let out a guffaw.

"We're going to win, friends. The Devil isn't invincible, for it was Satan himself gave me the sign! Satan stealing Hazelton's soul kept me from handing him my own, praise God! And I had a revelation. Do you know what it was? Can you guess? Of course you can, for it's written in the Good Book bigger than any billboard you see from the Interstate: You must be born again, praise Jesus! And I accepted Christ as my personal Savior and I was saved!"

A hymn exploded, lifting people from their seats in surprise. As the collection plates were passed, Fitzwater accepted a towel from a pretty robed girl and mopped his face, a tent-circuit James Brown. Refreshed, he got down to business.

"Friends, I know Satan's put doubts in some of you. It's his job! And he doesn't take coffee breaks or long lunches, neither. That old snake has whispered in your ears, 'How do you know he's saved? How do you know Brother Atwood has really accepted Jesus Christ as his personal Savior?' Well, I'm prepared to answer those doubts tonight. You've all heard about this Hit List killer what's been going around murdering men in God's name. You all know that a certain reporter has decided I would make a good victim."

"No!" cried dozens in the crowd. "We love you, Atwood!"

Fitzwater held up his hands in protest.

"Well, maybe I would. Maybe, if I was standing up here preaching trash, maybe I would deserve death and eternal damnation. But I say to you, I have been born again, and I'll place my life on the line to prove it!"

The lights in the Coliseum dimmed to a single spotlight trained directly on Fitzwater.

"I have invited this killer, this miserable, unfortunate man, to come here tonight and witness God's love firsthand. I have said, Come see for yourself the joy of accepting Jesus Christ into your heart. And I pray he's here. Why, he may be sitting next to you at this very minute."

There was a nervous rustling in the dark crowd.

197

"I say to you, inheritor of the stain of Cain, see my happiness in being saved and feel the love of Christ. It's there, it's waiting for you. If I'm not speaking truth, may you smite me down. Take my life if I lie. Strike me down!"

Fitzwater threw his arms wide in invitation. The invisible congregation held its breath in fearful waiting. Seconds ticked by, a minute, and no shots rang out. Fitzwater dropped his arms, his smiling, sweaty face resolutely reverential.

"If I, the most miserable man on earth, have been saved, anyone can. Each and every one of you here tonight can be born again! All you have to do is ask! All you have to do is pray to Him and say, Save me, Jesus! Christ, save me from Satan!"

"Christ, save me from this asshole," said someone behind Pete.

"Sheila?" Pete asked, trying to make her out in the darkness. "Where are you? What are you doing here?"

"Right here, and I'm working. What about you?"

"Searching for redemption." He reached out and grasped her hand.

"I'm going to ask people in the crowd to step forward and be born again," Fitzwater said, his voice an ecstasy of righteous control. "I'm going to pick out Christians at random and ask them to testify for Christ. And friends, brothers and sisters, if enough of you step forward, if all of us believe, I'm going to ask the killer to come forward and join us in Christ. So I ask you now: Are you willing to be saved?"

"Yes!" roared the crowd.

"Are you ready to be saved?"

"Yes!"

"Then make your choice for Jesus!"

Spotlights overhead began cutting through the auditorium like searchlights scanning for perpetrators.

Speaking of perpetrators, what if Pete's suspicion was correct and Hazelton was the Hit List killer? Was it over? Had the killing stopped without a tidy conclusion, no killer in custody, no assurance but time that the spree was finished? Or with Hazelton gone, was there another prime suspect that Pete should concentrate on? Like a vicious ex-cop who hated him.

The spotlights continued to flicker over the rows of ready Christians, finally settling on a mousy-looking woman with hunched shoulders and a pillbox hat. She look terrified. An attendant hurried over with a microphone and held it up to her quivering lips.

"Are you ready to be born again?" Fitzwater asked her.

"Yerp," she chirped, petrified.

"Then stand and be saved!"

She stood up, and the crowd clapped and cheered as the attendant helped her to the stage, where Fitzwater placed her next to himself.

"Make your choice for Jesus!" he called again, and again the spotlights sought another lamb to cut from the herd, this time choosing a blubbery young man, who boomed his readiness and lumbered to the stage faster than the scurrying attendant.

"I'm going to be picked," Pete told Sheila.

"That's paranoid," she said. A grandmotherly type was chosen.

"Do you remember when you were in school and the teacher asked a question you didn't know the answer to, and he looked around for someone to choose, and you knew, you were absolutely sure that he would pick you? I'm next."

The spotlights danced and swirled and, one by one, came to rest on Killharney. The attendant thrust a microphone at him.

"Are you ready to be born again?" the evangelist asked, not knowing or caring who had been selected, for Fitzwater's calls to salvation shook with the blind exaltation of power.

Pete stood and took the microphone in his hand.

"That depends, Brother Atwood," he said, and Fitzwater glared peevishly toward the source of the skepticism. "It depends on whether you still like to suck shit."

Fitzwater gaped in horror at the blasphemy, then saw who chance had chosen him to save and dropped as if shot.

"I still get goosebumps when I think of those spotlights all stopping on you," Sheila said. "Jesus, your neck's tight. Relax."

"Umph," Pete grunted into the pillow as her fingers probed the knots of muscle roped around his neck. He hadn't had this good a rubdown since Saint Bonaventure's, where the old welterweight who ran the training room had made his back crack like a drum tattoo.

"Does that sort of intuition happen to you often?"

"Not often. Sometimes my gut starts to crawl and I know things. Or think I do. I've been wrong."

"Did I tell you someone from the *Enquirer* called every reporter at the *Apple,* offering a hundred dollars for the name of the woman the killer was referring to on the radio show?"

"That's appalling."

"Certainly was."

"I would have held out for double that."

"I told him two-fifty or don't waste your breath."

Pete smiled and felt himself loosen under Sheila's massage. It was the first time they had been back together since making love that one afternoon, and it felt comfortable, welcoming, good.

On her television, a group of implausibly handsome fishermen drank beer around a campfire that would have incinerated a trout in ten seconds. The news came back on, and Melissa Sanchez's voice spoke over the footage of Fitzwater being helped into a long black limousine by several of his ecclesiastical flunkies.

"Brother Atwood Fitzwater left under his own power tonight after collapsing during a religious revival he was holding at the Coliseum. Aides for Fitzwater maintain that the preacher succumbed to heatstroke in the middle of his sermon and vowed to sue the Port Authority, which owns the building, over what they maintained was inadequate air conditioning. They pointed out that the Coliseum is slated to be razed this year."

The cameras cut back to Sanchez looking both concerned and dubious.

"Reports from inside the Coliseum, however, indicate that Fitzwater's collapse followed a confrontation between him and reporter Pete Killharney. Killharney could not be reached for comment at this time."

"And how did you know about that service entrance?" Sheila asked, giving him a slap on the butt as she got up and turned off the TV.

"I watched the Coliseum being built. A garage where I used to fence hubcaps and hood ornaments when I was a kid was torn down to make way for it, so I took an interest in the project. One of my first columns was about the number and variety of bribes needed to get the eyesore finished near schedule."

"Has your old neighborhood changed totally since you grew up there?"

"Hell's Kitchen is one of those semi-slums that are always trading one set of poor for another. When I left, the Italians had taken over above Fiftieth Street, and after the war the Hispanics and blacks began nibbling around the edges. Nowadays it's the Asians everyone swears are ruining the area."

"And you left because your parents died."

Killharney nodded.

"How did it happen, Pete?"

"One at a time," he said shortly.

"And it has to do with the McCann family?"

Outside, an ambulance raced toward one of the East Side hospitals, its siren howling. Sheila returned to the bed and resumed her backrub.

"What did your cousin the cop say about the tail?" Pete asked, not answering her question.

"Definitely not NYPD. You didn't answer my question."

"Did you ever meet Kreutzer's chief of security, an old police captain named Steptoe?"

"Never. And I guess you don't want to talk about it, because your neck just knotted up like a Boy Scout exhibition."

He turned over and kissed her hands.

"My dad drove a bus for the city," he said. "A good, steady job, courtesy of McCann's Huron Democratic Club. One evening he had a heart attack while driving down Fifth Avenue, and his bus skidded out of control and crushed a group of prominent socialites outside the Pierre.

"I heard about the accident and hopped on my bike and was there in minutes. And I saw my dad's face blue and covered with blood from the shattered windshield, and some big asshole in a tuxedo was slapping him, trying to sober him up. I figure my father died while being slapped around during a coronary.

"Not counting Dad, which they didn't, three people

202

died, including the City Council president, and someone had to pay. So first they spread the slander that my father was drunk on the job. Then, because all Irish are drunks, hundreds of O'Briens and Carrolls and Sweeneys were purged from the city payroll. Hundreds of families went hungry and cold just because they were Irish.

"And Charles McCann, head of the clan and protector of the Celts in the city, was too busy betting his inheritance on the horses to raise a murmur of protest over the pogrom. The only active step he took during the whole vendetta was to have my family illegally evicted from our tenement.

"My mother was shattered by it, widowed and homeless within a week. I'll always remember her glazed eyes as we waited a whole day in front of the McCann brownstone for someone to come out and help us. A cop eventually chased us away. We spent the next three nights on the street, sleeping in alleys, eating garbage, begging. A priest finally put us up temporarily in the damp basement of his church.

"Both Mom and my baby sister caught a chill from that modest act of charity, then pneumonia, and both died, and my brother and I spent the rest of our childhood in orphanages and foster homes, all because of one powerful man's indifference and others' thirst for revenge. One night when I was twelve, after a beating by my foster father, I vowed never to permit the powerful to brutalize or neglect innocents with impunity. And I've never forgotten."

Her eyes glistening, Sheila came to him and gathered his head to her breast, and Pete felt his own eyes sting from tears. The orphan in him tightened against the solace, then something in him let go, and he stopped struggling, and they held each other in silent understanding. Pain and love acknowledged, they embraced in that small hollow of comfort that couples create when they discover they belong to each other.

"I have to go," Pete finally said. Sheila nodded, took his hand, led him to the door.

"When this is all over with, when the danger's passed, could we start over?" she asked.

"I'd like that."

"Be careful," she said, kissing him.

"Don't worry," he promised, and opened the door. It was covered with a dripping cross of blood.

Nine

What's a euphemism for eating shit?

Pete searched for an uncensorable description of the Coliseum confrontation. It didn't help that the night before a psychopathic killer had given his lover's door a bloodbath while Pete spilled his life story inside. At least the horror had gotten Sheila a police escort in exchange for Pete's silence about the lurid vandalism. Dombowski had fallen for the bluff. "You're going to print this when I put on a dress and cruise Christopher Street, Killharney, but the squad car's hers anyway."

"Mr. Killharney, into my office at once, please!" Wilson summoned him.

"What?" asked Pete, notebook in hand.

"Watch," Wilson ordered.

A head shot of Melissa Sanchez filled the TV screen behind the editor's desk. She looked as available as ever, with an added edge of excitement to her eyes and voice that hadn't been there the night before.

"Early this morning, a cassette and a hand drawing were dropped off at the 'Newsmakers' studio. We have every reason to believe they're from the Hit List killer. It appears the killer wants to open a dialogue with me."

"How the hell do you have a dialogue with a cassette?" Wilson muttered. It was probably a fake, Pete told himself. Another copycat.

"We bring you, live and exclusively, the Hit List killer," Melissa proclaimed, and the camera zoomed in on a blowup of the drawing, a crudely drawn corpse with X's for eyes and a huge dagger protruding from the head. The knife handle was labeled KILL and the body lettered with the rest of Pete's name, HARNEY. By the effigy's feet lay ten graves, five filled, five open. Gravestones identified living and dead; Hazelton's had been smeared with a bloody cross and slashed repeatedly.

"Missy," a voice hissed, halfway between a sigh and a whisper, and Pete froze in recognition. "It's up to you now." A pause for labored breathing. "Killharney." The voice quivered with hate. "He spared Hazelton. He hid Hazelton's soul from me. Undead, undead," the killer groaned as if in awful pain. There was more labored breathing. "Killharney. All this time I listened, and followed, and he's Satan!"

The last word was screamed, and the hairs stood stiffly on the back of Killharney's neck.

"Satan!" the killer continued to scream. "Blackness! Lies! Lies!"

The howl choked on its own rage, and sobs continued for almost a minute before the killer could control himself again.

"Cleansed," the voice then whispered. "All . . . shall . . . be . . . wiped . . . clean. 'The lion is come up from his thicket, and the destroyer is on his way.' You can count on me, Missy."

On cue, Sanchez reappeared on the screen, eyes cast downward in a pose of solemn attention. She looked up and batted her eyelashes meaningfully. "More after this," she said.

Wilson and Killharney looked at each other, the space between them charged with a foreboding stillness that the nattering stream of TV ads did nothing to fill. Wilson turned off the set.

"Ms. See," he called to his secretary. She entered the office, eyes wide. She had heard. "Please arrange a meeting of the city staff at eleven."

She left, and the two men faced each other again.

"I don't know what to do," Killharney admitted.

"Do your job," the editor replied through a scowl of concern.

"Killharney, you got a phone call," someone said from a safe distance. "It's Dombowski."

"It's him, isn't it?" the detective asked when Pete came on the line.

"It's him."

"Thought so. That shit about the lion coming from his thicket was from Jeremiah. I looked it up."

"You always keep a Bible by the phone?"

"If I was you, I'd keep one with a bulletproof cover next to my heart. What do you want to do?"

"I want protection for my ex-wife and daughter."

"You got it," pledged the detective. "What about yourself?"

"A reporter with a police escort is about as useful as a hooker at Club Med."

"Wise up, Killharney. Reporters act like they got some special immunity, and you don't. This nut's a butcher, and he doesn't fuck around. You want protection, you got it."

"I'll let you know. Has Washington tracked down the killer's fingerprints you sent them yet?"

"It's a mess, no." Dombowski sighed pessimistically.

207

"You know something funny? I'm listening to that cassette, and I swear I know that voice from somewhere. The guy's probably some wacko from Omaha and he reminds me of like my next door neighbor or someone."

"You got a lot of mass murderers on your block?"

"Fuck you," the detective said, "and be careful."

"Something's up," said Bisceglia as he passed Pete's desk. "Murchison's here."

In Wilson's office, the editor and publisher were engaged in impolite discussion. Scots-tinged obscenities overrode Wilson's inaudible rebuttals, and the fight ended with the editor's exit to the elevator, his departure a dignified march that everyone watched with silent alarm.

"Staff meeting now, step to it," Murchison bellowed cheerfully from the vacated office.

Reporters eyed each other with cynical acceptance, gathered up notebooks and cigarettes and coffee, and filed into the conference room designed to hold half their number. Hoping to preserve some measure of anonymity, Pete lingered in the back, while up front Murchison paced furiously, sucking on his Dunhills as he brainstormed the crisis facing them.

"The story's getting away from us," he said. "Until this morning, people had to read the *Apple* for their Hit List news. We have to regain that edge, that momentum. Pete, front and center, lad."

An aisle of the unchosen gladly opened, and Pete found himself facing his animated publisher.

"Who's the target, I ask you? Not some faceless psychopath. Not some busty newscaster who's been handed the undeserved break of her career. You're the target, Peter. You're the story. Ideas!" he demanded.

"I found the quote," Bisceglia said. "It's from Jeremiah. We could play up the religious angle."

"Do you think our readers are all priests?" Murchison said.

"Then how about tying in last night's Coliseum story with the Bible quote as lead?" offered Rossetti.

"I like it. Now we're selling papers. Keep going."

"If Pete's going to be the focus, how about a layout featuring him?" the art director suggested.

"I like that too. Maybe a centerfold with his bio bordered by the murder weapons. Perhaps rerun the victims' morgue shots around it. Play with it."

"Better save something for the obit," Pete put in.

"They'll reread it," the publisher said.

Pete caught Sheila staring at him with fear-haunted eyes, her knuckles clenched white in an effort to keep from trembling.

"Angus, everything you're suggesting makes me a more attractive kill," Pete objected with uncharacteristic caution.

"You're right. Absolutely right. But Angus Murchison has taken precautions. Lads, introduce yourself to Mr. Killharney."

A couple of well-dressed linebackers, who reminded Pete of Marchetti's front line, broke through the thin protection of reporters and stuck out thick-wristed hands to shake.

"Tony Lamp," said one.

"Jimmy Queen," said the other.

"These are your new and true friends," said Angus, and turned to one of the secretaries taking dictation. "Get this down. 'Sir Angus Murchison, publisher of the *New York Apple*, has hired two bodyguards to provide twenty-four-hour protection for star columnist Peter Killharney.' Let's see, 'At his own personal expense, Sir Angus has rented a suite at the Waldorf-Astoria to accommodate Mr. Killharney and his guards until the homicidal maniac threatening the columnist's life has been caught by the police.' Rossetti, tony that up for me a bit, would you please?"

"Sure, Mr.—Sir Angus."

"The Waldorf, I'm impressed," said Pete.

"Don't be. The paper keeps a room at the Sheraton that should fit the three of you with a roll-away."

As the staff chuckled at the parsimony, Pete noticed that Sheila looked immensely relieved.

"Thanks, Angus, I appreciate the protection," he lied.

"That's enough for a start. But I want more, and I want it daily, and I want it hot. This story's a reporter's dream, and it must—it *will*—stay at the *Apple* where it belongs. Get on it, lads!"

Murchison swept out of the conference room, leaving behind a staff exasperated by its own enthusiasm. For the publisher was right; it was a reporter's dream, and visions of bylines and scoops danced in all their eyes. Except Killharney's. He turned to Sheila and found himself staring at the muscle-humped shoulder of one of his new companions. He turned in the other direction and faced the tie knot of the second. Sandwiched between them, he could already guess who would wind up with the roll-away.

"Say, do either of you snore?" he inquired.

"Yup," said one.

"Affirmative," said the other.

"Well, so do I. Maybe we could work up a trio."

"Funny," said one.

"Ha," said the other.

Pete asked himself just how bad death could be.

"You're scared of him, aren't you?" said the good-looking man on TV.

"Call," said Killharney.

"You don't know what it's like," replied the beautiful

210

woman, fearfully shaking her elaborate blond hair. "When the law's rotten, there's no one to turn to for help."

"Pair of jacks," said Tony from one side of Pete.

"I've taken precautions," the handsome man said.

"Beats me," said Jimmy from the other.

Three thuggish-looking cops burst in on the couple. A fat man wearing a badge entered and smiled evilly. Pete flipped over his down card and doubled the ace already showing.

"Dealt the fabled ace in the hole," he said. "Bullets takes it."

"Did you say precautions?" the fat man sneered, and stepped out of the way to let a corpse fall into the room. The woman screamed, the good-looking man looked worried, and a toothpaste ad came on.

As he raked in the sixty-cent pot, Killharney regarded his own precautions. The bodyguards reminded him of bookends: silent, functional, and stupid as stone. Even locked in the small hotel room made smaller by the roll-away bed, they covered both flanks.

"Say, boys, how about a drink?" Pete said.

"I'll call room service," Jimmy offered.

"I meant in the bar."

"Gee, Mr. K., I don't think that's a good idea," said Tony.

"Right," Pete agreed, and five minutes later he was safely shelved between them at a secure corner table of the Sheraton cocktail lounge, with Cokes all around. The decor denied the possibility of filth or passion, but outside the shrinking circle of action permitted him, Pete felt the presence of murder. He carried with him a palpable sense of danger, of festering menace growing, preparing to strike. The cassette had merely made it official.

Who are you?

The hissing threats gave Pete, like Dombowski, an

unexplained sense of the familiar. He tried to remember, tried to imagine someone with Kreutzer's ruthlessness, Melissa's ambition, Steptoe's viciousness, Baumann's amorality. Steptoe was certainly capable of the murders, but he lacked motive, and Killharney had known him too long to believe he really had the makings of a psychopath. Steptoe wasn't crazy, he was just one mean son of a bitch.

No, the pieces refused to coalesce. What was clear was that Killharney had been targeted for extinction. The options were equally obvious: he could wait to die or he could strike back. Killharney opened his notebook and began to write.

The Doughboy has taken charge of the defenses and is a sight out of the history books. The helmet still fits, its steel rim lending ferocity to the bloodshot eyes beneath. But the shirt wouldn't button on an order from Pershing, and one side droops from his accumulation of good-conduct ribbons and the Purple Heart. "Where do you think the other leg went?" he asks, pointing from medal to empty trouser leg.

Yes, the patrons of Killharney's Bar can recognize risk. Even the reluctant Swede has volunteered to stack sandbags. The front window has disappeared behind a foot of Jones Beach's finest, and the door's been backed by two automobile seats retrieved from a wreck on the FDR Drive. At the rear, the heavy artillery, a Gatling gun of obvious antiquity, perches atop the bar. (The morning line has it nine to five that it won't fire a round before jamming.)

But no caviling. The Doughboy's done his best. Precautions have been taken, for now there is no question:

War has been declared.

The killer has declared himself. Six murders aren't enough. The habit of killing has taken hold and he cries, 'More blood!' My blood. But after me there will be others, assuredly, because the killing will continue until he's run to ground and locked away forever.

I know. I'm harping on the obvious just when things are getting interesting again. Now there's a new titillation: the killer's gone video! You've read about him, you've heard him on the radio, and now he's live on TV. Hey, and he's an artist too!

It makes me puke.

I can't pretend my own hands are clean. I'm part of the business of selling news. I use fear and tragedy and degradation in my trade. For instance, I spoke with Hazelton right before his suicide, and I'll never know whether or how much my questions helped drive him off that church steeple.

Killharney paused and reread the confession. In the column, it didn't scorch his soul as it had when hoarded inside as his own awful secret. There are no secrets. Live that truth.

So this isn't facile sanctimony I'm trying to peddle today. It's sanity.

We're a society held together by that flimsiest of conventions, the rule of law. It's the glue that binds us in amity, or at least armistice. And murder flouts this rule; it shreds the fundamental assumptions that permit us the freedom to louse up our lives as we choose. To the extent that this butcher has weakened the rule of law, we are all his victims. The killer has spit in our eye.

What can be done?
The killer can be caught.

As Pete wrote the sentence, he had a sudden, certain vision of vanity, his killer's overweening ego daring the police with the variety and brutality and predictability of his murders. That was it, the killer's own blind spot, and Killharney poked at it with the sharp stick of ridicule.

Don't fall for the media hype. And if you still believe that religious garbage, I've got a bridge for you cheap. (Which one? asks the Swede, interested. Your pick, Swede.) No, this isn't some omnipotent avenger. This is just another perpetrator for Homicide to track down. There are clues. There are leads. The killer will be caught.

I've been declared a marked man. I don't believe it. I think it's the bluster of a desperate man consumed by his hate and his hunger for blood. Besides, I've taken precautions. Hiram the Bartender, who has never been closer to a horse than the rail at Belmont, has lent me a cavalry saber won in a crap game forty years back. So I'm ready. I only pray the police catch him before I do.

Finished, Killharney looked up at his real-life precautions and noticed them patiently rolling the melting cubes in their empty glasses as they surveyed the Sheraton bar for mass murderers.

"What do you say to a nightcap, fellas?" he offered, holding up a five.

"Sure thing, Mr. K.," said Tony. "Your turn to fetch, Jimmy."

Jimmy grunted in agreement, swallowed the five in

a hand built to grip a football, and walked to the bar with the rolling gait of a weightlifter who spends time on his thighs.

"Killharney!" called a thin, pimply youth with bottle-thick glasses that magnified the intense, gleaming eyes behind them. His right arm came up, and Pete, petrified, could already feel the bullet separating his ribs. The bodyguard swiveled around in horror and lunged for the outstretched hand, stopping himself just before he would have crushed bones. For the hand was empty. The boy wanted to shake with Pete.

"I, I want to, to t-tell you how m-much I a-a-a-admire your column."

"Thank you very much," Pete said, shaking hands, his whole body swimming in sweat.

"I also w-want to tell you n-n-not to b-blame yourself for these k-k-killings," the youth managed to say. "You're doing the r-r-right thing, so keep giving them h-h-h-hell."

"Okay. I will. Thanks," Pete said.

Praise and consolation successfully delivered, the teenager shuffled off, beaming with pleasure, leaving Pete touched but still soaked from panic.

"What was that all about?" asked Jimmy, back with the Cokes.

"Some nut," Tony said. "Keep an eye on him."

"Roger."

"He's all right," Killharney said, and both professionals regarded him with exasperated condescension.

"Mr. K., John Lennon's assassin asked for his autograph before shooting him," Tony pointed out. "You take care of the writing and leave the protecting to us, all right?"

"All right," Pete said.

But it wasn't all right. If he couldn't trust his instincts about people, if humanity disappeared beneath a sea of indiscriminate suspicion, then he was naked, defenseless, entirely dependent on his bookends for protection. After the scare with the stutterer, it was obvious they weren't enough. And after this new column ran, the killer would come for him. Pete knew it. He just didn't know what to do about it. But he knew that if he did nothing, he would die.

The column worked.

"Mr. Killharney! The killer's talked again!" Wilson's assistant called from the editor's vacated office the day after the piece ran.

Wilson himself hadn't been seen since Murchison's pep talk, and the rumors had him variously fired, demoted to editing *Sheep Shearing Quarterly*, or having resigned over some unknown point of honor. As Pete entered the editor's office, he was surprised how much he missed the usual anxiety churned up by having to face Wilson's contempt and integrity.

"There has been a startling new development in the Hit List murders story," proclaimed Melissa Sanchez on all three office TVs. She looked thrilled. "Twenty minutes ago the Hit List killer called this station and talked to me and answered my questions. We have this dramatic conversation on tape, so you, our viewers, are getting the news as it's happening, right here on 'Newsmakers.' For you, now, the Hit List killer."

The camera zoomed on Melissa, intently pressing her earplug for better reception, then pulled back enough to take in a backdrop graphic of the grave-filled drawing.

"This is Melissa Sanchez, 'News . . .' "

"Missy," hissed the killer, cutting her off. "No prints."

"Prince?" asked Sanchez.

"I leave no prints," the voice whispered. "The prophet shall become wind."

Hoarse breathing filled the tape.

"Tell me why you're doing this," Melissa prompted. "Tell me why you're killing."

"I am weary," he panted, "with holding in." Then, louder, "I am full of the fury of the Lord."

Pete's phone began to ring.

"Is there anything I can do for you?" Sanchez asked.

"Killharney!" the killer screamed. "I want Killharney! I will punish all! All must die!"

"Hello? Hello?" Melissa called out. The backdrop faded and the live Sanchez said, " 'All must die.' What does that mean? Stay tuned to 'Newsmakers.' "

His phone was still ringing. Pete walked over and picked it up.

"You goddamn lying son-of-a-bitch!" screamed Dombowski. "You promised to keep quiet about those fingerprints."

"I did."

"You call having the killer throw it in my fucking face on TV quiet?"

"I didn't write about them. I didn't talk about them."

"Jesus Christ," grumbled the detective, his anger deflating into something closer to despair. "This psycho's got me spooked. I feel like he's looking over my shoulder, watching every goddamn move I make. Listen, are those two guards enough? You want the full treatment?"

"They crimp my style as it is."

"So would a forty-four slug, or a noose, or whatever new twist he's thought up just for you. Christ, we gotta nab this fucker before he takes out the one reporter who ever quoted me accurately."

"I didn't think you cared."

"Fuck you."

"That's how you always end our chats."

"It beats 'Amen' and a shovelful of dirt," the cop said, and hung up.

How did the killer find out about the missing prints? Who knew about them? Dombowski's office. Washington. Sheila. Himself. But no cop, city or federal, would broadcast a gross procedural error; it went against the unspoken code that kept all mistakes in-service. And Sheila? Killharney looked over at her working at her desk. He didn't know the rest of her life away from him, who her friends were, what unrevealed desire or ambition drove her.

No. He couldn't believe it. It hurt too much even to consider.

Which left himself. Hit Man Killharney. Killharney the celebrity, whose every move, public and private, was apparently now watched.

Or listened to.

He knew where to look. Keeping the cradle buttons pressed down, Pete unscrewed his phone's earpiece and exposed the small listening device, its wire antenna trailing from it like the tail of some electronic sperm. He contemplated the bug with a grin of mirthless determination, then carefully put the phone back together. He had found his edge.

"We just heard the news," said Tony, as the bodyguards bracketed him protectively.

"I think we should be real careful from now on," Jimmy said to Tony's nodding assent. "No more cocktail lounges, okay?"

"Don't worry about me, boys," Pete comforted them. "I'm not planning anything more dangerous than some stud poker."

"Now you're talking," said Jimmy.

"When you're dealt an ace in the hole, you have to play the hand, right?"

"Copacetic, Mr. K.," Tony said with encouraging dimness.

And to ante up, I'll have to ditch you both, Pete didn't bother to add.

Panic is the predator's friend. It paralyzes his prey, making the kill easy and sure. But what if the predator panics? What if he sees the shadow of a closing net? Would he freeze in dumb acceptance of his fate? No, he would strike out at any opening left. A predator would seek freedom by blind, ferocious attack.

"Oh, brrrrr! Brrrrr! Forget about spring today. It's going to be cold, cold, cold," the weatherman on the hotel's TV predicted, shivering extravagantly.

"This guy's great," said Tony, cleaning his gun.

So to catch this killer, there had to be a closing net, and there had to be bait to lure him toward the only apparent opening, where the real trap should be laid. Killharney had no doubt who was the tastiest chum available.

"Ready when you are, Mr. K.," said Tony, holstering his .38.

Pete led his personal parade through the Sheraton's characterless lobby, detouring to the row of public phones to lay the trap.

"County Cork. We don't open till ten."

"And close at nine. Seamus, I have a big favor to ask."

"For you, anything," the bartender said, and proved it.

The second call was to his friend Larry Sisko, head of operations at Grand Central. The third was to Herlihy, at home.

"I'll set it up," the police inspector said to Killharney's proposal, "but promise to be careful until then. The killer's already smelled out one trap."

"He didn't smell it out," Pete insisted. "He knew every detail beforehand. And I'd rather take the risk now than let him kill me at his pleasure next month, or year."

"We are who we are," Herlihy said, "but the angels still need you, so stay out of sight till the party starts."

At the office, he cast the net from the bugged phone at his desk.

" 'Newsmakers,' " announced a bored male voice.

"Melissa Sanchez, please. Pete Killharney calling."

"Ms. Sanchez is unavailable at the moment," the man said, clearly disbelieving him. "Please leave a message and she'll get back to you."

"Who the hell are you?"

"David Untermeyer," the man said, as if that explained everything.

"Well, David, let me repeat for the hard of hearing and terminally blow-dried. This is Pete Killharney of the *Apple* calling. Ms. Sanchez wants to speak with me, she lusts to speak with me, and I am taking time out from perhaps my last minutes on earth to oblige her. Now if you don't play fetch, and quickly, I'm not calling back, I'm not appearing on her show as she so fervently desires, and your job is fucking out the window when they find out, from me, that you're the reason why."

A pause.

"You have to be Killharney," he finally said. "No one else talks like that. Hold on."

"So sweet of you to call," Melissa soon purred over the tapped phone line. "But I have to break your heart. I'm booked this afternoon doing promos."

"What about tomorrow night?"

"Some of us work nights," she said.

Pete surprised himself by resisting the cheap shots.

"Right. I've decided to take your advice and get

smart. I want to appear on your show tomorrow night. If the offer still stands, that is."

"But of course."

"Aren't you going to ask me why?"

"Sure. Why?"

"To reveal the identity of the Hit List killer."

"I can't believe it!" she cried. "Who is it?"

"Tomorrow night. And I have one ground rule. You can promote my appearance, but not one word why. There's a killer gunning for me. I don't want him to know his luck's run out."

"I think I can get my producers to agree to that."

"Knew I could count on you, Missy," Pete said. Almost as an afterthought, he decided to float a trial balloon over the wired phone. "By the way, do you know Kreutzer's chief of security, an ex-cop named Steptoe?"

"Not really," she said carefully. It sounded like a lie. "Is there some reason I should?"

"Depends on what you're into. Tomorrow night."

The trap had been set and the net cast to close tomorrow night. Now it was time to dangle the bait.

"What the hell do you want?" Dombowski demanded when Pete made the last of the day's bugged calls.

"I couldn't sleep. I have fears for my personal safety."

"About fucking time."

"I want to take you up on the protection offer, but I'd like to keep this between the two of us. I'm going on Melissa Sanchez's show tomorrow night, and I'm wondering if you could meet me at the County Cork, say at seven, and walk me over to the show."

"Jesus Christ, you want me to nursemaid you now?"

"It's important. I'll buy."

"Hell shit," the detective muttered. "Bring plenty of cash."

"Thanks. I owe you."

"You'll pay," Dombowski promised.

"Next stop Grand Central, boys," Pete told his bodyguards, and ten minutes later Killharney was leisurely reading the arrivals and departures board in the station's main concourse as Jimmy and Tony twitched nervously by his side.

"See anything you like?" asked Tony.

"No, not really," Pete said. He wondered if the tail Marchetti had told him about was hidden in the anonymous stream of travelers rushing around them. Or if the seminary spy was likewise looking on. Or the killer. Whoever the audience, it was time to disappear.

"You know what we need?" Pete said. "We need some snacks for the hotel room, so we don't have to go out or anything."

"Great idea," said Jimmy, relieved at Killharney's caution. "There's that small deli across from the newsstand over there."

"Super."

Tony stood watchfully by the front as Jimmy waited in line at the deli counter in back. Pete made a circuit around the crowded aisles before rejoining Tony up front.

"I hope he gets cheddar cheese," Pete said, handing him a party-size bag of potato chips. "Would you go back and ask Jimmy to pick up some cheddar?"

"No problem," the bodyguard said. Tony headed back and Pete slipped out the front, threading through the crowded concourse to the "Employees Only" door by the Amtrak ticket window. The door opened at first knock, and Larry Sisko, head of Grand Central operations, quickly locked it behind them.

"You're either really out of shape or damned scared," Larry said. "You're sweating like a sow in heat. This way."

He led Pete up three flights of stairs and along a corridor to a tarnished brass door.

"This next stretch is the only publicly visible part of today's tour. Ready for a thrill?"

He opened the door and stepped into a flood of light. They made their way across a walkway of translucent glass sandwiched between the double layers of window that covered the entire west face of Grand Central Terminal. Forty feet below, the main concourse pulsed and writhed with people, any one of whom could casually glance up and see Killharney defenselessly framed in the late-morning light. Pete felt like a walking purloined letter.

Once across the walkway, Sisko guided him downward through the maze of corridors and staircases connecting the levels beneath the terminal. They paralleled a dark section of track, where unseen air brakes hissed percussively, to the repair door Sisko had told him about earlier that day. He handed Pete a huge, rusted skeleton key.

"Watch out for subways. If you see one coming, make friends with the wall."

"I hear you. Thanks, Larry."

"Take care of yourself," Sisko said, and left Killharney to finish his vanishing act alone.

Pete unlocked the door and slowly descended a slimy staircase, feeling his way in the near total darkness. A thin edge of light outlined the bottom door, and Pete gratefully pushed against it. It didn't budge. He began to feel foolish about this elaborate escape. He pushed again. It didn't budge.

"Open, goddamn it!" he cried, heaving his whole weight against it. He and the door both swung open just as a subway thundered by in an explosion of hammering steel. A foot from his head, car after car hurtled past. Then, just as suddenly, the subway was gone and Pete was alone in the dark, silent tunnel.

"Jesus, Mary, and Joseph," he said. A rat squealed

223

three inches from his ear. He jumped, and the darkness thrummed with the patter of many tiny rodent feet. He decided not to linger.

Killharney trotted up the tracks to the platform of the next subway station and caught the Number seven Flushing train to Shea Stadium, where he spent a chilly afternoon watching the Mets score a close win over the visiting Cardinals. After the game, he booked a room at a nearby motel and watched the "Newsmakers" network hype his scheduled appearance every thirty minutes throughout the evening.

He'll come, Pete told himself. His vanity and viciousness would compel him to leap at the only opening left him.

Tomorrow night, someone would try to murder him.

"Glad you could make it," Herlihy greeted him as Pete entered the County Cork. The inspector was comfortably perched on the stool normally inhabited by Svenson. Behind the bar, Seamus looked distinctly stouter than Pete remembered him.

"Bulletproof apron," the bartender explained, seeing his stare. "All the best barkeeps are wearing them."

"You give new meaning to the term 'fashion plate,'" Pete said, then added seriously, "You don't have to do this. You don't have to be here."

The old Irishman spread his hands magnanimously. "This is my bar. Where else would I be?"

"So what now?" Pete asked Herlihy.

"According to your plan, we wait until the killer walks through the door and we arrest him."

"Super," Pete said, and retired with the police inspector to the back booth.

At seven o'clock, Lieutenant Dombowski, looking furious, walked through the door.

"Why the fuck is this place staked out?" he bellowed as he steamed up to Pete, then saw Herlihy and his mouth dropped open.

"What tipped you off?" asked the inspector.

"One of the SWAT team sharpshooters was buying smokes around the corner. Once I started looking, I saw them everywhere. You expecting a Russian invasion?"

"No, we're expecting the Hit List killer," said Herlihy. "Why don't you join us?"

Pete ordered a beer for Dombowski, and the three men settled back to wait for the Hit List killer to make his move.

Customers came in, were served by Seamus, drank, and left, and were replaced by others. Some Pete knew by sight as regulars or semi-regulars. Some stared at him with blank looks or the mild curiosity of drinkers checking out the turf. None tried to kill him.

In an hour, Killharney began to feel the sucking pull of despair. There was no contingency plan. He had assured everyone, including himself, that the killer would show. But if not? If not, then the killer would confront him at some other time and place of his own careful choosing and slaughter him.

"I canceled bowling for this shit," Dombowski said. "I think the waitress working the lanes has a crush on me, and instead I'm sitting in some dive, watching two guys' beards grow."

Christ, what if Pete had to go on "Newsmakers" at eleven and tell a million interested viewers he was just kidding?

"Killharney, you got a phone call," one of the plain-clothes detectives said.

"Pete, the killer just called the paper looking for you," Vinnie Bisceglia blurted excitedly, when Killharney picked up the phone. "He said you'd find who you're looking for at Grand Central. And he quoted Jeremiah again: 'Displayed as a curse, and an astonishment, and a hissing, and a reproach.' "

"Jesus, that's a bad sign," Pete said, feeling control over events slipping away from him. "Have you notified the police?"

"Murchison said to call you first and meet you there with a car in case you need to follow up."

"Okay. Call the cops. I already have a couple of them keeping me company, and we'll all rendevous by the information desk. I'll cancel 'Newsmakers'; it looks like I've caused enough trouble already tonight. Oh, and tell the cops to look up when they enter the concourse."

"What's the story?" Herlihy asked.

"It looks like we're about to find either the killer or another victim," Pete said. "My money's on the victim."

When they got to Grand Central, there was already a circle of onlookers craning their necks upward at the window walkway Pete had crossed just yesterday. Through the grimy glass they could see a lump sprawled in the middle, already receiving Forensics' careful attention. Bisceglia came over to meet them.

"Who is it?" Herlihy asked him.

"Steptoe. Garroted."

"What?" Pete cried. His suspects were all dying. He felt like a walking kiss of death.

"Now why the hell would someone want to snuff Steptoe?" Dombowski asked. "The guy was an asshole, but he wasn't famous."

I fingered him, Pete came close to confessing, then stopped to consider a radical thought: But so what? What if he himself wasn't the continuing inspiration for these killings? What if Killharney was really only filling a small part in a plan no one had yet guessed? His mentioning Steptoe's name over the bugged phone may or may not have made a difference. Until he uncovered the killer, there wasn't time to waste on possibly misplaced guilt. And Pete felt time running out. On himself? No, on the killer's true target.

"Vinnie, why don't we take a drive to Connecticut? I want to break the news of Steptoe's loss to Kreutzer in person."

"Let me hitch a ride," Dombowski said. "There's a few questions I'd like to ask Kreutzer about his employee, like what the hell did Steptoe find out that got him killed."

Pete glanced up at the walkway, where Steptoe was being crammed into a body bag. " 'A little knowledge is a dangerous thing,' I think Pope said. It looks like whatever Steptoe found out wasn't enough to keep him alive."

"Don't make the same mistake," Herlihy said.

Pete had forgotten how dark it could get in the country. Their headlights provided the sole illumination in the moonless night, and the blackness surrounding them seemed limitless and dreadful.

"I got a bad feeling," Dombowski said. "Maybe I should have rung up the Staties to check things out before we drove up."

"The way it's been going, the killer probably had that possibility worked into the schedule." Pete said. "Whoever he was planning to kill tonight is already dead. Slow down, Vinnie. The entrance is right around the next curve."

The car swung into the driveway, casting light on the darkened gatehouse and open gates. Something was wrong.

"Those gates should be locked," Pete said. "And we should already be surrounded by guards pointing guns at us."

Dombowski hopped from the car as he pulled his service revolver. He knocked on the gatehouse door while standing carefully to one side, then eased the door open and felt for a switch. The house lit up as he hurled himself through the entrance. There was a long pause.

"We've got trouble," he finally said from inside.

The reporters rushed in to see Dombowski dangling a phone receiver with its cord cut in his free hand. He was standing over a body dressed in the Kreutzer security uniform.

"Phone's dead. So's he. Another garroting. Someone's into quiet killing tonight."

"What do you suppose is waiting for us up at the house?" Vinnie asked nervously.

"More death," Pete said. "Let's go."

They got back into the car and sped up to the main mansion. On approach, everything appeared tranquil. The house had a normal amount of lights shining, and the poolhouse was a brilliant box of smooth aqua. The only thing out of place in the picture of slumbering wealth was a body by the open front door. Once again, the cop was first out.

"Another security guard," Dombowski said, feeling for a pulse and finding none.

"Oh my God! Oh, thank God someone's come!" Stephanie Kreutzer cried as she recognized Pete. She ran out the door and into his arms, and he held the slight ex-ballerina as she quaked hysterically.

"I—I found the body just lying there, and the phone doesn't work, and then I heard a shot down by the pool-house, where Helmut should be swimming, but no one's in the water, and I was afraid to go down there or call out, and, and—"

"Mrs. Kreutzer, I'm Lieutenant Dombowski, NYPD. Where is everyone? Your help?"

"It's the cook and the butler's night off. The other help aren't live-in. I—I'm alone and something terrible's happened down there, I'm sure of it."

"Vinnie, why don't you stay with Mrs. Kreutzer?" Pete said, gently transferring the terrified woman from one set of arms to another. "We'll check out the poolhouse."

They took a shortcut down the daffodil-carpeted hill, and the sweet smell of flowers and the spongy spring earth gave the approaching danger a sense of unreality. Messy death seemed out of place in such a peaceful setting. As they neared the poolhouse door, they could see a body slumped by the diving board at the far end.

"Kreutzer?" Dombowski asked.

"No, I don't think so. He looks way too tall from here." Pete looked toward the inert form in the tan raincoat. A more positive identification was difficult from a distance because the man's face was a messy mask of blood.

They warily entered the brightly lit poolhouse. The only sound was the hum of the circulating pumps. The water was absolutely still. There was the smell of cordite, and evacuation, and gas.

"Mr. Kreutzer," Dombowski called out. "Mr. Kreutzer, it's the police. Are you there?"

Receiving no answer, they walked up one side of the Olympic-size pool to the corpse. Half his face had been obliterated by a gunshot blast, and a Bulldog .44 lay next to his side where he had dropped it. Pete looked at the remaining features. There was something familiar about the fading smirk that had been the man's last expression. Pete was sure he had seen him before.

"Friend of yours?" Dombowski asked. "Maybe president of your fan club? I think that might be what's left of the Hit List killer."

Pete stared at the source of so much violence. There was nothing left to fasten his anger onto. At the end of the trail of bodies was a faceless corpse, whose own self-inflicted death seemed as horrible as those he had caused. Instead of relief that the killings had come to a fitting conclusion, Killharney felt his usual sadness and denial. It couldn't be over.

Pete sniffed the air. The smell of gas was growing. He looked toward the kitchenette attached to the pool-house. Someone was lying by the stove, head stuck in the oven, and Pete recognized Kreutzer's bathrobe. The body's arms were tied behind his back with wire. His hands were missing. There was a bloody mass next to the body in which Pete could see a fingernail, a knuckle, and a bloody ball peen hammer.

"I think he crossed off one last Hit List member before shuffling off this mortal coil," Pete said, pointing toward the kitchenette.

"Do you smell gas? I smell gas." Dombowski walked to the doorway and surveyed the carnage. "Jesus, talk about symbolic fucking murder. The JDL's going to love hearing about a suspected ex-Nazi getting gassed."

"Helmut! Helmut!"

Pete looked up and saw Stephanie Kreutzer sprinting their way, a panting Bisceglia trailing behind her. Pete ran for the far poolhouse door to head her off as Dombowski stepped into the kitchenette.

Suddenly Killharney acquired an expanding halo of light, and there was a roar, a hammering wave of noise that turned the air hard and hostile, and Pete floated through chaos to an oblivion the color of swimming-pool blue.

Part Three

Ten

"Dumb."

"Daddy?"

"Dombowski."

"Daddy! Go tell my mom, Michael. Oh, Daddy!"

Killharney opened his eyes. One eye. The other was blind or bandaged. His pretty daughter, Peg, was sitting by what was obviously a hospital bed, looking at him with enormous concern and a tentative glimmer of relief. He felt no pain. In fact, he felt nothing at all, but there was a high-pitched drone in his ears through which the rest of reality struggled to be heard. It seemed he was in the grip of some giant, well-monitored hangover.

"Must have tied one on," he mumbled.

"What?"

Pete had the suspicion he was pretty doped up. Words dribbled from his mouth, sounding wrapped in flannel. And why else hadn't he already checked to see if the rest of him was still attached?

"How's it going, Peg?" he asked, his working eye reconnoitering the hospital sheet for bulges where hands, legs, and feet were supposed to be. Everything seemed in place. His first thought returned.

"What about Dombowski?" he asked.

Peg bit her lip, unschooled at bad tidings.

"You look a mess," his ex-wife greeted him as she breezed into the private room. Peg gratefully made way for her.

"Hi, Marge. Great. You look." He was definitely drugged.

"Margaret was worried you would wind up a rutabaga."

"Mom!"

"I told her it would be a step up the great chain of being for you. Still, you have been out, what, almost two days now."

"Dombowski," he persisted through the numbed droning.

"He's dead," Marge told him. "Instantly, they say."

He shouldn't have died, Pete thought, not Dombowski. I was the one meant to blow up, not a homicide cop who was supposed to be bowling.

"There's something else," Margie said, unusually tentative. Oh God, it's Sheila, Pete thought. "Seamus had a stroke last night. He's in a coma. The doctors, the doctors say he probably won't . . ."

Margie faltered, old memories of Irish kindness dissolving her stoic façade. Pete was stunned. With all the murders, he hadn't considered the possibility of a normal tragedy. He reached out and pinched a pleat of her skirt.

"Thank you for coming," Pete said. "I know how much you liked him, and he you. Could you send mass cards?"

"I'll take care of it," his ex-wife said, glad to assume a responsible role. "There's a policeman waiting for you outside, an Inspector Herlihy. Have I met him before?"

"St. Patrick's," Pete said.

"Cathedral or day?"

"Both. He's the one who returned your purse after that slash-and-snatch gang jostled you by the sacristy back in '72."

The explanation exhausted him, and the droning took on the quality and effectiveness of a runaway chainsaw inside his skull.

"Yes, that's right, I remember now. He was a nice man."

"Side of the angels," Pete said, and passed out.

He woke again at night. Or had gone blind in the other eye as well. No, he could see stars through the window. Someone was sitting by his bed. A nurse or a nun. Sheila? No. No one was there. A dream. A ghost. It didn't matter. He went under again.

"Good morning, Mr. Killharney. Six o'clock. Time for birds and patients to start tweeting."

His good eye shot open at the reveille sounded by a very real nurse cheerfully clattering about the room, opening blinds, scanning his chart, shaking down a thermometer while she wheeled the blood-pressure apparatus into place.

"Didn't anyone tell you I was in a coma?" Pete asked.

"Well, I'm sorry to interrupt it, but I must get my readings, and you have to choose your menu for the day."

She thrust the thermometer into his mouth and a meal card into one hand, and wrapped the pressure sleeve around his other arm.

"Ummph," he retorted, then realized he was beginning to hurt. All over. Proves you're alive, he told himself. Himself was unappreciative.

"You're a very lucky man," the nurse told him. "The doctor will be in to see you after breakfast."

She left, but the pain remained, and grew stronger,

asserting its primacy over his consciousness. He had yet to ask about the eye, which throbbed in time to his pulse beneath a quilt of bandages.

What else did Killharney feel? Grief? Guilt? Unceasing remorse? No, right now his inner world consisted of searing, physical pain. Pete knew guilt would wait its turn. And grief? Oh, Seamus, don't die. Not you too. A quiet knock on the door set off a pounding echo inside his skull.

"You look almost alive," Herlihy greeted him with his typical note of pleasant surprise.

"Sorry I stood you up yesterday," Pete said.

"You needed the sleep. The last time I saw you, the night of the explosion, blood was oozing from your ears and a six-inch splinter was sticking out of your cheekbone. Bisceglia was quite concerned, forgetting the thickness of the average Irish skull. He was the one fished you out of the pool, by the way. Fought fire and flood to keep you with us."

Bisceglia saved his life? Herlihy saw Pete's shock.

"Isn't it amazing, people's potential for noble acts? He was brave when it counted, and there's no better definition I know for a hero." The inspector turned solemn. "You heard about Dombowski?"

"I'm so sorry, Francis. I feel so filled, so filthy with death."

"A tragic night. Three guards dead, plus Steptoe, plus Kreutzer."

"So that was Kreutzer in the oven."

"As far as we can tell. Forensics says the killer had wrapped both himself and Kreutzer in a sheath of plastic explosive set with a pressure fuse. When the gas from the oven exploded, both bodies were practically atomized. The widow identified a few odd bits of hair and scarred skin."

"So," Pete updated the arithmetic of death, "five Hit

List members murdered, a sixth dead from suicide, plus Dombowski, two other cops, three security guards, and Steptoe. That brings the body count to thirteen."

"Fourteen," Herlihy corrected him. "You left out the Hit List killer. Did you recognize him, Peter? Do you know who he was?"

Killharney tried to remember the corpse by the diving board, but the killer's features retreated from recall. Tall, medium build, brown hair, a frozen smirk, a stranger who Pete thought looked familiar.

"You know, I may have seen him tailing me once or twice. I have a vague memory of him watching me outside the church that Hazelton attended. But other than that . . ." Pete shook his head. The Hit List killer had turned out to be the unknowable lone psychopath, "the null hypothesis," as Brendan had aptly termed it. Surely nothing Pete had done had helped change anything.

"Well, whoever he was, he's history now," Herlihy said. "It's over, Peter."

There was a knock on the door, and a fistful of red tulips preceded Sheila McGrath into the hospital room.

"I think these might be blowing my cover," she said, handing the flowers to Killharney. "The nurses are beginning to doubt I'm a brain surgeon."

"A speedy recovery," Herlihy said to Pete as he got up to leave. "And my best to your Uncle George, Miss McGrath." Sheila stared after him, then back to Pete.

"There are no secrets," he said.

Silence filled the room. Into it flowed the sounds of New York going to work, sirens and horns and the chatter of traffic, a shout, a snatch of music, a gunshot or backfiring car. Pete wondered what hospital he was in. He wondered about Sheila. The silence grew.

"Pretty flowers," he said at last. "They remind me of spring."

"Oh, it is spring. It's so beautiful this morning," she

replied, the words rushing from her in a clumsy torrent of relief. "The air is fresh and soft, and everything's green and new and alive. And *you're* alive! I was so worried when you wouldn't wake up. But here you are, and, and . . ."

"And it's over."

"Yes, finally. I'm so glad. I was so scared," she admitted in a low voice. He held her hand and together they listened to the sounds of normal life come to them through the hospital window.

The therapeutic torture of hospital routine slowly returned Killharney to irksome normality. Needles were stuck in him, bedpans swapped, dressings changed. The doctors told him that trauma from the splinter wound had impinged on the optic nerve, but that his bandaged eye should regain its full vision after the swelling subsided. And they also told him to expect headaches from the concussion. And maybe a blackout or two.

Bisceglia came by for a visit, uncertain how much to presume upon his heroics. Both of his hands were wrapped in bandages.

"Todd pulled off the takeover," he said, ignoring the reason they were meeting in a hospital room. "Camden Fabricators is now a subsidiary of American Wrapper."

"Vinnie, let's talk straight," Pete said. "I don't remember anything after the explosion, but I do know I'm alive and you're the reason why. Thank you for saving my life."

Bisceglia waved away the gratitude with one of his gauze-covered mitts. "It happened so fast, I didn't think what I was doing. I was talking with the Kreutzer woman, trying to calm her down, and I mentioned about how Steptoe's murder had worried us, and she went crazy.

Tore herself out of my arms and ran down the hill toward you guys, screaming her husband's name."

"I remember that, and me running to intercept her."

"That explains why after the explosion I could see you floating in the pool near the door. All I had to do was haul you out and drag us away. I just wish I could have gotten to Dombowski before the roof collapsed in flames."

"There wouldn't have been anything to get. He was at the center of the explosion. How did you burn yourself?"

Bisceglia blushed. "I grabbed the safety rails on the pool steps like a well-trained jerk, and blistered both hands. Don't tell anyone. I'm letting people imagine that I moved burning timbers to get to you or something."

"You don't need the embellishment. What you did was damned brave."

"Well, it wasn't much," Vinnie said, still uncomfortable in his role as hero. "Oh, some colorful acquaintances have been asking after you: Joey Dee, Fiji, a Manny, no last name. All very solicitous. One even asked if you were still buying Hit List tips."

"It's nice to feel wanted."

"And the whole city room says get well and hurry back," Bisceglia added. "I just wanted to stop by and, you know . . ."

"Sure. Thanks for coming."

Bisceglia quickly left to avoid more expressions of gratitude, and Killharney settled back with his pain. Get well and hurry back. Hurry back to what?

Murchison sent flowers addressed to "Yesterday's News," which was true. Even his own paper had relegated the postmortems to page ten. He was no longer news, which both relieved and perversely depressed him. He had hated celebrity, yet enjoyed being the center of the storm. He supposed being an invalid was a good transitional state. After all, without the patient there was no one to visit.

"Hi, Daddy, you're looking good. You're not really, with that yukky bandage and no eyebrows or anything, but I'm supposed to say cheerful stuff." Peg got the greeting out in one breath, her vivacity released from the chains of worry.

"You're looking good enough for us both," he flattered her, and almost got a blush for his effort.

"Who was that woman?"

"What?"

"The redhead who waited with us while you were in your coma?"

"Sheila McGrath. She's a fellow reporter at the paper."

"Some fellow. Mommy didn't like her. Said she looked slutty. I think she's jealous. You going to marry her?"

"I've been kind of busy lately, getting blown up and all," he said. "But how's your love life? I remember some boy's name mentioned when I was waking up."

"Michael," she murmured through her hair. "He— I—he's nice." She tossed her hair back from her pretty face just as her mother used to do, and Pete's heart tightened with love and regret.

"I'd like to meet him."

"You will. He's picking me up next time I visit. He doesn't like me wandering the streets of New York alone."

"Loving concern makes fools of us all. You like him?"

"Sure," she said, hiding behind her hair once more. This time Pete was sure she was blushing. People get murdered, have strokes, lose their drive or dreams, and still first love and other simple miracles continue. "I guess I gotta go now."

"Give me a kiss. You want to autograph my eye?"

"Oh yuk, Daddy. Get better. I love you."

Peg left Killharney with his heart open to love and

possibility. Instead, shame and guilt and dread rushed in and swamped his conscience. Herlihy said it was over, and Pete had repeated it to Sheila. But he knew it was only the start. People had died because of his empty words. Punishment followed. The rest of his life, he knew, would be spent carrying a burden of blood whose weight, just hefted, already seemed intolerable.

"Oh my God, I am heartily sorry for having offended Thee," he prayed to the empty room, and emptiness answered him.

The next day, James McNaughton Wilson himself called on Killharney. It was the first time Pete had seen his editor since that still-unexplained fight with Murchison, and one of the very few times he had ever seen him outside the confines of the *Apple*'s art-deco edifice. Wilson was dressed with a formality sixty years out of fashion: ancient three-piece flannel suit complete with gold watch fob, derby, spats, and a gold-handled walking stick.

"You don't look very sick to me," he sniffed, and sat stiffly on the bedside chair as if ready at any moment to terminate such foolishness. "I hope you're at least getting a column or two out of this torpor."

"Pretty dry material, Chief," Pete said, gesturing to the totally impersonal room. He could make small movements today without undue repercussions.

"I should think so. How are you?"

"Mending. Except for my conscience, the prognosis is good for a complete recovery."

Why had he said that to Wilson?

"I'm glad to hear it," the editor replied, unperturbed by the confession, then shocked Pete by matching it. "I got a man killed once—was responsible for his death, that is."

"You?"

"When I was twenty-three. I wasn't careful enough about protecting the identity of a source. He died, and I've lived with the knowledge now for almost forty years."

"Jesus Christ," Pete said. He didn't want to hear this right now.

"Want to know the secret of how to beat the guilt?" Wilson asked, leaning forward conspiratorially. His spats creaked with the movement.

"Sure. Yeah."

"There isn't any," he replied. "You'll burn with shame whenever you consider your part in the Hit List killings. Shame will become your closest companion."

"You have the bedside manner of a hanging judge."

"You interrupt me. As I say, you will become familiar, even intimate with shame. But sooner or later you will notice that work has piled up alarmingly while you were sporting sackcloth and hair shirt, and you will take a short break from recrimination and get something done. You will work, and life will proceed."

"I seem to have missed a punchline somewhere in there."

"Yes, I can see that from your bovine stare of incomprehension. So let me make it simple for you. In your position, there are only two avenues open that don't lead to despair. I submit that work is one, and you should get the hell out of that bed and back to work as if your life depended on it, because it probably does. Enough cops and robbers, enough of the invalid life. Find a story, fill it with facts, then write it so a sixth-grader can follow your prose."

"You just want to get me within shouting distance."

"I quit."

"You what?"

"It's a transitive verb meaning to tender a resignation in light of mutually irreconcilable differences with current editorial policy and goals."

Pete couldn't believe it. Wilson as editor was a changeless landmark in his life. "Does this have something to do with Murchison wanting to publish the killer's letter to me?" he asked, hoping there was some way to restore order in his world.

"A catalyst. He intended to publish it without first getting your approval. I demurred. He insisted. I quit." Pete began to protest, but Wilson hushed him.

"Don't you dare denigrate my noble gesture. And we both know that my tenure was foredoomed the day he bought the paper. Murchison might once have needed me to establish his reputation in New York as a serious publisher, but my inexplicable fascination with hard news runs counter to every principle that has made him a wealthy man."

"Tits and titters."

"I hate alliteration," Wilson said, standing, "and I hate what the *Apple* will become, so I quit. I just hope my successor is able to prevail on you for an occasional piece of solid reporting."

"I've been thinking about that a lot lately," Pete said, "but I don't think you'll like my conclusion."

The editor consulted his pocket watch. "Try me."

"You've heard it before, but that doesn't stop it from being true: the news ignores life. Getting blown up has scorched off some of my typical acceptance of sensationalism. Fires, muggings, and mayoral proclamations have nothing to do with most people's daily reality. A sheet-metal worker lives with rivets and solder and a three-beer lunch Fridays, and whether he'll get lost again on his yearly hunting trip upstate. And goddamn it, he's worth writing about. He's as much news as the most recent murder or who pinched Farrah at Elaine's last night."

The editor didn't appear swayed.

"I know you preferred my investigative columns.

But I no longer want to, I no longer need to skewer the rich and powerful. I'm bored with them, and I'm tired of the fight. No more blood for this sinner."

"None?" Wilson asked with a trace of a smile.

"Well, maybe now and then, to keep the fuckers honest," Pete conceded.

Wilson smoothed the brim of his derby, then flicked a speck from the gold lion's head of his walking stick.

"In other reporters, I might diagnose a nascent Pollyanna syndrome, that malady which makes the sufferer think the world would be a better place if he only wrote happy news. But I'll spare you such suspicions. For you, I'll confine myself to a caution. Unless you're very good at what you're suggesting, you'll be very bad indeed. Good luck to you, Pete. You're one of the best reporters I've had the privilege to edit."

Wilson walked slowly to the door.

"Wait a minute," Pete called to him. "You said there were two avenues open. What's the other?"

James McNaughton Wilson looked at him with an expression of amused exasperation.

"Love, of course," he said, and left.

Sheila took him home. She packed his bags, helped him dress, had a taxi waiting, and half carried the weakened Killharney from his room to the cab.

"I've fallen to pieces," Pete gasped as he collapsed in the backseat.

"Save your breath," Sheila said. "I've got a surprise for you."

The surprise stopped him in awe at the door to his apartment. It was livable. He had left four white walls and little else. Sheila had transformed the sterile, characterless box by the discreet addition of colorful Egyptian rag rugs and a solid burgundy bedspread. And there were flowers everywhere, tulips on the table, daffodils by the bed, sprigs of blooming forsythia arched around the bathroom mirror.

"Check the fridge," she prompted.

The refrigerator was defrosted, defoliated, scrubbed, and stocked with milk, eggs, orange juice, cheese, fresh vegetables, even new bottles of ketchup, mustard, and mayonnaise.

"A get-well present," she said, then turned shy and uncertain. "I figured we could . . . you said that after it ended we could start over."

He looked into her green eyes shining with soft fire, and felt profoundly unworthy. Yet to say so now would spurn the gift of her heart, might spoil any hope of redemption. Some part of him loved this beautiful woman. He had to give that part time to triumph over injury and shame.

"Wilson visited me yesterday," Killharney said. "He told me there were two ways for me to get back on track. Work was one."

"And he wants you to cover the metropolitan beat for the *Baltimore Sun.*"

"The *Sun?*"

"They offered him a job the day after he resigned."

"That's great for him," Pete said. "But no, he only ordered me to get back to work. You can take the editor out of the *Apple*, but not the editor out of the man."

"So what was the other?" Sheila asked.

"Love."

He looked into her eyes until she had to blink the tears away.

"Yes, let's start over, Sheila." And he took her in his arms, and kissed her, and she clung to him, knees quivering with relief and passion.

"Where do you suppose we should start?" Pete asked, breathless.

"We'd better start on the bed, darling," Sheila said. "I don't think you have your strength back yet for gymnastics."

Three hours later, kept awake by a post-concussion headache, Pete watched Sheila dream. Her fists were curled around the covers, reminding him of Peggy, whom he often used to watch over late at night after coming home from covering a fire or fight.

How tangled the strands of love had become for Killharney. Peggy on the verge of womanhood, his ex-wife poised for marriage number two, and her possible replacement asleep by his side. At the threshold of what he promised was their new life, Pete felt dirty, guilty, forever exiled from the easy innocence of love. Some fucking springtime.

Sheila mewed but kept sleeping as he slipped from bed. He sat at the table, opened his notebook next to the jar of tulips, and began to write.

Our revels now are ended at Killharney's Bar, or the County Cork Bar and Grill on 48th and 8th, to strip away the tattered scrim and faded scenery of that exhausted conceit. The soul of the County Cork, cradle of my columns, haven filled with friends who drank and judged not, is dying.

Today I honor the dead and bury the past.

In all, fourteen men died in the course of what everyone calls the Hit List killings: Hit List members, cops, private guards, the Hit List killer himself. To the family and friends of all the victims, I send my deepest, forever unworthy regrets.

I would like to honor Detective Lieutenant Herman Dombowski, Homicide Division, NYPD. He was a good cop, mostly honest, usually fair. I say mostly and usually only because that's the best a good cop can do. The evil and degradation and unremitting vileness within which police conduct their professional lives is more awful than anyone who hasn't lived it can guess. I will not cheapen his memory with impossible superlatives. Dombowski was a good cop and a better man than most still walking the streets he gave his life trying to keep safe. All New Yorkers should mourn his loss.

I want also to honor a man who remains among the living, but by so tenuous a grip and in such hopeless condition that mercy bids us pray for his speedy ascendance to the Host of Angels waiting to welcome him. His name is Seamus O'Brien, known in this column as Hiram the Bartender (the Judaic alias tickled his Hibernian sense of humor). He ran the County Cork. He *was* the County Cork, as his last words reminded me. "This is my bar," he said. "Where else would I be?"

Are there saints among us still? I believe there are, and I count Seamus among their number.

He nursed me through my first and worst drunks. He listened to me rave for hours against injustice and greed and other tiresome realities that maddened me so in younger days. And when the future was inconceivable without the company of the girl who became my first wife, his graceful love for all women helped ease her into my often sordid life, helped us both see through his eyes that our love was acceptable, was good. He acted as counselor, comforter, friend, confessor, sage.

New York City is full of bartenders like Seamus O'Brien, men who tend their patrons with a depth of love and patience impossible to deserve. Seamus was mine, and he's dying. Farewell.

There remains only to bury the past. I now of-

247

ficially declare Hiram the Bartender, and the Dough-boy, the Swede, the Boss Tweed portrait, the Center Booth, the Terrible Corned Beef and Cabbage (a slander, by the way), the Hit List, and all other contents, characters, and appurtenances of said Kill-harney's Bar retired, finished, void, done. That part of my past dies with Seamus O'Brien.

From now on, I speak with my own voice. This life contains enough false fronts without my adding to the sham. What shame I share in the horror now finished, I'll face in my own name.

Permit me to introduce myself: male Caucasian, mid-forties, lapsed Catholic, decent small forward, pursued by Furies, surprised by love. My name is Peter Killharney. I'm a reporter.

He closed the notebook and began to cry. He cried for Seamus, and Dombowski, and for his favorite bar and his failed marriage, and he cried in shame and self-pity and cried until his ribs hurt and he no longer cared what he cried for.

Arms wrapped around his shaking body, and he turned and pressed his tear-soaked face against Sheila's warm belly.

"There, there," she said, gently patting his still quaking back. "It's over. It's all over now."

She held him and stroked him until his sobs lessened. Then she helped him back to bed, where he cried himself to sleep in her arms.

Eleven

"I still don't get it," Peg said, breaking the spell of Shakespeare that had followed them from the theater and into the surrounding filth of Times Square at night. "There wasn't any real reason for Othello's jealousy. Shakespeare never explained it, not really. I mean, the play's great and everything, and I thought James Earl Jones was super."

"Me too," said her boyfriend, Michael, squeezing her hand. The gesture sent ambiguous darts through Killharney.

"So many of the internal motives that direct our lives are irrational," Pete answered her. "My truth-telling compulsion wears the mask of virtue, but virtue can't explain it. Jealousy has no such convenient gloss. It's just ridiculous and horrible and blinds its victims to everything but its vicious circle of self-generated pain."

It was his turn to have his hand squeezed by Sheila, who had heard enough of Margie's late-marriage infidelities to recognize the autobiography in Killharney's description.

The four turned onto Forty-second Street and passed under a movie marquee for *Cheerleader Orgy*, rated "Triple XXX Wet." As they strolled down the Deuce toward Grand Central Terminal, voices in doorways pushed smoke and crack and gold-looking jewelry, using spiels as subtle as unbaited fishhooks. Still cushioned by the elegance of Shakespeare, the double-daters easily ignored the pimps and hustlers and garbage and drunks.

"Did you tell your dad about Muffy?" Michael asked. The teenagers giggled together.

"It's embarrassing, Daddy, but Muffy really has the hots for you. God, I mean, my own father!" Then Peg caught herself as she realized Sheila might not find the idea so ludicrous. Peg hurried on with her story. "Talk about crazy, but Muffy's convinced the guy who got blown up that night wasn't the Hit List killer. She says the circumstances all point to the killer pulling a switch with another body. Morbid."

Sheila hugged Pete tightly. They had entered into an unspoken pact not to discuss the killings, and here was his motormouth daughter, gossiping blithely about the unspeakable.

"Interesting conjecture," he said evenly, "but I was never much for yesterday's news."

They entered Grand Central, and Pete steered them toward the correct departure gate.

Then he remembered.

"Is everything all right?" Sheila asked him. Pete noticed he was gripping her arm with a fierceness that was probably painful.

"I—no, yes. Fine," he sputtered incoherently.

"Thank you for the play, Daddy, and it's nice meeting you, Sheila, outside a hospital and everything."

"And you, Peg," she replied. "I haven't been on a double date since I was sixteen."

Both women began to blush for different reasons, and the teenagers turned and walked to their train, still holding hands.

"Nice kids," Sheila said, watching them with a smile on her face. Pete said nothing. She looked at him with concern. "What's the matter?"

"That night you met me in the County Cork—how long had Judge Sanderson been dead when you saw him hauled up from the sewer?"

"Pete, don't."

"It's important."

"The coroner placed time of death as between eight and eight-thirty P.M."

"And you talked to the killer around nine."

"Yes."

"And came to see me around ten-thirty."

"Pete, stop it."

"Between about seven o'clock and the time we left the bar together, the man who blew up at Kreutzer's poolhouse was sitting ten feet from me. He had been tailing me all evening."

"That can't be."

"I'm certain of it. When you started to cry that night, he smirked at us, and he died with that same smirk on what was left of his face. He couldn't possibly have killed Sanderson."

"But if he didn't, he's not—"

"Let me get you a cab."

"Pete, please, no," Sheila pleaded as he walked her to the taxi stand.

"I'm the only person who could have noticed, and I wasn't supposed to see the body. The real killer's made a mistake, and he knows it. He'll be coming after me."

"No."

"He'll be coming after me," Pete repeated, "and I

251

have to figure out who he is and stop him before he succeeds."

"You will." Tears formed in her eyes. "But in the meantime, don't mess up that apartment or I'll kill you."

She got into a cab, crying and brave, and the taxi pulled away, leaving him alone and scared and determined.

"I'm going to nail the fucker," Killharney announced to the almost empty street. A nearby bag lady, camped over a steam vent, woke up and looked at him as if he were nuts.

The *Apple*'s city room idled in nocturnal tranquility. Killharney had always been soothed by the steady chatter of the wire-service printers, and the sight of other reporters busy at their shared craft made him feel less alone, less exposed. He felt both now, but most of all, he felt the reporter's ageless thrill of breaking a story. He had his lead. For the smirking man, as Pete now thought of him, had an ironclad alibi for the Sanderson murder: Killharney himself.

Fact: The smirking man did not kill Sanderson.

Fact: The man who killed Sanderson also killed Murry and Bengelsdorf and Kreutzer and perhaps Lopiccolo.

Conclusion: New York hadn't been in the grip of a bloody rampage by some Bible-spouting psycho taking inspiration from Pete's columns. No, a clever killer had fit himself into certain events and conditions, had used Pete and Lopiccolo and the smirking man and God knows who else to commit a murder, which he then hid among other murders, with pursuit sidetracked by yet more murders.

Then who was the true target, the one all the rest had died to disguise?

Killharney pulled out a legal pad and drew a chain of three circles, more of his brother Brendan's clarifying algebra:

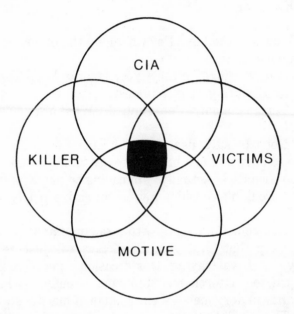

The question was, which victim did the smirking man link the killer to? Underneath the VICTIMS circle, Pete wrote the names of the victims:

Lopiccolo
Murry
Bengelsdorf
Sanderson
(Hazelton)
Kreutzer

He crossed out Hazelton, the suicide. He crossed out Lopiccolo, the victim who may have been killed by someone else. The shortened list read:

Murry
Bengelsdorf
Sanderson
Kreutzer

Who was the key? For whom did the others all die?
The phone rang.

"Pete, darling, it's Lilly, your favorite Deep Throat," said the *Apple*'s gossip columnist.

"Tempt me not," Pete replied. "What are you doing home?"

"Don't be silly, dear boy. I'm calling from Maxim's. I love to have a phone brought to my table. It makes me feel so essential. Actually, I'm calling to play Cupid."

"I wouldn't consider myself an active player right now."

"Not you. I'm sitting with a talented and *très* sexy man. Stop that! Not you, Pete. Serge is just getting frisky. As I was saying, this occasional gentleman has long carried a torch for Stephanie Kreutzer, who we know has undergone a recent change of marital status."

"That's a delicate way of saying her husband's been splattered into unrecognizable bits."

"I'm a delicate woman. What I want from you is a reading as to how distraught the widow Kreutzer seemed. How long before Serge and the rest of society might expect her reappearance?"

"The last time I saw her, she was running toward her husband's corpse, screaming his name."

"That doesn't sound hopeful. However, Vinnie Bisceglia did tell me it was hearing about that odious Steptoe's death that truly set her off. If she was keening over the wrong man, then Serge's suit might stand a quicker chance of proceeding."

"Lilly, your capacity for thinking the worst of people

puts mine to shame. Tell me, is this Serge going to chase after all the Hit List widows and go with whoever's willing to bankroll his adoration?"

"Interesting suggestion. Gloria Sanderson is a Van Rensselaer, and they've had money since people spoke Dutch at dinner. But no, Serge is a romantic gigolo. Frankly, I think you and Stephanie would have made a lovely couple. She wouldn't even have to change the monograms."

"As I said, I'm sort of busy."

"So am I, darling. Kisses to Sheila."

Pete hung up and stared distractedly at his circles. If millions could sponsor romance, what motive was strong enough to fuel a dozen gruesome homicides? He intersected the chain with a circle he labeled MOTIVE and listed under it:

Greed
Love
Power
Fear

Greed wasn't helpful; all four had brimmed with it. Love? I love my wife, Kreutzer had said, but how could that realistically translate into a murder spree? Every victim held power, though some held more than others. Murry, for instance, had Congressional say in foreign affairs, intelligence, and international commerce.

Wait.

Something was coming clearer. Pete looked at the short list of victims. At the top was Murry, the killer's first incontestable victim, the congressman who had sat on the Intelligence Oversight Committee that monitored clandestine operations. And there was a definite professionalism surrounding the killings—the bugs and tails

and break-ins—that seemed unlikely even for a moti-
vated amateur.

Pete drew yet another circle to intersect VICTIMS
and labeled it CIA. What else linked the CIA to the
victims? What else did the Agency know?

They probably knew the man whose fingerprints were
sent to Washington for identification. And that man was
supposed to be the Hit List killer. And the Hit List killer
was supposed to be the smirking man.

Which meant the CIA knew who the smirking man
was. Did they know who the killer was as well?

Killharney regarded his circles again. He would have
to connect CIA to SMIRKING MAN. Then he realized the
smirking man was himself a victim. Pete crumpled the
paper and on a new sheet redrew his circles so they all
linked together:

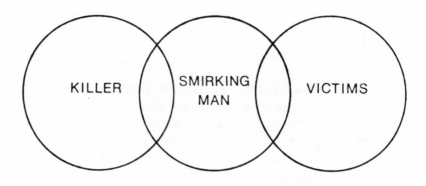

Close.

Oh yes, Killharney was close. He darkened the small
part where the four circles overlapped and asked the
payoff question: What motive connected both the killer
and the CIA to the victims?

Answer: Fear. What if Murry had uncovered some intelligence secret that endangered the killer, that exposed him to the greatest fear of all, the fear of imminent death? If the killer feared nothing so much as becoming a victim himself . . .

And there it was. All the circles converged. Peg's friend Muffy had it half right. There had been a switch of bodies before the poolhouse explosion. Except *two* bodies had been switched.

The car that met the 6:00 A.M. shuttle flight did not take Killharney to CIA headquarters in Langley, Virginia. Instead, it dropped Pete off at a nondescript office building near Capitol Hill, and he was told a floor and room number for the meeting. Baumann himself answered the door.

"Welcome to Washington, Mr. Killharney," he said, showing him through a suite of unoccupied rooms to a practically bare office in back.

"This isn't Langley," Pete said.

"The CIA represents less than ten percent of intelligence appropriations."

"So you're not CIA?"

"I was expecting your call sooner or later," Baumann said, ignoring the question. "I have a very high opinion of you. Quite a fan, actually. You mentioned you wanted to see me about—let me get this right—revolution and authentication. Why don't we take them in that order?"

"How long was Kreutzer a double agent?"

"We have to presume ever since entering the country, very likely since after the Russian army conquered Hungary during World War II. Ex-Nazis didn't go on living if they couldn't prove their utility."

"And how long have you known?"

Baumann smiled noncommittally.

"But Murry tipped him off," Pete prompted.

"Unwittingly, yes. He heard rumors about Kreutzer from his contacts with the Nicaraguan Contras. Unfortunately, he passed the information along to us through an unreliable source."

"So Kreutzer killed him."

"Or had him killed. It's skilled labor, shooting a congressman in public and getting away with it. Of course, Kreutzer didn't need to search far for the necessary talent; he already had an expert on staff."

"I take it you're referring to the late ex-Captain Stephen Steptoe."

"Whose history of making suspects disappear we first learned from reading your column. We've had our eye on Steptoe ever since he took over Kreutzer's security. That's how we knew he had developed a fondness for the Bulldog forty-four, the gun that killed Murry. The coincidence was enough for us to activate an agent in place on the security force."

"You mean you had an agent there all along and . . . wait a minute: the smirking man," Pete said. Baumann looked puzzled. "At Kreutzer's poolhouse, the stand-in for the Hit List killer died with a smirk on what was left of his face."

"I see. Yes, he was ours."

"And those were his fingerprints that were sent to Washington for identification," Pete said. "You lost them because they would have blown your agent's cover."

"No, we held on to them because the killings continued. Why Bengelsdorf? Why Sanderson? A check of duty assignments showed the agent allegedly tailing you during both those murders. To be honest, we had to sidetrack and determine whether he had soured on us drastically."

"Do you often have this particular personnel problem?"

"About as often as you have someone murdering your enemies for you," Baumann replied. "We concluded instead that the agent's cover had already been blown. Someone associated with the Hit List killings had planted his fingerprints at a murder scene to contact us."

"I missed something there. Who was contacting you?"

"Steptoe. Obviously Kreutzer was blackmailing him. Even a bad cop wouldn't kill a congressman except under enormous pressure. But there was something more going on. Far too many people were murdered just for the sake of an alibi. And when Sanderson was strangled, two cops were also shot. How could one man kill three people with two different weapons at the same time?"

"Kreutzer got in the act himself," Pete said, finally unravelling what turned out to be a double trail of murder and murderers. "He strangled Sanderson, then Steptoe, then two security guards at the estate. Because he liked it. He liked killing. Steptoe may have played triggerman, but Kreutzer's the real Hit List killer."

"Exactly. Steptoe must have come to the same conclusion. We figure sending those fingerprints was his way of letting us know there was going to be one last Hit List murder. He thought he could get Kreutzer before Kreutzer got him."

"And that was fine with you."

"Kreutzer's a traitor whose usefulness as a double agent had been fatally compromised. Yet, thanks to Murry's clumsy patriotism, we couldn't move on him ourselves without risking the efficacy of other sources."

"So you did nothing."

"At the time, inaction seemed a course with much to recommend it."

"Except your inaction cost your agent's and Steptoe's and the guards' lives, not to mention whoever the poor stiff was who blew up in the oven. I should have guessed it wasn't Kreutzer because of the severed and pulverized hands. Kreutzer's missing finger couldn't have been quickly duplicated; it takes too long for scar tissue to form."

"Very observant. I'm impressed."

"I'm outraged," Killharney shot back. "You also got a hell of a good cop killed. Dombowski's dead because you did nothing."

"A tragic misjudgment."

"I call it official complicity in mass murder."

"What do you want, Mr. Killharney?"

"I want Kreutzer caught. For once in his life, I don't want him slipping out some back door, most particularly one you might leave open for him. I want Kreutzer arrested, tried according to the criminal codes of the states of New York and Connecticut, and sent to prison for the rest of his natural days." Pete tossed an envelope on the desk between them.

"What's this?"

"A Xerox copy of today's column. I thought I'd ask for authentication before it ran. I just got it."

Baumann opened the envelope and carefully scanned the copy, which was titled PLAYING PATTY-CAKE WITH A KILLER.

"You can't publish this," Baumann said when he finished.

"Fuck you and everyone like you."

"I understand your anger, but I can't permit it. It might very well jeopardize national security."

"It might jeopardize the job security of some licensed sociopaths who consider mass murder a miscalculation. I want Kreutzer caught, and this column's my insurance. And it's on its way to press. In a few hours you'll have senators and CBS and scared White House staffers all demanding to know why you protected the killer of a United States congressman."

For the first time, Baumann's confidence broke. He took off his glasses and polished them with a meticulous attention that didn't quite mask the tremor in his hands. "Perhaps we can help each other. Would you believe me if I told you we've been trying to locate Kreutzer for over two weeks?"

"I wouldn't believe you if you said birds fly. But I do believe you can stop him from escaping the country. You keep him here and the police will catch him quickly enough. In fact, Inspector Herlihy of the New York City Police Department is waiting for your call. I told him to anticipate unparalleled interdepartmental cooperation."

"He'll get it," Baumann said resignedly. "But permit me a word of caution. Your insurance doesn't cover mad dogs, and this one really has slipped his leash. Kreutzer is a desperate, probably deranged man. Anyone who knows or gets near him now is in enormous danger. Until he's in custody, I suggest you find a safe place and stay there. Because if Kreutzer finds you first, you're dead."

As soon as he got back to New York, Pete called his paper from a phone booth at La Guardia.

"Is it printing?" he asked Vinnie Bisceglia.

"It's already on the trucks. Murchison ordered a special edition at twice the press run, swearing to give back his knighthood if it didn't sell out. By the way, Melissa Sanchez has left you three messages this morning. She wants to do a follow-up on the Hit List widows. I took one of the calls and she blathered to me about the Dutch Van Rensselaers."

Killharney went cold. So that was who'd planted the bug on his phone, probably while visiting Bisceglia the day he saw them together. And no one had thought to remove it because the tapper was supposed to be dead. Pete recalled Baumann's warning that anyone who knew or got near the killer was in enormous danger. Missy.

"You still there?" Vinnie asked.

"Not for long," Pete said. "Do me a favor and stay close to Sheila till this wacko is caught."

"She's two desks away and sends her love."

"I'll deliver mine in person, but there are two other women I have to see first."

"Pete, you're looking more dishy than ever," Melissa said as she welcomed him into her office.

"And you look as pneumatic as always. How's your love life?"

"You're indiscreet but a mind reader. I've got this new toy I'm just dripping to try."

"Electronic?" She looked at him suspiciously, and he continued, "That's your bug on my phone, isn't it?"

"I told you I played hardball," she said defensively.

"I'm curious. Which one were you fucking, Kreutzer or Steptoe? Which one gave you the bug to plant?"

"No one gave me—"

"And just what the hell did you think when the killer announced that he knew those fingerprints had been mislaid the day after Dombowski and I quarreled about it on my phone?"

A glimmer of fear appeared in her eyes. "A leak somewhere," she said. "Helmut told me it happened all the time."

"So Kreutzer was the john. You went too far, Melissa, way too far. It wasn't enough for you, trading some saps a little pussy for an inside line. You had to try and rig the game, and all along you were feeding the Hit List killer the knowledge he needed to keep killing."

"What are you talking about?"

"I'm talking about your being an accessory to first-degree murder. The Hit List killer isn't dead. Neither is Kreutzer. And it's no coincidence, because Helmut Kreutzer's the true Hit List killer. Congratulations, Missy, you've been balling a mass murderer."

"I don't believe you," Melissa said, and began to hiccup.

"Believe this: you need police protection. Kreutzer has killed often and gladly. You know him, you're a loose end, and he'll surely kill you if he has the chance."

Sanchez nodded dumbly, not registering his words, seeing instead the certain ruin of her career, so he grabbed her by the shoulders and shook her. She started to moan through her hiccups, an almost sexual groaning. Missy still liked it rough.

"Get help, Melissa. Call the police and tell them everything you know, so they can catch him before he kills again."

Killharney turned and walked away.

"You can't leave now," she wailed, and hiccuped.

"Social obligation. I have to pay a belated condolence call."

The guardhouse was empty, and Pete entered the Kreutzer estate unchallenged. Fruit trees dotted the grounds with sweet-smelling puffs of pink and white, and the daffodil hill had been replanted with tulips to parody the progression of the seasons. Killharney parked the rental car in front of the main house, and as he regarded the surrounding beauty, a sudden, deep stab of spring fever made him envy the other worlds he didn't inhabit, the worlds where spring was lived, not visited, where peace was the norm, not this deceptive façade he was about to strip bare to its murderous core.

"Pete Killharney to see Mrs. Kreutzer," he told the butler through the front door opened a reluctant six inches.

"On what matter shall I say, sir?"

"Murder. Go tell her, it'll make your day."

The door closed, and remained closed for minutes before the butler returned.

"Please follow me."

As Killharney was led through the mansion's maze of rooms, he noticed that the Matisse he had admired earlier was missing, and a full set of Louis Vuitton luggage was parked at the foot of the main staircase.

"A quick getaway," he remarked.

"I beg your pardon?"

"A beautiful day," Pete amended. The butler stopped at French doors leading into an attached greenhouse filled with mutilated roses. At the other end, dressed in black to the tie holding her ponytail, Stephanie Kreutzer was hacking at a bush in glorious bloom. Pruned clusters blanketed the path. The butler vanished. Shrugging, Killharney strode through the floral carnage, grinding petals into the floor.

"A novel way to deal with grief," Pete said.

She spun toward him with a look of terror and dread, and in turning she raked her arm across the thorns of the plant she was destroying. The terror subsided when she saw who it was.

"What are you doing here?" she demanded weakly, ignoring the blood welling from the wounds.

"Murder. Didn't the butler tell you? I came to talk about murder, and just in time, too. It looks like you're planning to leave."

"Yes, yes I am. I've put the house on the market. This was Helmut's home, really," she said, staring at the pruning shears in her hand.

"You mean *is*. Present tense. This is Helmut's home."

"That's not funny."

"Murder isn't."

"Please go, or I'll call the police," she said, and tried to brush past Killharney, but her skirt caught on more thorns, forcing her to stop and extricate herself.

"Don't bother, they're on their way. However, you might want your lawyer on hand to help get the best deal possible."

"What are you talking about?" she asked, tearing herself free with a tug that shredded the skirt.

"Same subject. Murder. It's funny, you're the second woman I've explained this to this morning. Do you know Melissa Sanchez? That TV newswoman with the big—"

"I know who she is," Stephanie Kreutzer said bitterly, unconsciously folding trembling arms across her dancer's chest.

"It's all come undone, Mrs. Kreutzer. The police know your husband's the Hit List killer. And they know you helped him fake his own death. You were very convincing, by the way. Especially after you heard the news of Steptoe's murder, when you ran toward the poolhouse, knowing it was about to explode."

The memory dissolved her pretense. "He wasn't supposed to die," she said, weeping softly. "I don't know how that monster found out about us, but he didn't have to kill Stephen." Teardrops dappled the carpet of decapitated blooms. Through the greenhouse windows Pete saw a cavalcade of six police cars speeding up the driveway, lights flashing.

"Killing's a hard habit to break," he said as he saw Inspector Herlihy step out of the lead car and sniff the spring air appreciatively. "I'm just glad I got here before he added you to his list."

Killharney let two policemen take custody of the broken woman and joined Herlihy at the front door. Pete pried off a crushed rose that had stuck to his shoe, and handed it to his old friend. "She loves him not."

"You really think Kreutzer might still be here?" Herlihy asked as they watched two dozen police dressed in flak jackets methodically surround the house and fan out through the grounds.

"If he can't be found, maybe he hasn't gone anywhere."

An engine fired up somewhere nearby, and a helicopter rose from the woods and quickly ascended beyond the effective range of the shots fired at its retreat.

"That man has more moves than a thousand-dollar whore," Herlihy said.

"A million-dollar whore should," Pete replied.

"You shouldn't be playing with bombs, an amateur like yourself," Red Ethel scolded him, safely bunkered behind her paper barricades that crammed the Municipal Research Center.

"I've retired from being a Trotskyite," Pete said. But not from being a reporter, for here he was, working on a follow-up story instead of lying low till Kreutzer was caught.

"That revisionist. Tell me, with all the victims part of the power elite, do you suppose your killer could have been a Marxist?"

Pete laughed ruefully. "Only by convenience. He was a Nazi and a Communist and a CIA front man, and whatever else it took to stay alive and prosper. Kreutzer's the Hit List killer, Ethel, and he's still alive."

"Kreutzer! And to think I already celebrated his death day."

"So did he, I bet. That's why I'm here. I thought I'd check out his will, find out how much he came close to keeping after killing all those men. Has it been probated yet?"

"You came here to find out? You think while you were being blown up they maybe passed a law, Connecticut residents now have their wills probated in New York?"

"Good point. I must still be missing a step. But then what am I supposed to do with this?" he asked, holding up the customary chocolate-covered cherries. "Will you take it as a gift, or do I have to come up with another way to bribe you?"

"I'll give you bribes. The mafioso Marchetti was indicted this morning. Income-tax evasion, RICO-statute conspiracy to commit fraud, and attempted subornation of a grand jury proceeding. He tried to bribe one of the jurors."

"Let's take it as a sign. As Herlihy would say, the angels are in the ascendant today."

"Will they catch him this time?" Ethel asked worriedly. "Will Kreutzer finally pay for his crimes?"

For the first time Pete saw the ancient, fragile woman Red Ethel would be if fear ever mastered her spirit. "He'll be caught, I promise. This morning I turned over the last rock he could have hidden behind."

"You're a lackey of the bourgeois press, but you're still a good man," the old radical said, starting to sniffle. "So get out of here and let a silly woman cry in peace."

Killharney kissed her grudgingly tendered cheek, and left her dabbing at her eyes and tearing the cellophane wrapping off the candy box.

Halfway across the mosaic-faced lobby, the sense of being watched that he had felt here months before returned like a fragment from a recurring dream. Or nightmare, for that was the day Lopiccolo died, the day it all began. Pete scanned the inner courtyard, its portals mostly opening onto dark cul-de-sacs, but his only company was a tarnished brass eagle nesting on the radiator cage in the corner. He shook off the fear, squinting up at the spring sunlight being strangled by the murky skylight four floors above. This was nature as New Yorkers knew it, grudging and grimy.

As Killharney took out his pen and notebook to write down the image, a throaty chuckle reverberated from somewhere around the courtyard's perimeter.

"So close to death and still scribbling."

Kreutzer! Sweat burst from every inch of Pete's skin, and the notebook slipped from his hand to the floor. Where was the voice coming from? To the left, not too high up.

"No doubt you'll be scratching away while they tighten down your coffin lid, Mr. Killharney."

The voice had changed location, now between him and the front exit. Stall, Pete ordered himself. Keep him talking till you think of something clever to save your sorry Irish ass.

"Why did you fly to New York, of all places?" Pete called out. "Every cop in the city is looking for you."

"Fly? For once, don't be stupid. That was my butler in the helicopter. I rode in the trunk of your car. It was so convenient, I thank you. Not only is New York where I find the friends to help me disappear, but this way I also get to dispose of you on my way out."

Kreutzer seemed to be circling, toying with him till he decided to pounce. Counter it. Throw off his timing.

"Don't bank on either one," Pete said. "You obviously haven't seen my column this morning."

"That's one chore I give up gladly, reading your grubby trash to plot out the Hit List charade. It pleased Steptoe to destroy your reputation, but except for the killings, I found it all tiresome."

"Baumann doesn't. Why, just this morning your good buddy was telling me how much he admired my work."

Silence meant Pete had scored a hit. Press it.

"Of course, that was before he found out I was blowing the whistle on your faked death," Pete said with a casual insolence he hoped hid his terror. "My column persuaded him to pull the plug on you. You're officially overboard, Kreutzer."

"A pitiful bluff," Kreutzer said, surprisingly close. The Hit List killer now seemed to be on the same floor as Pete. "And Baumann's masters are not my only friends."

"You think either side's going to waste time and talent to hide a mass murderer? You're dead meat. Hell, I'm probably the only one who wants you alive, and that's only so you'll go to jail for the crimes you committed."

Pete took a step backward toward the courtyard's exit to the basement stairs. His memory told him the corridors down there dead-ended at the antique elevator, but perhaps he could hide in one of the side rooms and ambush the maniac. It sounded like a crummy plan.

"Jail?" Kreutzer asked, directly behind him. Pete pivoted around. No sign of the killer. "I thought you hated me, and all you wanted was to see me in jail?"

Kreutzer was now somewhere to the right. Pete took another step toward the basement.

"That's where convicted killers grow old and die. And what I hate are the types of private, purchased betrayals by which you've managed to evade judgment. You always found someone who was willing to be bought. Well, I went public with the truth this morning, and no one can buy off a million angry men."

"Truth!" Kreutzer cried. "How I despised it when you prattled on about truth and crimes and such rubbish. What does the truth matter when you're dead, answer me that!"

Kreutzer sounded suddenly like he was losing control. Pete thought he might be able to sprint through the exit to the basement before the madman could get off a shot.

"I will survive this! I will find some safe place and start over, and soon I buy any truth I wish. But first I kill you!"

That was Pete's exit cue. He hurled himself through the pillars flanking the staircase, but something snared him by the throat in midair. It jerked him to a complete stop, and Killharney found himself dangling from a ribbon of torment that was quickly choking him to death. Black spots filled his vision. A dark roar of pain swamped his power to resist. The basement loomed beneath him, a quick dumping ground for his body.

No!

Pete tightened his grip on the ballpoint pen still in his hand and desperately, blindly stabbed backward. A shriek filled the courtyard, the stranglehold released, and Pete staggered over the top of the stairs, his ankle twisting as he cascaded down the hard marble steps. He lay dazed on the basement floor, gasping for breath, his right thumb bent all the way back, his ankle sprained or broken.

A bloodied, enraged Helmut Kreutzer appeared at the top of the stairs, Pete's pen protruding from one eye.

"You never stop hurting me!" he howled and yanked the pen from his punctured eye. Blood poured from the wound, painting the killer's face in a mask of blood. "You won't even die right."

Kreutzer pulled out a huge gun, and Pete leaped to his feet. Or tried to. The ankle gave, and he collapsed back helplessly to the floor. The Hit List killer started down the stairs, blood spilling on each step, and smiled triumphantly through his own agony.

"Once more I say good-bye to an enemy," he said, panting, spitting blood from his mouth with every word. "You want the truth? I live. You die."

Looming over the crippled reporter, Kreutzer lifted the gun and sighted down the barrel. Mother Mary hear our prayers. Killharney sank under a flood of screaming blood.

Epilogue

It was a beautiful June day, sunny and warm, a light breeze rustling the bright new leaves on the trees, a day designed for weddings and graduations and other ceremonies of hope.

"Hell of a day for a funeral," muttered Hanratty, watching the hearse at the head of the procession wind through the acres of headstones that covered Valhalla, New York. They passed two other burials in progress. "You're in the wrong line of work, Svenson," he told the sandhog. "Your water tunnel might never get dug, but those guys got a guaranteed job as long as people keep dying."

"And they keep dying," Svenson said. "You got any more of that after-shave I smell?"

Hanratty handed him the bottle and, taking turns, they emptied the pint of bad scotch by the time the cortege reached its destination. As the simple casket was maneuvered into the machine-dug pit, the mourners assembled themselves around the grave. Peggy, propped up by her boyfriend, was quietly and steadily sobbing.

Margie looked stern as she stood with her lawn-care fiancé, who studied the cemetery's landscaping with professional interest. Hanratty and Svenson flanked Seamus's sister. She sniffed disdainfully.

"You could have sprung for Johnny Walker Black," she whispered.

Pete, of course, was with Sheila.

The priest recited the words of the burial ceremony from memory as he commended the immortal soul of Seamus Matthew O'Brien to his Creator in the name of God the Father, the Son, and the Holy Spirit. The ritual handful of dirt was tossed onto the coffin, and the mourners moved away from the grave as cemetery workers took over to finish the job.

Margie steered her new man toward Killharney for the obligatory introduction.

"Pete, this is Bob Granger, my intended. Bob, Pete Killharney, my sordid past. Jesus, Pete, you look worse every time I see you."

Which was true. Bruises mottled his face and neck where he had hit his head falling down the stairs, and he walked with a cane.

"I just found out the phrase was 'hard-hitting reporter,' instead of 'hard-hit.' Congratulations, Bob," Pete said, and stuck out his right hand with its taped thumb. Margie's fiancé gingerly shook the undamaged fingers.

"Hey, Pete, is it true they're going to give that woman a medal?" Hanratty asked as he joined the group. By now his breath could qualify as a flammable substance.

"The mayor wanted to, but Red Ethel turned him down. She told him she wouldn't be a dupe for ruling-class propaganda."

"She told the mayor that?" Margie asked.

"Who would have thought a little old lady would be

toting a straight razor in her handbag?" Granger marveled.

"For forty years," Pete said. "It belonged to her late husband. Ethel always kept it sharp."

"She sure as hell knew what to do with it," Svenson exclaimed in boozy admiration. "Ear to ear in a single slice. Kreutzer was maggot bait before he hit the floor."

"Charming conversation," said Margie.

"Oh, Daddy, he was such a kind man!" Peggy wailed as she wrapped her father in a teary embrace. Pete held her as she cried for Seamus, and her tears reminded them all of the sadness that had brought them together. Killharney squinted hard at the sun. Hanratty dabbed at moist eyes with an unhealthy-looking handkerchief. Only the strangers to Seamus's gentle devotion remained dry-eyed, and they regarded their loved ones with the puzzled helplessness of the unaffected comforter. After enough tears had been shed, Killharney released his daughter to her boyfriend and took Sheila's arm. The group stood silently in awkward limbo between mourning and regular life until Margie broke the silence.

"Well, it's too nice a day to spend hanging around here. We're going down to the Botanical Gardens to see the roses in bloom. You two want to join the party?"

"No, I don't think so," Pete said. He had seen enough roses recently. "Thanks for the invitation, though. And good luck to you both on your marriage."

"Well, they say it's better the second time around. And considering the first . . ." Margie let the sentence hang unfinished, and hauled away her catch. The teenagers waved good-bye and followed, holding hands.

Sheila squeezed Killharney's good hand. They walked without speaking in the other direction, along a path bordered by blossoming rhododendron and flame azalea. At the top of a small rise, next to a tomb that had been spray-painted "DEMONS '69," they turned to each other and carefully embraced.

"I love you," he declared. Sheila nodded, smiling unsteadily, then looked down, unable to speak. Pete lifted her head and kissed away salty tears.

"This is a hell of a place to ask," he said, "and if I try the bended knee, I'll never make it back up. But, Sheila, will you marry me?"

She took a step back and regarded her suitor.

"Definitely damaged goods," she said. "Tell you what, buy me a cup of coffee and I'll consider all offers."

"Does that mean yes?"

She smiled and hooked her arm in his, and they strolled silently through the graveyard toward the future.